The Everyman Wodehouse

P. G. WODEHOUSE

Nothing Serious

EVERYMAN

Published by Everyman's Library
Northburgh House
10 Northburgh Street
London EC1V 0AT

First published in the UK by Herbert Jenkins, 1950
Published by Everyman's Library, 2008

Typography by Peter B. Willberg

ISBN 978-1-84159-157-5

A CIP catalogue record for this book is available from the British Library

Distributed by Random House (UK) Ltd.,
20 Vauxhall Bridge Road, London SW1V 2SA

Typeset by AccComputing, North Barrow, Somerset

Printed and bound in Germany
by GGP Media GmbH, Pössneck

Nothing Serious

CONTENTS

A crusty roll, whizzing like a meteor out of the unknown, shot past the Crumpet and the elderly relative whom he was entertaining to luncheon at the Drones Club and shattered itself against the wall. Noting that his guest had risen some eighteen inches into the air, the Crumpet begged him not to give the thing another thought.

'Just someone being civil,' he explained. 'Meant for me, of course. 'Where did it come from?'

'I think it must have been thrown by one of those two young men at the table over there.'

The Crumpet gazed in the direction indicated.

'It can't have been the tall one with the tortoiseshell-rimmed spectacles,' he said. 'That's Horace Pendlebury-Davenport, the club Darts champion. If he had aimed at me, he would have hit me, for his skill is uncanny. It was Bingo Little. More cheese?'

'No, thank you.'

'Then shall we go and have our coffee in the smoking-room?'

'It might be safer.'

'You must make allowances for Bingo,' said the Crumpet as they took their seats, observing that his companion's expression was still austere. 'Until a few days ago a dark shadow brooded over his life, threatening the stability of the home. This has now passed away, and he is consequently a bit above himself. The shadow to which I allude was his baby's Nannie.'

'Is that young man a father?'

'Oh, rather.'

'Good heavens.'

'Bingo married Rosie M. Banks, the celebrated female novelist, and came a day when he had this baby. Well, Mrs Bingo did most of the heavy work, of course, but you know what I mean. And naturally the baby, on being added to the strength, had to have a Nannie. They fired her last week.'

'But why should the dispensing with her services give rise to such an ebullition of animal spirits?'

'Because she had once been Bingo's Nannie, too. That is the point to keep the mind fixed on. Mrs Bingo, like so many female ink-slingers, is dripping with sentiment, and this ingrowing sentiment of hers led her to feel how sweet it would be if the same old geezer who had steered Bingo through the diaper and early sailor suit phases could also direct the private life of the younger generation. So when a photograph in a woman's paper of Miss Rosie M. Banks, author of our new serial (Mrs Richard Little), brought Sarah Byles round on the run to ascertain whether this was the Richard Little she had groomed, it was not long before she was persuaded to emerge from her retirement and once more set her hand to the plough.'

'And your friend disliked the arrangement?'

'You bet he disliked the arrangement.'

The news, broken to Bingo on his return from the office – he is ye ed. of a weekly organ called *Wee Tots* (P. P. Purkiss, proprietor) devoted to the interests of our better-class babes and sucklings – got (said the Crumpet) right in amongst him. Sarah Byles had always lived in his memory as a stalwart figure about eight feet high and the same across, with many of the less engaging personal attributes of the bucko mate of an old-time hellship, and he feared for the well-being of his son and heir. He felt that the latter would be giving away too much weight.

'Golly, queen of my soul,' he ejaculated, 'that's a bit tough on the issue, isn't it? When I served under Nannie Byles, she was a human fiend at the mention of whose name strong children shook like aspens.'

'Oh, no, sweetie-pie,' protested Mrs Bingo. 'She's an old dear. So kind and gentle.'

'Well, I'll take your word for it,' said Bingo dubiously. 'Of course, age may have softened her.'

But before dressing for dinner he looked in on young Algernon Aubrey, shook him sympathetically by the hand and gave him a bar of nut chocolate. He felt like a kind-hearted manager of prize-fighters who is sending a novice up against the champion.

Conceive his relief, therefore, when he found that Mrs Bingo had not been astray in her judgment of form. Arriving on the morrow, La Byles proved, as stated, to be an old dear. In the interval since they had last met she had shrunk to about four feet ten, the steely glitter which he had always associated with her eyes had disappeared, and she had lost the rather unpleasant suggestion she had conveyed in his formative years of being on the point of enforcing discipline with a belaying pin. Her aspect was mild and her manner cooing, and when she flung her arms about him and kissed him and asked him how his stomach was, he flung his arms about her and kissed her and said his stomach was fine. The scene was one of cordial good will.

The new régime set in smoothly, conditions appearing to be hunkydory. Mrs Bingo and Nannie Byles hit it off together like a couple of members of a barber-shop quartette. Bingo himself felt distantly benevolent towards the old dug-out. And as Algernon Aubrey took to her and seemed at his ease in her society, it would not be too much to say that for a day or two everything in the home was gas and gaiters.

For a day or two, I repeat. It was on the evening of the third day, as Bingo and Mrs Bingo sat in the drawing-room after dinner all happy and peaceful, Bingo reading a mystery thriller and Mrs Bingo playing solitaire in the offing, that the former heard the latter emit a sudden giggle, and always being in the market for a good laugh inquired the reason for her mirth.

'I was only thinking,' said Mrs Bingo, now guffawing heartily, 'of the story Nannie told me when we were bathing Algy.'

'Of a nature you are able to repeat?' asked Bingo, for he knew that red hot stuff is sometimes pulled when the girls get together.

'It was about you pinning the golliwog to your Uncle Wilberforce's coat tails when he was going to the reception at the French Embassy.'

Bingo winced a little. He recalled the episode and in particular its sequel, which had involved an association between himself, his uncle and the flat side of a slipper. The old wound had ceased to trouble him physically, but there was still a certain mental pain, and he was of the opinion that it would have been in better taste for Nannie Byles to let the dead past bury its dead.

'Ha, ha,' he said, though dully. 'Fancy her remembering that.'

'Oh, her memory's wonderful,' said Mrs Bingo.

Bingo returned to his mystery thriller, and Mrs Bingo put the black ten on the red jack and that, you would have said, was that. But Bingo, as he rejoined Inspector Keene and resumed with him the search for the murderer of Sir Rollo Murgatroyd, who had been bumped off in his library with a blunt instrument, experienced a difficulty in concentrating on the clues.

Until this moment the signing on the dotted line of his former bottlewasher had occasioned in him, as we have seen, merely a concern for his wee tot. It had not occurred to him that he himself was in peril. But now he found himself filled with a growing uneasiness. He did not like the look of things. His had been a rather notably checkered childhood, full of incidents which it had taken him years to live down, and he trusted that it was not Nannie Byles's intention to form an I-Knew-Him-When club and read occasional papers.

He feared the worst, and next day he was given proof that his apprehensions had been well founded. He was starting to help himself to a second go of jam omelette at the dinner-table, when his hand was stayed by a quick intake of the breath on the part of Mrs Bingo.

'Oh, Bingo, darling,' said Mrs Bingo, 'ought you?'

'Eh?' said Bingo, groping for the gist.

'Your weak stomach,' explained Mrs Bingo.

Bingo was amazed.

'How do you mean, weak stomach? My stomach's terrific. Ask anyone at the Drones. It's the talk of the place.'

'Well, you know what happened at that Christmas party at the Wilkinsons when you were six. Nannie says she will never forget it.'

Bingo flushed darkly.

'Has she been telling you about that?'

'Yes. She says your stomach was always terribly weak, and you *would* overeat yourself at children's parties. She says you would stuff and stuff and stuff and go out and be sick and then come back and stuff and stuff and stuff again.'

Bingo drew himself up rather coldly. No man likes to be depicted as a sort of infant Vitellius, particularly in the presence of a parlourmaid with flapping ears who is obviously drinking it all in with a view to going off and giving the cook something juicy to include in her memoirs.

'No more jam omelette, thank you,' he said reservedly.

'Now, that's very sensible of you,' said Mrs Bingo. 'And Nannie thinks it would be ever so much safer if you gave up cigarettes and cocktails.'

Bingo sank back in his chair feeling as if he had been slapped in the eye with a wet sock.

A couple of days later things took a turn for the worse. Returning from the office and heading for the nursery for a crack with Algernon Aubrey, Bingo met Mrs Bingo in the hall. It seemed to him that her manner during the initial embracings and pippippings was a little strange.

'Bingo,' she said, 'do you know a girl named Valerie Twistleton?'

'Oh, rather. Pongo Twistleton's sister. Known her all my life. She's engaged to Horace Davenport.'

'Oh, is she?' Mrs Bingo seemed relieved. 'Then you don't see much of her now?'

'Not much. Why?'

'Nannie was saying that you made yourself rather conspicuous with her at that Christmas party at the Wilkinsons. She says you kept kissing her under the mistletoe. She says you used to kiss all the little girls.'

Bingo reeled. It was the last picture a husband would wish to be built up in his wife's mind's eye. Besides, a chivalrous man always shrinks from bandying a woman's name, and he was wondering what would happen if this loose talk were to come to the ears of Horace Davenport, the Drones Club's leading Othello.

'She must be thinking of someone else,' he said hoarsely. 'I was noted as a child for my aloofness and austerity. My manner towards the other sex was always scrupulously correct. Do you know what the extraordinary ramblings of this Byles suggest to me?' he went on. 'They suggest that the old blister is senile and quite unequal to the testing office of ministering to Algy. Boot her out is my advice and sign on someone younger.'

'You would prefer a young nurse?'

Bingo is no fool.

'Not a *young* nurse. A sensible, middle-aged nurse. I mean to say, Nannie Byles will never see a hundred and seven again.'

'She was fifty last birthday, she tells me.'

'She tells you. Ha!'

'Well, anyway, I wouldn't dream of letting her go. She is wonderful with Algy, and she looks after your things like a mother.'

'Oh, very well. Only don't blame me when it's too late.'

'When what's too late?'

'I don't know.' said Bingo. 'Something.'

As he went on to the nursery to pass the time of day with Algernon Aubrey, his heart was leaden. No question now of his ignoring his peril. He could not have been better informed regarding it if the facts had been broadcast on a nation-wide hook-up. A few more of these revelations from this voice from the past and he would sink to the level of a fifth-rate power. Somehow, by some means, he told himself, if his prestige in the home was to be maintained, he must get rid of this Nannie.

The woman knew too much.

As a matter of fact, though he would not have cared to have the thing known, his prestige at the moment was quite rocky enough without having any Nannies nibbling at the foundations. A very serious crisis was impending in his domestic affairs, threatening to make his name a hissing and a byword.

When Bingo receives his envelope from *Wee Tots* on the first of the month, it is too often his practice, in defiance of Mrs Bingo's expressed wishes, to place its contents on the nose of some horse of whose speed and resolution he has heard good reports, and such horses have a nasty habit of pausing half-way down the stretch to pick daisies. And this had happened now. A mistaken confidence in Sarsaparilla for the three o'clock at Ally Pally had not only cleaned him out but had left him owing his bookie ten quid. This tenner would have to be coughed up in the course of the next few days, and tenners in this iron age are hard to come by.

He had explored every avenue. He had bought a ticket for the club Darts sweep with his last ten bob, but had drawn a blank. He had tried to touch P. P. Purkiss for an advance of salary, but P. P. Purkiss had said that it was foreign to the policy of *Wee Tots* to brass up in advance. It really began to look as if he would be forced to the last awful extreme of biting Mrs Bingo's ear, which would mean that he might hear the last of it somewhere round about the afternoon of their golden wedding day, but scarcely before then.

It was a pretty poignant position of affairs, and what made Bingo so frightfully sick about it all was that if he had been the merest fraction of a second slippier when the hat for the Darts sweep was circulating, he would have been on velvet, for he would have secured that sweep's most glittering prize. He had started to reach out for a ticket, and just as his fingers were about to close on it Oofy Prosser had reached out ahead of him and scooped it in. And that ticket, when opened, had been found to contain the name of Horace Davenport.

Horace Davenport is a bird, who, while lacking many of the other qualities which go to make a superman, has always thrown a beautiful dart. Both at school and at the University his skill had been a byword among the sporting set, and the passage of the years had in no way diminished his accuracy. His eye was not dimmed nor his natural force abated, and anyone drawing his name in the sweep was entitled to regard the contents of the kitty as money in the bank. And this singular bit of goose, as I say, had fallen to the lot of Oofy Prosser, a bloke already stinking with the stuff. That was Oofy at the next table to us at lunch, the stout, pimpled chap. You probably noticed how rich he looked. That a fellow as oofy as Oofy should get the money seemed to Bingo a crime.

But the last thing he had anticipated was that the same reflection should have occurred to Oofy. Yet so it proved. He was in the club the morning before the Darts contest, and Oofy came up to him, looking, it seemed to Bingo, pensive. Though it is always hard to read the play of expression on Oofy's face, because of the pimples.

'What ho, Bingo,' said Oofy.

'What ho, Oofy,' said Bingo.

'I wonder, Bingo,' said Oofy, perking himself beside him and stroking the third pimple from the left in a meditative sort of way, 'if you have ever reflected how weird life is.'

Bingo agreed that life was pretty weird in spots, and Oofy said that what struck him about life – and he was a man who had gone into the thing – was that there was mismanagement somewhere.

'Gross mismanagement,' said Oofy. 'Well, as an instance of what I mean, take this Darts sweep. Think of all the eager, hard-up waifs who would have given their left eyeball to draw Horace

Davenport. And who gets him? I do. And what ensues? Horace is bound to win, so I spear thirty-three pound ten. What's the use of thirty-three pound ten to me? Do you know what my annual income is? No, I won't tell you, it would make you sick. It isn't right, Bingo,' said Oofy warmly. 'All wrong, Bingo. I shall give this ticket away. Would you like it, Bingo?'

Bingo, leaping in the air like a rising trout, said he would, and Oofy seemed to ponder. Then he said that giving Bingo the ticket might destroy Bingo's self-respect, and when Bingo urged very strongly that in his opinion the risk ought to be taken he pondered again.

'No,' he said at length, 'I should hate to have it on my mind that I had sapped a friend's self-respect. I will sell you this ticket, Bingo, for the nominal price of a fiver.'

A sharp cry of agony escaped Bingo. He had sufficient capital for the club luncheon at four-and-sixpence, but no more. Then an idea struck him.

'Will you hold it open for a couple of hours?'

'Certainly,' said Oofy. 'I shall be here till a quarter past one. Slip me the money then, and the ticket is yours.'

The idea that had struck Bingo was this. In his bedroom at home there was a set of diamond cuff-links, a present from Mrs Bingo on his last birthday, worth, he estimated, five pounds of any pawnbroker's money. What simpler than to secure these, thrust them up the spout, snaffle the Horace Davenport ticket, get his hooks on the thirty-three pounds ten, rush back to the pawnbroker's, de-spout the links and return to Position One? It would afford a masterly solution of the whole difficulty.

The Bingo residence, being one of those houses off Wimbledon Common, takes a bit of getting to, but he made good time there and sneaking in unobserved was able to present himself at the club at ten minutes past one. Oofy was still there. The five changed hands. And Bingo, who had stuck out for eight pounds ten at the pawnbroker's so as to have a bit of spending money, went off to the Savoy grill to revel. There are moments in a man's life when the club luncheon at four-and-sixpence is not enough.

And he had just got back to the office after the repast and was about to settle down to the composition of a thoughtful editorial on What Tiny Hands Can Do For Nannie, wishing that his own tiny hands could take her by the scruff of the neck and heave her out on her left ear, when Mrs Bingo rang up to say that, her mother having had one of her spells at her South Kensington abode, she was buzzing along there and would not be able to get home to-night.

Bingo said he would miss her sorely, and Mrs Bingo said she knew he would, and Bingo was preparing to toodle-oo and ring off, when Mrs Bingo uttered a sudden yip.

'Oh, Bingo, I knew there was something else. All this excitement about Mother put it out of my head. Your diamond links have been stolen!'

It was a pure illusion, of course, but Bingo tells me that as he heard these words it seemed to him that P. P. Purkiss, who was visible through the doorway of the inner office, suddenly started doing an Ouled Nail Stomach dance. His heart leaped sharply and became entangled with his tonsils. It was a matter of some moments before he was able to disengage it and reply.

'My links? Stolen? Absurd!'

'Well, Nannie says she was tidying your room just now and couldn't find them anywhere.'

Bingo was himself again.

'Nannie Byles,' he said sternly, 'is temperamentally incapable of finding a brass drum in a telephone booth. You are familiar with my views on that gibbering old fathead. Don't listen to a word she says.'

'Then you wouldn't advise sending for the police?'

'Certainly not. The police are busy men. It is not fair to waste their time.'

'Nannie says they would go round and make enquiries at all the pawnshops.'

'Exactly. And while they were doing it, what would happen? About fifty murders would be taking place and not a rozzer on duty to attend to them. One wishes sometimes that these Nannies had the rudiments of a civic conscience. Don't you worry about those links. I can tell you just where they are. They are ... no, I've forgotten. But it'll come back. Well, pip-pip, light of my life,' said Bingo, and rang off.

His first act on replacing the receiver was, you will scarcely be surprised to learn, to grab his hat and nip round to the Drones for a quick one; for despite the intrepid front he had put up the news that the A.W.O.L.-ness of those links had been discovered had shaken him to his foundations, and he was feeling a little like some Eliza who, crossing the ice, heard the baying of the pursuing bloodhounds.

But with the first sip of the restorative Reason returned to its throne, assuring him that there was absolutely no cause for alarm. The Darts tourney, Reason pointed out, was to take place to-morrow morning. He had the Horace Davenport ticket on his person. It followed then as doth the night the day, concluded Reason, that he would be able to restore the missing trinkets the moment he got home to-morrow afternoon.

He was just musing affectionately on Horace Davenport and feeling how fortunate he was in holding all rights to a dart hurler of his incomparable skill, when his attention was attracted by a deep sigh in his vicinity, and looking up he saw Horace approaching. And with a sudden sharp alarm he noted that something seemed to have gone wrong with the Davenport works. The other's face was pale and drawn and the eyes behind their tortoiseshell-rimmed glasses were like those of a dead fish.

'Stap my vitals, Horace,' he cried, deeply concerned, for naturally what he would have liked to see on the eve of the Darts tournament was a rosy-cheeked, bright-eyed Horace Davenport, full of pep, ginger and the will to win. 'You look a bit down among the wines and spirits. What's the matter?'

'Well, I'll tell you,' said Horace Davenport. 'You know Valerie Twistleton.'

'Yes.'

'You know I'm engaged to her.'

'Yes.'

'Well, that is where you make your ruddy error,' said Horace Davenport. 'I'm not. We have parted brass rags.'

'Why on earth?'

'Well, if you ask me, I think she loves another.'

'What rot!'

'I don't agree with you. We quarrelled about a mere trifle, and I maintain that no girl would have handed a man his hat for a trifle as mere as that, unless she had already decided to hitch on elsewhere and was looking out for a chance of giving him the gate.'

Bingo's tender heart was touched, of course, but he could not forget Horace's great mission.

'Too bad,' he said. 'But you mustn't brood on it, old man, or you'll go putting yourself off your stroke.'

'My stroke?'

'For the Darts binge to-morrow.'

'Oh, that? I shall not be competing,' said Horace dully. 'I'm going to scratch.'

Bingo uttered a quick howl like that of a Labrador timber wolf which has stubbed its toe on a jagged rock.

'Sker-ratch?'

'Exactly what Oofy Prosser said when I told him, in the same agitated voice. But I'm dashed if I can see why you're all so surprised,' said Horace. 'Is it likely, after what has happened, that I would be in any mood for bunging darts?'

A blinding light had flashed upon Bingo. I doubt if there are half-a-dozen fellows in the club, or ten at the outside, more capable than he of detecting funny business when such is afoot. He remembered now, what he ought to have remembered before, that Oofy, despite his colossal wealth, had always been a man who would walk ten miles in tight shoes to pick up even the meanest sum that was lying around loose.

At the thought of how the subtle schemer had chiselled him out of that fiver his soul blazed in revolt, and it was with an eloquence of which he had not supposed himself capable that he now began to plead with Horace Davenport to revise his intention of scratching for the Darts tournament. And so moving were the words in which he pictured the ruin which must befall him, should the other remove his name from the list of competitors, that Horace's better self awakened.

'This opens up a new line of thought,' said Horace. 'I didn't know Oofy had sold you that ticket. Well, to oblige you, Bingo, I will go through the hollow formality of entering the arena. But build no hopes on that. You can't aim darts when your heart is broken. My eyes will be so dim with unshed tears that I doubt if I'll he able to get a single double.'

As if the word 'double' had touched a chord in his mind, he moved off in the direction of the bar, and Bingo, clutching his head in both hands, started to think more tensely than he had ever thought in his puff.

There is no gainsaying the truth of Horace's parting words. If there is one thing calculated to take the edge off a fellow's form in an athletic contest, it is unrequited love. He recalled the time in his own bachelor days when a hopeless yearning for a girl whose name he had forgotten had ruined his putting touch for several weeks. What was needed here first and foremost, therefore, was some scheme for reconciling these two sundered hearts. The re-insertion of the love light in Valerie Twistleton's eyes would put Horace Davenport right back in mid-season form and the ticket bearing his name would once more be worth thirty-three quid of the best and brightest.

And it ought not, he felt, to be so dashed difficult to get that love light resuming work at the old stand. What Horace had said about Valerie having given him the air because she loved another he regarded as the purest apple-sauce. Honoured from time to time with the girl's confidence, he knew that she looked on the Darts wizard as a king among men. Obviously what had occurred was what is technically known as a lovers' tiff, and this he was convinced could be set right by a few well-chosen words from a polished man of the world.

Why, then, should he not get Valerie on the 'phone, ask her out for a bite of supper, and having lushed her up as far as his modest resources would permit plead with her to forgive and forget?

Bingo is a chap who knows a ball of fire when he sees one, and that this idea was a ball of fire he had no doubts whatever. He sped to the telephone booth, established communication, and a few minutes later the deal had been clinched. The girl checked up immediately on his proposition of a slab of supper, and suggested Mario's popular restaurant as the *mise en scène*.

'Okay, Valerie, old crumpet,' said Bingo, infinitely relieved. 'Eleven-fifteen at Mario's then.'

So far so good. A smooth bit of work. But it did not take Bingo long to realize that before the revels could begin there was one rather tricky hurdle to be surmounted. Nannie Byles, like the night, had a thousand eyes; and some pretty adroit manœuvring would be required if he was to get out of the house without her spotting him. He had no desire to be called upon to explain to Mrs Bingo on her return what he had been doing oozing off the premises in the soup and fish at half-past ten p.m. The statement that he had been on his way to give Valerie Twistleton a morsel of supper in her absence would, he felt, not go any too well.

Thinking quick, he saw the policy to pursue. Immediately upon arrival he touched the bell and desired the parlourmaid to inform La Byles that he would be glad of a word with her. And when the latter hove alongside, she found him lying on the sofa, a limp, interesting figure.

'Oh, Nannie,' he said, speaking faintly, 'I think I had better not come and hobnob with Algernon Aubrey to-night. I have a strange all-overish feeling, accompanied by floating spots before the eyes, and it may be catching. Explain the circumstances to him, give him my best and say I shall hope to see him to-morrow. I, meanwhile, will be popping straight up to bed and turning in.'

Well, of course, the Byles wanted to 'phone Mrs Bingo and summon medical aid and all that, but he managed to head her off and they eventually settled for a basin of gruel and a hot-water bottle. When these had been delivered at the bedside, Bingo said, still speaking faintly, that he didn't want to be disturbed again as his aim was to get a refreshing sleep.

After that everything was pretty smooth. At about ten-thirty he got up, hopped out of the window, eased himself down the water-pipe, was fortunate enough after waiting a short while at the garden gate to grab a passing taxi, and precisely at eleven-fifteen he alighted at the door of Mario's. And a few minutes later along blew Valerie Twistleton looking charming in some soft, clinging substance which revealed the slender lines of her figure, and the show was on.

Since the days when he had kissed her under the mistletoe at the Wilkinson's Christmas party there had come to exist between Bingo and this girl one of those calm, platonic friendships which so often occur when the blood has cooled and passion waned. Their relations now were such that he would be able to talk to her like a kindly elder brother. And as soon as he had headed her off from ordering champagne by persuading her that this wine is better avoided, causing as it does acidity and often culminating in spots, it was like a kindly elder brother that he jolly well intended to talk to her.

On his way to the restaurant he had debated whether to lead up to the subject of Horace by easy stages, but when they were seated at their table with a bottle of sound and inexpensive hock between them he decided to skip preliminaries and snap straight into the agenda.

'Well, I met your future bread-winner at the Drones this morning,' he said. 'We might drink a toast to him, what, with a hey nonny nonny and a hot cha-cha. Horace Davenport,' said Bingo, raising his glass.

A quick frown disfigured Valerie Twistleton's delicate brow. The state of Bingo's finances had precluded the serving of oysters, but had these been on the bill of fare you would have supposed from her expression and manner that the girl had bitten into a bad one.

'Don't mention that sub-human gargoyle's name in my presence,' she replied with considerable evidence of feeling. 'And don't allude to him as my future bread-winner. The wedding is off. I am through with Horace Pendlebury-by-golly-Davenport, and if he trips on a banana skin and breaks his bally neck, it will be all right with me.'

Bingo nodded. With subtle skill he had got the conversation just where he wanted it.

'Yes, he rather gave me to understand that there had been a certain modicum of rift-within-the-lute-ing, but he did not go into details. What seemed to be the trouble?'

A brooding look came into Valerie Twistleton's eyes. She gnashed her teeth slightly.

'I'll tell you,' she said. 'He had come round to our house and we were in the drawing-room chatting of this and that, and I happened to ask him to lie down on the floor and let Cyril, my cocker spaniel, nibble his nose, which the little angel loves. He said he wouldn't, and I said, "Oh, come on. Be a sport", and he said "No, he was blowed if he was going to be a stooge for a cocker spaniel". It ended with my digging out his letters and presents and handing them to him, together with the ring and his hat.'

Bingo t'ck-t'ck-t'ck-ed, and the girl asked him what he was t'ck-t'ck-t'ck-ing about.

'Wasn't I right?' she demanded passionately. 'Wasn't I ethically justified?'

Bingo started to be the kindly elder brother.

'We must always strive,' he urged, 'to look at these things from the other chap's point of view. Horace's, you must remember, is a sensitive, high strung nature. Many sensitive, high strung natures dislike being the supporting cast for cocker spaniels. Consider for a moment what his position would have been, had he agreed to your proposal. The spaniel would have hogged all the comedy, leaving him to all intents and purposes painted on the back drop. Not a pleasant situation for a proud man.'

If Valerie Twistleton had been a shade less pretty, one would say that she snorted.

'As if that was the trouble! Do you think I can't read between the lines? He just grabbed at that spaniel sequence as a pretext for severing diplomatic relations. Obviously what has happened is that he has gone and fallen in love with another girl and has been dying for an excuse to get rid of me. I wish you wouldn't laugh like a pie-eyed hyæna.'

Bingo explained that his reason for laughing like a pie-eyed hyæna was that he had been tickled by an amusing coincidence. Horace Davenport, he said, had made precisely the same charge against her.

'His view is that your affections are engaged elsewhere and that your giving him the bum's rush on account of his civil disobedience *in re* the cocker spaniel was simply a subterfuge. I happened to jot down his words, if you would care to hear them. "I maintain," said Horace, "that no girl would have handed a man his hat for a trifle as mere as that, unless she had already decided to hitch on elsewhere and was looking out for a chance of giving him the gate".'

The girl stared, wide-eyed.

'He must be crazy. "Decided to hitch on elsewhere", forsooth.

If I live a million years, I shall never love anyone but Horace. From the very moment we met I knew he was what the doctor had ordered. I don't chop and change. When I give my heart, it stays given. But he's not like me. He is a flitting butterfly and a two-timing Casanova. I'm sure there's another girl.'

'Your view, then, is that he is tickled pink to be freed from his obligations?'

'Yes, it is.'

'Then why,' said Bingo, whipping the ace of trumps from his sleeve, 'was he looking this morning when I met him at the Drones like a living corpse out of Edgar Allan Poe?'

Valerie Twistleton started.

'Was he?'

'You bet he was. And talking about his heart being broken. Have you ever seen those "before taking" pictures in the patent medicine advertisements?'

'Yes.'

'Horace,' said Bingo. 'He looked like a stretcher case in the last stages of lumbago, leprosy, galloping consumption and the botts.'

He paused, and noted that a misty film had dimmed the incandescence of his companion's eyes. Valerie Twistleton's lips were trembling, and the bit of chicken which she had been raising to her mouth fell from her listless fork.

'The poor old slob,' she murmured.

Bingo saw that the moment had come to sew up the contract. Striking while the iron is hot is, I believe, the expression.

'Then you will forgive him?'

'Of course.'

'All will be as it was before?'

'If anything, more so.'

'Fine,' said Bingo. 'I'll go and call him up and tell him. No doubt he will be round here with his foot in his hand within ten minutes of getting the glad news.'

He had sprung to his feet and was about to dash to the telephone but the girl stopped him.

'No,' she said.

Bingo goggled.

'No?' he repeated. 'How do you mean, no?'

She explained.

'He must have at least a couple of days in which to brood and yearn. So that the lesson can sink in, if you see what I mean. What one aims at is to get it firmly into his nut that he can't go chucking his weight about whenever he feels like it. I love him more than words can tell, but we must have discipline.'

Bingo was now stepping around like a cat on hot bricks. His agony was, as you may imagine, considerable.

'But the Darts tournament is to-morrow morning.'

'What Darts tournament?'

'The Drones Club's annual fixture. For a Horace with his mind at rest it is a sitter, but for a heartbroken Horace not a hope. If you don't believe me, let me quote his own words. "You can't aim darts when your heart is broken," he said, and I wish you could have heard the pain and anguish in his voice. "My eyes will be so dim with unshed tears", he said, "that I doubt if I'll be able to get a single double".'

'Well, what does a potty Darts tournament matter?'

And Bingo was just drawing a deep breath before starting in to explain to her in moving words just how much this Darts tournament mattered to him, when the top of his head suddenly came off and shot up to the ceiling.

That is to say, he felt as if it had done so. For at this moment there came to his ears, speaking loudly and authoritatively from the direction of the door, a voice.

'Don't talk to me, young man,' it was saying. 'I keep telling you that Master Richard is in here somewhere, and I insist on seeing him. He has a nasty feverish cold and I have brought him his woolly muffler.'

And there on the threshold stood Nannie Byles. She was holding in her hand a woolly muffler bearing the colours of the Drones Club and looking in an unfriendly way at some sort of assistant head waiter who was endeavouring to bar her progress into the restaurant.

I don't know if you ever came across a play of Shakespeare's called Macbeth? If you did, you may remember that this bird Macbeth bumps off another bird named Banquo and gives a big dinner to celebrate, and picture his embarrassment when about the first of the gay throng to show up is Banquo's ghost, all merry and bright, covered in blood. It gave him a pretty nasty start, Shakespeare does not attempt to conceal.

But it was nothing to the start Bingo got on observing Nannie Byles in his midst. He felt as if he had been lolling in the electric chair at Sing-Sing and some practical joker had suddenly turned on the juice. How the dickens she had tracked him here he was at a loss to imagine. It could scarcely have been by the sense of smell, and yet there didn't seem any other explanation.

However, he didn't waste much time musing on that. This, he perceived, was a moment for rapid action. There was a door just behind where he had been sitting, which from the fact that waiters had been going in and out he took to be the entrance to the service quarters. To press a couple of quid into Valerie Twistleton's hand to pay the bill with and leave her flat and do a swan dive backwards and shoot through this emergency exit and slip a friendly native half a crown to show him the way to the street was with him the work of an instant.

Five minutes later he was in a taxi, bowling off to The Nook, Wimbledon Common. Forty minutes later he was shinning up the water-pipe. Ten minutes later, clad in pyjamas and a dressing-gown, he was at the telephone trying to get Horace.

But Horace's number was the silent tomb. The girl at the exchange said she had rung and rung and rung, and Bingo said Well, ring and ring and ring again. So she rang and rang and rang again, but there was still no answer, and eventually Bingo had to give it up and go to bed.

But it was by no means immediately that he fell into a dreamless sleep. The irony of the thing was like ants in the pants, causing him to toss restlessly on the pillow.

I mean to say, he had so nearly clicked. That was the bitter thought. He had achieved the object which he had set out to achieve – viz, the bringing together of the sundered hearts of V. Twistleton and H. Davenport, but unless he could get Horace on the 'phone in the morning and put him abreast before the Darts tourney began, all would be lost. It was a fat lot of consolation to feel that a couple of days from now Horace Davenport would be going about with his hat on the side of his head, slapping people on the back and standing them drinks. What was of the essence was to have him in that condition to-morrow morning.

He brooded on what might have been. If only he had been able to give Valerie Twistleton the heart-melting talk he had been planning. If only Nannie Byles had postponed her appearance for another quarter of an hour. Bingo is a pretty chivalrous chap and one who, wind and weather permitting, would never lay a hand upon a woman save in the way of kindness, but if somebody at that moment had given him a blunt knife and asked him to skin Nannie Byles with it and drop her into a vat of boiling oil, he would have sprung to the task with his hair in a braid.

The vital thing, he was feeling, as he at last dozed off, was to be up bright and early next day, so as to connect with Horace in good time.

Which being so, you as a man who knows life will not be surprised to hear that what happened was that he overslept himself. When he finally came out of the ether and hared to the telephone, it was the same old story. The girl at the exchange rang and rang and rang, but there was no answer. Bingo tried the Drones, but was informed that Horace had not yet arrived. There seemed nothing for it but to get dressed and go to the club.

By the time he got there the Darts tourney would, of course, be in full swing, and he could picture the sort of Horace Davenport that would be competing. A limp, listless Horace Davenport, looking like a filleted sole.

It was hardly worth going in, he felt, when he reached the club, but something seemed to force him through the doorway: and he was approaching the smoking-room on leaden feet, when the door opened and out came Barmy Fotheringay-Phipps and Catsmeat Potter-Pirbright.

'A walkover,' Barmy was saying.

A sudden irrational hope stirred in Bingo's bosom like a jumping bean. It was silly, of course, to think that Barmy had been speaking about Horace, but the level of form at the Drones, except for that pre-eminent expert, is so steady that he could not picture any of the other competitors having a walkover. He clutched Barmy's coat sleeve in a feverish grip.

'Who for?' he gasped.

'Oh, hullo, Bingo,' said Barmy. 'The very chap we wanted to see. Catsmeat and I have collaborated in an article for that paper of yours entitled "Some Little-Known Cocktails". We were just going round to the office to give it to you.'

Bingo accepted the typewritten sheets absently. In his editorial capacity he was always glad to consider unsolicited contributions (though these, he was careful to point out, must be submitted at their authors' risk), and a thesis on such a subject by two such acknowledged authorities could scarcely fail to be fraught with interest, but at the moment his mind was far removed from the conduct of *Wee Tots*.

'Who's it a walkover for?' he said hoarsely.

'Horace Davenport, of course,' said Catsmeat Potter-Pirbright. 'He has been playing inspired Darts. If you go in quick, you may be able to catch a glimpse of his artistry.'

But Bingo was too late. When he entered the smoking-room, the contest was over and Horace Davenport, the centre of an eager group of friends and admirers, was receiving congratulations, a popular winner – except with Oofy Prosser, who was sitting in a corner pale and haggard beneath his pimples. Seeing Bingo, the champion detached himself and came over to him.

'Oh, hullo, Bingo,' said Horace, 'I was hoping you would look in. I wanted a word with you. You remember that broken heart of mine? Well, it's all right. Not broken, after all. A complete reconciliation was effected shortly before midnight last night at Mario's.'

Bingo was amazed.

'You came to Mario's?'

'Thanks to you,' said Horace Davenport, massaging his arm gratefully. 'I must mention, Bingo, that after I had told you about my broken heart yesterday, I suddenly remembered that there were one or two things about it which I had forgotten to touch on. So I came back. They said you had been seen going to the 'phone booth, so I pushed along there. You had left the door ajar, and picture my horror on hearing you talking to Valerie and making an assignation with her at Mario's.'

'I simply wanted—' began Bingo, but Horace continued.

'I reeled away blindly. I was distraught. I had been telling myself that Valerie was being false to me with another, but I had never for an instant suspected that this snake in the grass was my old friend Richard Little, a chap with whom when at school I had frequently shared my last acid drop.'

'But listen. I simply wanted—'

'Well, I said to myself "I'll give them about half an hour, and then I'll go to Mario's and stride in and confront them. This," I said to myself, "will make them feel pretty silly." So I did. But when I got there, you had legged it and were not there to be confronted. So I confronted Valerie.'

'Listen, Horace, old egg,' said Bingo, insisting on being heard, 'I simply wanted to shoot a bit of nourishment into her for mellowing purposes and then plead your cause.'

'I know. She told me. She said you had talked to her like a kindly elder brother. What arguments you used I cannot say, but they dragged home the gravy plenteously. I found her in melting mood. We came together with a click, and the wedding is fixed for the twenty-third *prox*. And now, Bingo,' said Horace, looking at his watch, 'I shall have to be leaving you. I promised Valerie I would drop in directly the Darts contest was over and let her cocker spaniel nibble my nose. The animal seems to wish it, and I think we all ought to do our best to spread sweetness and light, even at some slight personal inconvenience. Good-bye, Bingo, and a thousand thanks. I can give you a lift, if you are coming my way.'

'Thanks,' said Bingo, 'but I must collect that thirty-three pound ten. After that I have one or two little things to do, and then I must be nipping home.'

Bingo reached The Nook in good time. And he had replaced the links in their box and was about to leave his bedroom, when Mrs Bingo shoved her head in the door.

'Why, Bingo darling,' she said, 'aren't you at the office?'

'I just popped back to see you,' explained Bingo. 'How's your mother?'

'Much better,' said Mrs Bingo. She seemed distrait. 'Bingo, darling,' she said after a bit of a pause, revealing the seat of the trouble, 'I'm a little worried. About Nannie.'

'About Nannie?'

'Yes. When you were a child, do you remember her as being at all . . . eccentric?'

'Eccentric?'

'Well, the most extraordinary thing happened last night. Where were you last night, Bingo?'

'I went to bed early.'

'You didn't go out?'

Bingo stared.

'Go *out*?'

'No, of course you didn't,' said Mrs Bingo. 'But Nannie declares that at about half-past ten she was walking in the garden getting a breath of fresh air, and she saw you jump into a cab—'

Bingo looked grave. He gave a low whistle.

'Started seeing things, eh? Bad. Bad.'

'— and she says she heard you tell the driver to go to Mario's.'

'Hearing voices, too? Worse. Worse.'

'And she followed you with your woolly muffler. She had to wait a long time before she could get a cab, and when she got to the restaurant they wouldn't let her in, and there was a lot of trouble about that, and then she found she had no money to pay the cab, and there was a lot of trouble about that, too, and I think in the end she must have lost her temper a little or she would never have boxed the cabman's ears and bitten that waiter.'

'Bit a waiter, did she?'

'She said she didn't like his manner. And after that they sent for the police and she was taken to Vine Street, and she telephoned to me to come and bail her out. So I went round to the police station and bailed her out, and she told me this extraordinary story about you. I hurried home and peeped in at your door, and there you were, fast asleep of course.'

'Of course.'

Mrs Bingo chewed the lower lip.

'It's all very disturbing.'

'Now there, with all due deference to you, my talented old scrivener,' said Bingo, 'I think you have missed the *mot juste*. I would call it appalling. Let me tell you something else that will make you think a bit. You remember all that song and dance she made about my links having been stolen. Well, I've just been taking a look, and they're in their usual box in the usual place on the dressing-table, just where they've always been.'

'Really?'

'I assure you. Well,' said Bingo, 'suit yourself, of course, but I should have thought we were taking a big chance entrusting our first-born to the care of a Nannie who is loopy to the eyebrows and constantly seeing visions and what not, to make no mention of hearing voices and not being able to see a set of diamond cuff-links when they're staring her in the face. I threw out the suggestion once before, and it was not well received, but I will make it again. Give her the push, moon of my delight. Pension her off. Slip her a few quid per and a set of your books and let her retire to some honeysuckle-covered cottage where she can't do any harm.'

'I believe you're right.'

'I know I'm right,' said Bingo. 'You don't want her suddenly getting the idea that Algernon Aubrey is a pink hippopotamus and loosing off at him with her elephant rifle, do you? Very well, then.'

A general meeting had been called at the Drones to decide on the venue for the club's annual golf rally, and the school of thought that favoured Bramley-on-Sea was beginning to make headway when Freddie Widgeon took the floor. In a speech of impassioned eloquence he warned his hearers not to go within fifty miles of the beastly place. And so vivid was the impression he conveyed of Bramley-on-Sea as a spot where the law of the jungle prevailed and anything could happen to anybody that the voters were swayed like reeds and the counter proposal of Cooden Beach was accepted almost unanimously.

His warmth excited comment at the bar.

'Freddie doesn't like Bramley,' said an acute Egg, who had been thinking it over with the assistance of a pink gin.

'Possibly,' suggested a Bean, 'because he was at school there when he was a kid.'

The Crumpet who had joined the group shook his head.

'No, it wasn't that,' he said. 'Poor old Freddie had a very painful experience at Bramley recently, culminating in his getting the raspberry from the girl he loved.'

'What, again?'

'Yes. It's curious about Freddie,' said the Crumpet, sipping a thoughtful martini. 'He rarely fails to click, but he never seems able to go on clicking. A whale at the Boy Meets Girl stuff, he is unfortunately equally unerring at the Boy Loses Girl.'

'Which of the troupe was it who gave him the air this time?' asked an interested Pieface.

'Mavis Peasmarch. Lord Bodsham's daughter.'

'But, dash it,' protested the Pieface, 'that can't be right. She returned him to store ages ago. You told us about it yourself. That time in New York when he got mixed up with the female in the pink négligée picked out with ultramarine lovebirds.'

The Crumpet nodded.

'Quite true. He was, as you say, handed his portfolio on that occasion. But Freddie is a pretty gifted explainer, if you give him time to mould and shape his story, and on their return to England he appears to have squared himself somehow. She took him on again – on appro., as it were. The idea was that if he proved himself steady and serious, those wedding bells would ring out. If not, not a tinkle.

'Such was the position of affairs when he learned from this Peasmarch that she and her father were proposing to park themselves for the summer months at the Hotel Magnifique at Bramley-on-Sea.'

Freddie's instant reaction to this news was, of course (said the Crumpet), an urge to wangle a visit there himself, and he devoted the whole force of his intellect to trying go think how this could be done. He shrank from spending good money on a hotel, but on the other hand his proud soul scorned a boarding-house, and what they call an *impasse* might have resulted, had he not discovered that Bingo Little and Mrs Bingo had taken a shack at Bramley in order that the Bingo baby should get its whack of ozone. Bramley, as I dare say you have seen mentioned on the posters, is so bracing, and if you are a parent you have to think of these things. Brace the baby, and you are that much ahead of the game.

To cadge an invitation was with Freddie the work of a moment, and a few days later he arrived with suitcase and two-seater, deposited the former, garaged the latter, kissed the baby and settled in.

Many fellows might have objected to the presence on the premises of a bib-and-bottle juvenile, but Freddie has always been a good mixer, and he and this infant hit it off from the start like a couple of sailors on shore leave. It became a regular thing with him to take the half-portion down to the beach and stand by while it mucked about with its spade and bucket. And it was as he was acting as master of the revels one sunny day that there came ambling along a well-nourished girl with golden hair, who paused and scrutinized the Bingo issue with a genial smile.

'Is the baby building a sand castle?' she said.

'Well, yes and no,' replied Freddie civilly. 'It thinks it is, but if you ask me, little of a constructive nature will result.'

'Still, so long as it's happy.'

'Oh, quite.'

'Nice day.'

'Beautiful.'

'Could you tell me the correct time?'

'Precisely eleven.'

'Coo!' said the girl. 'I must hurry, or I shall be late. I'm meeting a gentleman friend of mine on the pier at half-past ten.'

And that was that. I mean, just one of those casual encounters which are so common at the seashore, with not a word spoken on either side that could bring the blush of shame to the cheek of modesty. I stress this, because this substantial blonde was to become entangled in Freddie's affairs and I want to make it clear at the outset that from start to finish he was as pure as the driven snow. Sir Galahad could have taken his correspondence course.

It was about a couple of days after this that a picture postcard, forwarded from his London address, informed him that Mavis and her father were already in residence at the Magnifique, and he dashed into the two-seater and drove round there with a beating heart. It was his intention to take the loved one for a spin, followed by a spot of tea at some wayside shoppe.

This project, however, was rendered null and void by the fact that she was out. Old Bodsham, receiving Freddie in the suite, told him that she had gone to take her little brother Wilfred back to his school.

'We had him for lunch,' said the Bod.

'No, did you?' said Freddie. 'A bit indigestible, what?' He laughed heartily for some moments at his ready wit; then, seeing that the gag had not got across, cheesed it. He remembered now that there had always been something a bit Wednesday-matinee-ish about the fifth Earl of Bodsham. An austere man, known to his circle of acquaintants as The Curse of the Eastern Counties. 'He's at school here, is he?'

'At St Asaph's. An establishment conducted by an old college friend of mine, the Rev. Aubrey Upjohn.'

'Good Lord!' said Freddie, feeling what a small world it was. 'I used to be at St Asaph's.'

'Indeed?'

'Absolutely. I served a three years' sentence there before going on to Eton. Well, I'll be pushing along, then. Give Mavis my love, will you, and say I'll be round bright and early in the morning.'

He buzzed off and hopped into the car again, and for the space of half an hour or so drove about Bramley, feeling a bit at a loose end. And he was passing through a spot called Marina Crescent, a sort of jungle of boarding-houses, when he became aware that stirring things were happening in his immediate vicinity.

Along the road towards him there had been approaching a well-nourished girl with golden hair. I don't suppose he had noticed her – or, if he had, it was merely to say to himself 'Ah, the substantial blonde I met on the beach the other morning' and dismiss her from his thoughts. But at this moment she suddenly thrust herself on his attention by breaking into a rapid gallop, and at the same time a hoarse cry rent the air, not unlike that of the lion of the desert scenting its prey, and Freddie perceived charging out of a side street an elderly man with whiskers, who looked as if he might be a retired sea captain or a drysalter or something.

The spectacle perplexed him. He had always known that Bramley was bracing, but he had never supposed that it was as bracing as all this. And he had pulled up in order to get a better view, when the substantial blonde, putting on a burst of speed in the straight, reached the car and hurled herself into it.

'Quick!' she cried.

'Quick?' said Freddie. He was puzzled. 'In what sense do you use the word "Quick"?' he asked, and was about to go further into the thing when the whiskered bird came dashing up and scooped the girl out of the car as if she had been a winkle and his hand a pin.

The girl grabbed hold of Freddie, and Freddie grabbed hold of the steering wheel, and the whiskered bird continued to freeze on to the girl, and for a while the human chain carried on along these lines. Then there was a rending sound, and the girl and Freddie came apart.

The whiskered bozo regarded him balefully.

'If we weren't in a public place,' he said, 'I would horsewhip you. If I had a horsewhip.'

And with these words he dragged the well-nourished girl from the scene, leaving Freddie, as you may well suppose, quite a bit perturbed and a long way from grasping the inner meaning.

The recent fracas had left him half in and half out of the car, and he completed the process by alighting. He had an idea that the whiskered ancient might have scratched his paint. But fortunately everything was all right, and he was leaning against the bonnet, smoking a soothing cigarette, when Mavis Peasmarch spoke behind him.

'Frederick!' she said.

Freddie tells me that at the sound of that loved voice he sprang six feet straight up in the air, but I imagine this to be an exaggeration. About eighteen inches, probably. Still, he sprang quite high enough to cause those leaning out of the windows of Marina Crescent to fall into the error of supposing him to be an adagio dancer practising a new step.

'Oh, hullo, darling!' he said.

He tried to speak in a gay and debonair manner, but he could not but recognize that he had missed his objective by a mile. Gazing at Mavis Peasmarch, he noted about her a sort of rigidity which he didn't like. Her eyes were stern and cold, and her lips tightly set. Mavis had inherited from her father that austere Puritanism which makes the old boy so avoided by the County, and this she was now exuding at every pore.

'So there you are!' he said, still having a stab at the gay and debonair.

'Yes,' said Mavis Peasmarch.

'I'm here, too,' said Freddie.

'So I see,' said Mavis Peasmarch.

'I'm staying with a pal. I thought I'd come here and surprise you.'

'You have,' said Mavis Peasmarch. She gave a sniff that sounded like a nor'easter ripping the sails of a stricken vessel. 'Frederick, what does this mean?'

'Eh?'

'That girl.'

'Oh, that *girl*?' said Freddie. 'Yes, I see what you mean. You are speaking of that girl. Most extraordinary, wasn't it?'

'Most.'

'She jumped into my car, did you notice?'

'I did. An old friend?'

'No, no. A stranger, and practically total, at that.'

'Oh?' said Mavis Peasmarch, and let go another sniff that went echoing down the street. 'Who was the old man?'

'I don't know. Another stranger, even more total.'

'He said he wanted to horsewhip you.'

'Yes, I heard him. Dashed familiar.'

'Why did he want to horsewhip you?'

'Ah, there you've got me. The man's thought processes are a sealed book to me.'

'The impression I received was that he resented your having made his daughter the plaything of an idle hour.'

'But I didn't. As a matter of fact, I haven't had much spare time since I got here.'

'Oh?'

'The solution that suggests itself to me is that we have stumbled up against one of those E. Phillips Oppenheim situations.

Yes, that would explain the whole thing. Here's how I figure it out. The girl is an international spy. She got hold of the plans of the fortifications and was taking them to an accomplice, when along came the whiskered bird, a secret service man. You could see those whiskers were a disguise. He thought I was the accomplice.'

'Oh?'

'How's your brother Wilfred?' asked Freddie, changing the subject.

'Will you please drive me to my hotel,' said Mavis, changing it again.

'Oh, right,' said Freddie. 'Right.'

That night, Freddie lay awake, ill at ease. There had been something in the adored object's manner, when he dropped her at the hotel, which made him speculate as to whether that explanation of his had got over quite so solidly as he had hoped. He had suggested coming in and having a cosy chat, and she had said No, please, I have a headache. He had said how well she was looking, and she had said Oh! And when he had asked her if she loved her little Freddie, she had made no audible response.

All in all, it looked to Freddie as if what is technically called a lovers' tiff had set in with a good deal of severity, and as he lay tossing on his pillow he pondered quite a bit on how this could be adjusted.

What was needed here, he felt, was a gesture – some spectacular performance on his part which would prove that his heart was in the right place.

But what spectacular performance?

He toyed with the idea of saving Mavis from drowning, only to dismiss it when he remembered that on the rare occasions when she took a dip in the salty she never went in above the waist.

He thought of rescuing old Bodsham from a burning building. But how to procure that burning building? He couldn't just set a match to the Hotel Magnifique and expect it to go up in flames.

And then, working through the family, he came to little Wilfred, and immediately got a Grade-A inspiration. It was via Wilfred that he must oil back into Mavis's esteem. And it could be done, he saw, by going to St Asaph's and asking the Rev. Aubrey Upjohn to give the school a half-holiday. This kindly act would put him right back in the money.

He could picture the scene. Wilfred would come bounding in to tea one afternoon. 'Coo!' Mavis would exclaim. 'What on earth are you doing here? Have you run away from school?' 'No,' Wilfred would reply, 'the school has run away from me. In other words, thanks to Freddie Widgeon, that prince of square-shooters, we have been given a half-holiday.' 'Well, I'm blowed!' Mavis would ejaculate. 'Heaven bless Freddie Widgeon! I had a feeling all along that I'd been misjudging that bird.'

At this point, Freddie fell asleep.

Often, when you come to important decisions overnight, you find after sleeping on them that they are a bit blue around the edges. But morning, when it came, found Freddie still resolved to go through with his day's good deed. If, however, I were to tell you that he liked the prospect, I should be deceiving you. It is not too much to say that he quailed at it. Years had passed since his knickerbocker days, but the Rev. Aubrey Upjohn was still green in his memory. A man spiritually akin to Simon Legree and the late Captain Bligh of the *Bounty*, with whose disciplinary methods his own had much in common, he had made a deep impression on Freddie's plastic mind, and the thought of breezing in and trying to sting him for a half-holiday was one that froze the blood more than a bit.

But two things bore him on: (a) his great love, and (b) the fact that it suddenly occurred to him that he could obtain a powerful talking point by borrowing Bingo's baby and taking it along with him.

Schoolmasters, he knew, are always anxious to build for the future. To them, the infant of to-day is the pupil at so much per of to-morrow. It would strengthen his strategic position enormously if he dangled Bingo's baby before the man's eyes and said: 'Upjohn, I can swing a bit of custom your way. My influence with the parents of this child is stupendous. Treat me right, and down it goes on your waiting list.' It would make all the difference.

So, waiting till Bingo's back and Mrs Bingo's back were turned, he scooped up Junior and started out. And presently he was ringing the front door bell of St Asaph's, the younger generation over his arm, concealed beneath a light overcoat. The parlourmaid showed him into the study, and he was left there to drink in the details of the well-remembered room which he had not seen for so many years.

Now, it so happened that he had hit the place at the moment when the Rev. Aubrey was taking the senior class in Bible history, and when a headmaster has got his teeth into a senior class he does not readily sheathe the sword. There was consequently a longish stage wait, and as the minutes passed Freddie began to find the atmosphere of the study distinctly oppressive.

The last time he had been in this room, you see, the set-up had been a bit embarrassing. He had been bending over a chair, while the Rev. Aubrey Upjohn, strongly posted in his rear, stood measuring the distance with half-closed eyes, preparatory to bringing the old malacca down on his upturned trousers seat. And memories like this bring with them a touch of sadness.

Outside the French window the sun was shining, and it seemed to Freddie that what was needed to dissipate the feeling of depression from which he had begun to suffer was a stroll in the garden with a cigarette. He sauntered out, accordingly, and had paced the length of the grounds and was gazing idly over the fence at the end of them, when he perceived that beyond this fence a certain liveliness was in progress.

He was looking into a small garden, at the back of which was a house. And at an upper window of this house was a girl. She was waving her arms at him.

It is never easy to convey every shade of your meaning by waving your arms at a distance of forty yards, and Freddie not unnaturally missed quite a good deal of the gist. Actually, what the girl was trying to tell him was that she had recently met at the bandstand on the pier a man called George Perkins, employed in a London firm of bookmakers doing business under the trade name of Joe Sprockett; that a mutual fondness for the Overture to *Zampa* had drawn them together; that she had become deeply enamoured of him; that her tender sentiments had been fully reciprocated; that her father, who belonged to a religious sect which disapproved of bookmakers, had refused to sanction the match or even to be introduced to the above Perkins; that he – her father – had intercepted a note from the devout lover, arranging for a meeting at the latter's boarding-house (10, Marina Crescent) and a quick wedding at the local registrar's; and that he – she was still alluding to her father – had now locked her in her room until, in his phrase, she should come to her senses. And what she wanted Freddie to do was let her out. Because good old George was waiting at 10, Marina Crescent with the licence, and if she could only link up with him they could put the thing through promptly.

Freddie, as I say, did not get quite all of this, but he got enough of it to show him that here was a damsel in distress, and he was stirred to his foundations. He had not thought that this sort of thing happened outside the thrillers, and even there he had supposed it to be confined to moated castles. And this wasn't a moated castle by any means. It was a two-story desirable residence with a slate roof, standing in park-like grounds extending to upwards of a quarter of an acre. It looked the sort of place that might belong to a retired sea captain or possibly a drysalter.

Full of the old knight-errant spirit, for he has always been a pushover for damsels in distress, he leaped the fence with sparkling eyes. And it was only when he was standing beneath the window that he recognized in the girl who was goggling at him through the glass like some rare fish in an aquarium his old acquaintance, the substantial blonde.

The sight cooled him off considerably. He is rather a superstitious sort of chap, and he had begun to feel that this billowy curver wasn't lucky for him. He remembered now that a gipsy had once warned him to beware of a fair woman, and for a moment it was touch and go whether he wouldn't turn away and ignore the whole unpleasant affair. However, the old knight-errant spirit was doing its stuff, and he decided to carry on as planned. Gathering from a quick twist of her eyebrows that the key was in the outside of the door, he nipped in through the sitting-room window, raced upstairs and did the needful. And a moment later she was emerging like a cork out of a bottle and shooting down the stairs. She whizzed into the sitting-room and whizzed through the window, and he whizzed after her.

And the first thing he saw as he came skimming over the sill was her galloping round the lawn, closely attended by the whiskered bloke who had scooped her out of the car in Marina Crescent. He had a three-pronged fork in his possession and was whacking at her with the handle, getting a bull's-eye at about every second shot.

It came as a great surprise to Freddie, for he had distinctly understood from the way the girl had twiddled her fingers that her father was at the croquet club, and for a moment he paused, uncertain what to do.

He decided to withdraw. No chivalrous man likes to see a woman in receipt of a series of juicy ones with a fork handle, but the thing seemed to him one of those purely family disputes which can only be threshed out between father and daughter. He had started to edge away, accordingly, when the whiskered bloke observed him and came charging in his direction, shouting the old drysalters' battle cry. One can follow his train of thought, of course. He supposed Freddie to be George Perkins, the lovelorn bookie, and wished to see the colour of his insides. With a good deal of emotion, Freddie saw that he was now holding the fork by the handle.

Exactly what the harvest would have been, had nothing occurred to interfere with the old gentleman's plans, it is hard to say. But by great good fortune he tripped over a flower-pot while he was still out of jabbing distance and came an impressive purler. And before he could get right side up again, Freddie had seized the girl, hurled her over the fence, leaped the fence himself and started lugging her across the grounds of St Asaph's to his car, which he had left at the front door.

The going had been so good, and the substantial blonde was in such indifferent condition, that even when they were in the car and bowling off little came through in the way of conversation. The substantial blonde, having gasped out a request that he drive her to 10, Marina Crescent, lay back panting, and was still panting when they reached journey's end. He decanted her and drove off. And it was as he drove off that he became aware of something missing. Something he should have had on his person was not on his person.

He mused.

His cigarette case?

No, he had his cigarette case.

His hat?

No, he had his hat.

His small change? . . .

And then he remembered. Bingo's baby. He had left it chewing a bit of indiarubber in the Rev. Aubrey Upjohn's study.

Well, with his nervous system still all churned up by his recent experiences, an interview with his old preceptor was not a thing to which he looked forward with anything in the nature of ecstasy, but he's a pretty clear-thinking chap, and he realized that you can't go strewing babies all over the place and just leave them. So he went back to St Asaph's and trotted round to the study window. And there inside was the Rev. Aubrey, pacing the floor in a manner which the most vapid and irreflective observer would have recognized as distraught.

I suppose practically the last thing an unmarried schoolmaster wants to find in his sanctum is an unexplained baby, apparently come for an extended visit; and the Rev. Aubrey Upjohn, on entering the study shortly after Freddie had left it and noting contents, had sustained a shock of no slight order. He viewed the situation with frank concern.

And he was turning to pace the floor again, when he got another shock. He had hoped to be alone, to think this thing over from every angle, and there was a young man watching him from the window. On this young man's face there was what seemed to him a sneering grin. It was really an ingratiating smile, of course, but you couldn't expect a man in the Rev. Aubrey's frame of mind to know that.

'Oh, hullo,' said Freddie. 'You remember me, don't you?'

'No, I do not remember you,' cried the Rev. Aubrey. 'Go away.'

Freddie broadened the ingratiating smile an inch or two.

'Former pupil. Name of Widgeon.'

The Rev. Aubrey passed a weary hand over his brow. One can understand how he must have felt. First this frightful blow, I mean to say, and on top of that the re-entry into his life of a chap he hoped he'd seen the last of years and years ago.

'Yes,' he said, in a low, toneless voice. 'Yes, I remember you. Widgeon.'

'F. F.'

'F., as you say, F. What do you want?'

'I came back for my baby,' said Freddie, like an apologetic plumber.

The Rev. Aubrey started.

'Is this your baby?'

'Well, technically, no. On loan, merely. Some time ago, my pal Bingo Little married Rosie M. Banks, the well-known female novelist. This is what you might call the upshot.'

The Rev. Aubrey seemed to be struggling with some powerful emotion.

'Then it was you who left this baby in my study?'

'Yes. You see—'

'Ha!' said the Rev. Aubrey, and went off with a pop, as if suffering from spontaneous combustion.

Freddie tells me that few things have impressed him more than the address to which he now listened. He didn't like it, but it extorted a grudging admiration. Here was this man, he meant to say, unable as a clerk in Holy Orders to use any of the words which would have been at the disposal of a layman, and yet by sheer force of character rising triumphantly over the handicap. Without saying a thing that couldn't have been said in the strictest drawing-room, the Rev. Aubrey Upjohn contrived to produce in Freddie the illusion that he had had a falling out with the bucko mate of a tramp steamer. And every word he uttered made it more difficult to work the conversation round to the subject of half-holidays.

Long before he had reached his 'thirdly', Freddie was feeling as if he had been chewed up by powerful machinery, and when he was at length permitted to back out, he felt that he had had a merciful escape. For quite a while it had seemed more than likely that he was going to be requested to bend over that chair again. And such was the Rev. Aubrey's magnetic personality that he would have done it, he tells me, like a shot.

Much shaken, he drove back to the Bingo residence, and the first thing he saw on arriving there was Bingo standing on the steps, looking bereaved to the gills.

'Freddie,' yipped Bingo, 'have you seen Algernon?'

Freddie's mind was not at its clearest.

'No,' he said. 'I don't think I've run across him. Algernon who? Pal of yours? Nice chap?'

Bingo hopped like the high hills.

'My baby, you ass.'

'Oh, the good old baby? Yes, I've got him.'

'Six hundred and fifty-seven curses!' said Bingo. 'What the devil did you want to go dashing off with him for? Do you realize we've been hunting for him all the morning?'

'You wanted him for something special?'

'I was just going to notify the police and have dragnets spread.'

Freddie could see that an apology was in order.

'I'm sorry,' he said. 'Still, all's well that ends well. Here he is. Oh no, he isn't,' he added, having made a quick inspection of the interior of the car. 'I say, this is most unfortunate. I seem to have left him again.'

'Left him?'

'What with all the talk that was going on, he slipped my mind. But I can give you his address, Care of the Rev. Aubrey Upjohn, St Asaph's, Mafeking Road, Bramley-on-Sea. All you have to do is step round at your leisure and collect him. I say, is lunch ready?'

'Lunch?' Bingo laughed a hideous, mirthless laugh. At least, that's what Freddie thinks it was. It sounded like a bursting tyre. 'A fat lot of lunch you're going to get. The cook's got hysterics, the kitchen-maid's got hysterics, and so have the parlourmaid and the housemaid. Rosie started having hysterics as early as eleven-thirty, and is now in bed with an ice pack. When she finds out about this, I wouldn't be in your shoes for a million quid. Two million,' added Bingo. 'Or, rather, three.'

This was an aspect of the matter which had not occurred to Freddie. He saw that there was a good deal in it.

'Do you know, Bingo,' he said, 'I believe I ought to be getting back to London to-day.'

'I would.'

'Several things I've got to do there, several most important things. I dare say, if I whipped back to town, you could send my luggage after me?'

'A pleasure.'

'Thanks,' said Freddie. 'You won't forget the address, will you? St Asaph's, Mafeking Road. Mention my name, and say you've come for the baby I inadvertently left in the study. And now, I think, I ought to be getting round to see Mavis. She'll be wondering what has become of me.'

He tooled off, and a few minutes later was entering the lobby of the Hotel Magnifique. The first thing he saw was Mavis and her father standing by a potted palm.

'Hullo, hullo,' he said, toddling up.

'Ah, Frederick,' said old Bodsham.

I don't know if you remember, when I was telling you about that time in New York, my mentioning that at a rather sticky point in the proceedings Freddie had noticed that old Bodsham was looking like a codfish with something on its mind. The same conditions prevailed now.

'Frederick,' proceeded the Bod, 'Mavis has been telling me a most unpleasant story.'

Freddie hardly knew what to say to this. He was just throwing a few sentences together in his mind about the modern girl being sound at heart despite her freedom of speech, and how there isn't really any harm in it if she occasionally gets off one from the smoking-room – tolerant, broad-minded stuff, if you know what I mean – when old Bodsham resumed.

'She tells me you have become entangled with a young woman with golden hair.'

'A fat young woman with golden hair,' added Mavis, specifying more exactly.

Freddie waved his arms passionately, like a semaphore.

'Nothing in it,' he cried. 'Nothing whatever. The whole thing greatly exaggerated. Mavis,' he said, 'I am surprised, and considerably pained. I should have thought that you would have had more trust in me. Kind hearts are more than coronets and simple faith than Norman blood,' he went on, for he had always remembered that gag after having to write it out two hundred times at school for loosing off a stink bomb in the form-room. 'I told you she was a total stranger.'

'Then how does it happen that you were driving her through the streets of Bramley in your car this morning?' said old Bodsham.

'Yes,' said Mavis. 'That is what I want to know.'

'It is a point,' said old Bodsham, 'upon which we would both be glad to receive information.'

Catch Freddie at a moment like this, and you catch him at his best. His heart, leaping from its moorings, had loosened one of his front teeth, but there was absolutely nothing in his manner to indicate it. His eyes, as he stared at them, were those of a spotless bimbo cruelly wronged by a monstrous accusation.

'Me?' he said incredulously.

'You,' said old Bodsham.

'I saw you myself,' said Mavis.

I doubt if there is another member of this club who could have uttered at this juncture the light, careless laugh that Freddie did.

'What an extraordinary thing,' he said. 'One can only suppose that there must be somebody in this resort who resembles me so closely in appearance that the keenest eye is deceived. I assure you, Bod – I mean, Lord Bodsham – and you, Mavis – that my morning has been far too full to permit of my giving joy rides to blondes, even if the mere thought of doing so wouldn't have sickened me to the very soul. The idea having crossed my mind that little Wilfred would appreciate it, I went to St Asaph's to ask the Rev. Aubrey Upjohn to give the school a half-holiday. I want no thanks, of course. I merely mention the matter to show how ridiculous this idea of yours is that I was buzzing about with blondes in my two-seater. The Rev. Aubrey will tell you that I was in conference with him for the dickens of a time. After which, I was in conference with my friend, Bingo Little. And after that I came here.'

There was a silence.

'Odd,' said the Bod.

'Very odd,' said Mavis.

They were plainly rattled. And Freddie was just beginning to have that feeling, than which few are pleasanter, of having got away with it in the teeth of fearful odds, when the revolving door of the hotel moved as if impelled by some irresistible force, and through it came a bulging figure in mauve, surmounted by golden hair. Reading from left to right, the substantial blonde.

'Coo!' she exclaimed, sighting Freddie. 'There you are, ducky! Excuse me half a jiff,' she added to Mavis and the Bod, who had rocked back on their heels at the sight of her, and she linked her arm in Freddie's and drew him aside.

'I hadn't time to thank you before,' she said. 'Besides being too out of breath. Papa is very nippy on his feet, and it takes it out of a girl, trying to dodge a fork handle. What luck finding you here like this. My gentleman friend and I were married at the registrar's just after I left you, and we're having the wedding breakfast here. And if it hadn't been for you, there wouldn't have been a wedding breakfast. I can't tell you how grateful I am.'

And, as if feeling that actions speak louder than words, she flung her arms about Freddie and kissed him heartily. She then buzzed off to the ladies' room to powder her nose, leaving Freddie rooted to the spot.

He didn't, however, remain rooted long. After one quick glance at Mavis and old Bodsham, he was off like a streak to the nearest exit. That glance, quick though it had been, had shown him that this was the end. The Bod was looking at Mavis, and Mavis was looking at the Bod. And then they both turned and looked at him, and there was that in their eyes which told him, as I say, that it was the finish. Good explainer though he is, there were some things which he knew he could not explain, and this was one of them.

That is why, if our annual tournament had been held this year at Bramley-on-Sea, you would not have found Frederick Widgeon in the ranks, playing to his handicap of twenty-four. He makes no secret of the fact that he is permanently through with Bramley-on-Sea. If it wants to brace anybody, let it jolly well brace somebody else, about sums up what he feels.

As the Oldest Member stood chatting with his week-end guest on the terrace overlooking the ninth green, there came out of the club-house a girl of radiant beauty who, greeting the Sage cordially drew his attention to the bracelet on her shapely arm.

'Isn't it lovely!' she said. 'Ambrose gave it me for my birthday.'

She passed on, and the guest heaved a moody sigh.

'Once again!' he said. 'I've never known it to fail. What on earth is the good of Nature turning out girls like that, seeing that before an honest man can put in his bid they have always gone and got an Ambrose attached to them? Or if not an Ambrose, a Jim or a Tim or a Fred or a Ned or a Mike or a Spike or a Percival. Sometimes I think I shall go into a monastery and get away from it all.'

'You admired my little friend?'

'She is what the doctor ordered.'

'It is odd that you should say that, for she is what the doctor got. She is the wife of our local medicine man, Ambrose Gussett.'

'I'll bet he isn't worthy of her.'

'On the contrary. You might say that he married beneath him. He is scratch, she a mere painstaking eighteen. But then we must remember that until shortly before her marriage she had never touched a golf club. She was a tennis player,' said the Oldest

Member, wincing. A devout golfer from the days of the gutty ball, his attitude towards exponents of the rival game had always resembled that of the early Christians towards the Ebionites.

'Well, anyway,' said the guest. 'I'm glad he remembers her birthday.'

'He will always do so. That is one date which is graven on his memory in letters of brass. The time may come when in an absent-minded moment Ambrose Gussett will forget to pronate the wrists and let the club head lead, but he will never forget his wife's birthday. And I'll tell you why,' said the Oldest Member, securing his companion's attention by digging him in the lower ribs with the handle of a putter.

Ambrose Gussett (the Sage proceeded) had been a member of our little community for some months before Evangeline Tewkesbury came into his life. We all liked Ambrose and wished him well. He was a pleasant clean-cut young fellow with frank blue eyes and an easy swing, and several of our Society matrons with daughters on their hands were heard to express a regret that he should remain a bachelor.

Attempts to remedy this, however, had come to nothing. Like so many young doctors with agreeable manners and frank blue eyes, Ambrose Gussett continued to be an iodoform-scented butterfly flitting from flower to flower but never resting on any individual bloom long enough to run the risk of having to sign on the dotted line.

And then Evangeline Tewkesbury arrived on a visit to her aunt, Miss Martha Tewkesbury, and he fell for her with a thud which you could have heard in the next county.

It generally happens around these parts that young men who fall in love look me up in my favourite chair on this terrace in order to obtain sympathy and advice as to how to act for the best. Ambrose Gussett was no exception. Waking from a light doze one evening, I perceived him standing before me, scratching his chin coyly with a number three iron.

'I love her, I love her, I love her, I love her,' said Ambrose Gussett, getting down to it without preamble. 'When in her presence I note a marked cachexia. My temperature goes up, and a curious burning is accompanied by a well-marked yearning. There are floating spots before my eyes, and I am conscious of an overpowering urge to clasp her in my arms and cry "My mate!"'

'You are speaking of—?'

'Didn't I mention that? Evangeline Tewkesbury.'

'Good God!'

'What do you mean?'

I felt it best to be frank.

'My dear Ambrose, I am sorry to give you pain, but Miss Tewkesbury is a tennis player. I have seen her with my own eyes leaping about the court shouting "Forty love", "Thirty all" and similar obscenities.'

He astounded me by receiving my words with a careless nod.

'Yes, she told me she played tennis.'

'And you still love her?'

'Of course I still love her.'

'But, Ambrose, reflect. A golfer needs a wife, true. It is essential that he has a sympathetic listener always handy, to whom he can relate the details of the day's play. But what sort of a life companion would a tennis player he?'

He sighed ecstatically.

'Just let me get this tennis player as a life companion, and you won't find me beefing. I love her, I love her, I love her, I love her, I love her,' said Ambrose Gussett, summing up.

* * *

A few days later I found him beside my chair once more. His clean-cut face was grave.

'Say, listen,' he said. 'You know that great love of mine?'

'Ah, yes. How is it coming along?'

'Not too well. Every time I call at her home, I find her festooned in tennis players.'

'Her natural mates. Female tennis players always marry male tennis players, poor souls. Abandon this mad enterprise, Ambrose,' I pleaded, 'and seek for some sweet girl with a loving disposition and a low handicap.'

'I won't. My stethoscope is still in the ring. I don't care if these germs are her natural mates. I defy them. Whatever the odds, however sticky the going, I shall continue to do my stuff. But, as I say, the course is heavily trapped and one will need to be at the top of one's form. Looking over the field, I think my most formidable rival is a pin-headed string bean of a fellow named Dwight Messmore. You know him?'

'By sight. She would naturally be attracted by him. I believe he is very expert at this outdoor ping-pong.'

'In the running for a place in the Davis Cup team, they tell me.'

'What is the Davis Cup team?'

'A team that plays for a sort of cup they have.'

'They have cups, do they, in the world – or sub-world – of tennis? And what are you proposing to do to foil this Davis Cup addict?'

'Ah, there you have me. I keep asking her to let me give her a golf lesson. I feel that in the pure surroundings of the practice tee her true self would come to the surface, causing her to recoil with loathing from men like Dwight Messmore. But she scoffs at the suggestion. She says golf is a footling game and she can't understand how any except the half-witted can find pleasure in it.'

'And that appalling speech did not quench your love?'

'Of course it didn't quench my love. A love like mine doesn't go around getting itself quenched. But I admit that the situation is sticky, and I shall have to survey it from every angle and take steps.'

It was not until several weeks had elapsed, a period in which I had seen nothing of him, that I learned with a sickening qualm of horror how awful were the steps which he had decided to take.

He became a tennis player.

It was, of course, as I learned subsequently, not without prolonged and earnest wrestling with his conscience that a man like Ambrose Gussett, playing even then to a handicap of two and destined in the near future to be scratch, had been able to bring himself to jettison all the principles of a lifetime and plunge into the abyss. Later, when the madness had passed and he was once more hitting them sweetly off the tee, he told me that the struggle had been terrific. But in the end infatuation had proved too strong. If, he said to himself, it was necessary in order to win Evangeline Tewkesbury to become a tennis player, a tennis player he would be.

And, inquiries having informed him that the quickest way of accomplishing this degradation was to put himself in the hands of a professional, he turned up his coat collar, pulled down the brim of his hat, and sneaked off to the lair where the man plied his dark trade. And presently he found himself facing a net with a racquet in his hand. Or, rather, hands, for naturally he had assumed the orthodox interlocking grip.

This led the professional to make his first criticism.

'You hold the racquet in one hand only,' he said.

Ambrose was astounded, but he was here to learn, so he followed out the instruction, and having done so peered about him, puzzled.

'Where,' he asked, 'is the flag?'

'Flag?' said the professional. 'But it isn't the fourth of July.'

'I can't shoot unless I see the flag.'

The professional was now betraying open bewilderment. He came up to the net and peered at Ambrose over it like someone inspecting a new arrival at the Zoo.

'I don't get this about flags. We don't use flags in tennis. Have you never played tennis? Never? Most extraordinary. Are there other games?'

'I play golf.'

'Golf? Golf? Ah, yes, of course. What they call cow-pasture pool.'

Ambrose stiffened.

'What *who* call cow-pasture pool?'

'All right-thinking men. Well, well, well! Well, listen,' said the professional. 'It looks to me as if our best plan would be to start right at the beginning. This is a racquet. This is the net. That is what we call a ball...'

It was toward the end of the lesson that a string-bean-like young man sauntered on to the court, and the professional turned to him with the air of one seeking sympathy.

'Gentleman's never played tennis before, Mr Messmore.'

'Well, he certainly isn't playing it now,' replied Dwight Messmore. 'Ha, ha, ha, ha, ha, ha ha,' he added, with scarcely veiled derision.

Ambrose felt the hot blood coursing in his cheeks, but all he could find to say was 'Is that so?' and the lesson proceeded to its end.

It was followed by others, every morning without respite, and at long last the professional declared him competent to appear in – if one may use the term – a serious game, at the same time counselling him not to begin too ambitiously. There was a cripple he knew, said the professional, a poor fellow who had lost both legs in a motor accident, who would be about Ambrose's form, always provided that the latter waited his opportunity and caught him on one of his off days.

But it was with no cripple that Ambrose Gussett made his first appearance. With incredible audacity he sought out Evangeline Tewkesbury and asked her for a game.

The fixture came off next day before an audience consisting of Dwight Messmore, who, though Ambrose gave him every opportunity of remembering another engagement elsewhere, remained on the side lines throughout, convulsed with merriment and uttering, in Ambrose's opinion, far more catcalls than were necessary. Having learned that morning that he had been selected to play in the Davis Cup team, whatever that may be, the man was thoroughly above himself. As early as the middle of the first set he was drawing audible comparisons between Ambrose and a cat on hot bricks, seeming to feel that the palm for gracefulness should be awarded to the latter.

When the game was over – 6–0, 6–0 – Ambrose inquired of Evangeline if she thought he would ever be a good tennis player. The girl gave him a curious look and asked if he had read any nice books lately. Ambrose mentioned a few, and she said that she had enjoyed them, too, and wondered how authors managed to think up these things. She was starting to touch on the new plays, when Ambrose, bluntly bringing up once more a subject which he had a feeling that she was evading, repeated his question.

Again the girl seemed to hesitate, and it was Dwight Messmore who took upon himself the onus of reply, sticking his oar in with insufferable heartiness.

'The problem which you have propounded, my dear fellow,' he said, 'is one which it is not easy to answer. A "good" tennis player, you say. Well, I feel sure that you will always be a moral tennis player, a virtuous, upright tennis player, but if you wish to know whether I think you will ever be able to make a game of it with a child of six, I reply No. Abandon all hope of reaching such heights. Console yourself with the reflection that you have great entertainment value. You are what I should call an amusing tennis player, a tennis player who will always be good for a laugh from the most discriminating audience. I can vouch for this, for I have been filming you from time to time with my ciné-kodak, and whenever I have run the result off at parties it has been the success of the evening. My friends are hard critics, not easy to please, but you have won them. "Show us Ambrose Gussett playing tennis," is their cry, and when I do so they guffaw till their eyes bubble.'

And scooping Evangeline up he led her off, leaving Ambrose, as you may well imagine, a prey to the most violent and disturbing emotions. If a patient had described to him the symptoms which he was experiencing, he would have ordered him cold compresses and a milk diet.

You will have no difficulty in guessing for yourself the trend his thoughts were taking. He was a doctor, and a doctor is peculiarly situated. He must be a dignified, venerable figure, to whom patients can show their tongues without secret misgivings as to his ability to read their message. And Ambrose, recalling some of his recent activities, could not but feel that a ciné-kodak record of these must lower, if not absolutely destroy, his prestige.

One moment in particular stood out in his memory, when in a fruitless effort to reach and return one of Evangeline's testing drives he had got his left foot entangled with his right elbow and had rolled over and over like a shot rabbit, eventually coming to rest with his head between his legs. Such a picture, exhibited to anything like a wide audience, might well ruin his practice irretrievably.

He woke from a troubled sleep next morning filled with a stern resolve. He had decided to confront Dwight Messmore and demand that film from him. So after a light breakfast he got in his car and drove to the other's residence. Alighting at the door with tight lips and a set face, he beat a sharp tattoo on it with the knocker. And simultaneously there came from within a loud cry, almost a scream, if not a shriek. The next moment the door opened, and Dwight Messmore stood before him.

'Holy smoke!' said Dwight Messmore. 'I thought it was an atom bomb.'

It was plain to Ambrose's experienced eye that the man was not in his customary vigorous health. He was wearing about his forehead a towel which appeared to have ice in it, and his complexion was a curious greenish yellow.

'Come in,' said Dwight Messmore, speaking in a hollow, husky voice, like a spirit at a *séance*. 'I was just going to send for you. Walk on tip-toe, do you mind, and speak very softly. I am on the point of expiring.'

As he led the way into the living-room, shuffling along like a Volga boatman, a genial voice with a rather nasal intonation cried 'Hello!', and Ambrose perceived a handsome parrot in a cage on the table.

'I didn't know you had a parrot,' he said.

'I didn't know it myself till this morning,' said Dwight Messmore. 'It suddenly arrived out of the unknown. A man in a sweater came in a van and left it. He insisted that I had ordered it. Damn fool. Do I look like a man who orders parrots?'

'Ko-ko,' observed the bird, which for some moments had taken no part in the conversation.

'Cocoa!' whispered Dwight Messmore with a powerful shudder. 'At a moment like this!'

He lowered himself into a chair, and Ambrose gently placed a thermometer in his mouth.

'Can we think of anything that can have caused this little indisposition?' he asked.

'Charcoal poisoning,' said Dwight Messmore promptly. 'I gave a little party last night to a few fellows to celebrate my making the Davis Cup team—'

'Did we drink anything?'

'Not a thing. Well, just a bottle or two of champagne, and liqueurs ... brandy, chartreuse, benedictine, curaçao, crème de menthe, kummel and so forth ... and of course whisky. But nothing more. It was practically a teetotal evening. No, what did the trick was that charcoal. As you are probably aware, the stuff they sell you as caviare in this country isn't caviare. It's whitefish roe, and they colour it with powdered charcoal. Well, you can't sit up half the night eating powdered charcoal without paying the penalty.'

'Quite,' said Ambrose. 'Well, I think our best plan will be to remain perfectly quiet with our eyes closed, and presently I will send us a little sedative.'

'Have a nut,' suggested the parrot.

'No nuts, of course,' said Ambrose.

It was only after Ambrose had returned to his car and was driving off to the Tewkesbury home in the hope of seeing Evangeline that it occurred to him that he had forgotten all about that film. Feeling, however, that there would be plenty of time to collect that later, he fetched up at *chez* Tewkesbury and was informed by Miss Martha that Evangeline was out.

'She's upset to-day,' said the adored object's aunt. 'Not ill, just in a temper. She's gone for a walk. She said it might make her feel better. She is very angry because nobody has remembered her birthday.'

Ambrose reeled. He had not remembered it himself. How he had come to allow so vital a date to slip his mind, he was at a loss to understand. He could only suppose that the strain of learning tennis had sapped his intellect.

'She is particularly annoyed,' proceeded Miss Tewkesbury, 'with Mr Messmore. She is passionately fond of birds, and Mr Messmore faithfully promised her a parrot for her birthday. Her birthday arrives, and what happens? No parrot.'

She was going on to speak further, but Ambrose was no longer there. With a brief 'Excuse me' he had shot from her presence as if Walter Hagen in his prime had driven him off the tee. His alert mind had seen the way.

Once again his knock on Dwight Messmore's door produced that loud cry that was almost a scream, if not a shriek. And once again the invalid presented himself, looking like a full page illustration from a medical treatise on bubonic plague.

'Ye gods!' he moaned. 'Must you? Rap, rap, rap. Tap, tap, tap. Are you a doctor or a woodpecker?'

'Listen,' said Ambrose. He had no time for these unmanly

complaints. 'It just occurred to me. We need perfect relaxation and repose, and we cannot enjoy perfect relaxation and repose if we are consistently hampered by parrots. I will take the bird off our hands.'

Although one would have said that such a thing was impossible, the look that came into Dwight Messmore's pea-green face made it seem almost beautiful.

'You will? You really will? Then heaven bless you, you Boy Scout of a physician! Take this bird, Gussett, and my blessing with it. Maybe in the days to come, when acquaintance has ripened into friendship and it feels justified in becoming confidential, it will reveal to you what it is that it expects people to have seen by the dawn's early light. So far it has maintained a complete reserve on the point. It just says "Oh, say have you seen by the dawn's early light?" and then stops and makes a noise like someone drawing a cork. After a brief interval for mental refreshment it then starts all over again at the beginning. Gosh!' said Dwight Messmore, having struggled with his emotion for a while. 'It's lucky you came along, you United States marine! I was very near the breaking point, very near. And, by the way,' he proceeded, 'as a fitting expression of my gratitude I am going to destroy those films I took of you playing – I use the word loosely – tennis. I feel that it is the least I can do. "Oh, say have you seen by the dawn's early light?" it says, and then the popping noise. Be prepared for this. Well, I will now take a short and, I anticipate, refreshing nap. Good-bye, Gussett. Don't forget your parrot.'

It was with a light heart that Ambrose returned to his car, dangling the cage on a carefree finger. And it was with a still lighter heart that, as he rounded a corner, he saw Evangeline coming along at a quick heel-and-toe. Her brow, he noticed, was overcast and her lips tightly set, but these were symptoms which he hoped very shortly to treat and correct.

Evangeline Tewkesbury was, indeed, in no sunny frame of mind. A queen accustomed to the homage of her little court, she could have betted her Sunday cami-knickers that her birthday would have found her snowed under with parcels and flowers, the gift of adoring males of her entourage, and she had imagined that on this important morning her telephone would never have stopped ringing. Instead of which, no parcels, no flowers, and out of the telephone not a yip. She might have been celebrating her birthday on some lonely atoll in the South Seas.

Could she have known that every male friend on her list was suffering, like Dwight Messmore, from too lavish indulgence in whitefish roe powdered with charcoal, she might have understood and forgiven. But she did not know, and so missed understanding and forgiveness by several parasangs. Her only feeling towards these faithless wooers was a well-marked urge to skin them all with a blunt knife and dance on the remains.

'Good morning, Miss Tewkesbury,' cried Ambrose gaily. 'Good morning, good morning, good morning. Many happy returns of the day. Happy birthday to you, happy birthday to you, in short. I have a little present here which I hope you will accept. Just a trivial parrot, but you may be able to fit it in somewhere.'

And, encouraged by the sudden softening of her eyes, he parked the car, stood on one leg and asked her to be his wife.

When he had finished, she stood silent for a space, and a close observer would have seen that a struggle was proceeding in her mind. She was weighing the pros and cons.

She had always liked Ambrose and admired his clean-cut

good looks. And the fact that he had remembered her birthday argued that he was kind, courteous and considerate; of the stuff, in short, of which good husbands are made. For a while the word 'Yes' seemed to be trembling on her lips.

And then, chillingly, there came into her mind the picture of this man as he had appeared on the tennis court. Could she, she asked herself, link her lot with that of such a super-rabbit? There rose before her a vision of that awful moment when Ambrose had got his left foot entangled with his right elbow.

'No, no, a thousand times no,' she told herself. Then aloud, with a remorseful sweetness which she hoped would rob the words of their sting: 'I'm sorry...I'm afraid...In fact...Well, you know what I mean.'

Ambrose, disjointed though her utterance was, knew but too well what she meant, and his eager face fell as if it, too, had got its left foot entangled with its right elbow.

'I see,' he said. 'Yes, I get your drift.'

'I'm sorry.'

'Don't mention it.'

'But you know how it is.'

'Oh, quite.'

There was a silence, broken only by the parrot asking one or both of them – it was impossible to say to whom the question was addressed – if they had seen by the dawn's early light. Despite his efforts to keep a stiff upper lip, Ambrose Gussett was showing plainly how deeply this stymie had gashed his soul. His aspect caused the girl's tender heart to bleed for him. She yearned for some means of softening the blow which she had been compelled to deliver.

And then she saw how this might be done.

'You used to speak,' she said, 'of giving me a golf lesson.'

Ambrose raised his bowed head.

'So I did.'

'Would you like to give me one now?'

Ambrose's sombre face lit up.

'May I really?'

'Do. I'll go and fetch my racquet.'

'You don't use a racquet.'

'Then how do you get the ball over the net?'

'There isn't a net.'

'No net. What a peculiar game.'

She was still sniggering a little to herself, for she was a girl with a strong sense of the ridiculous, when they came on to the practice tee.

'Now,' said Ambrose, having teed up the ball and placed the driver in her hands and adjusted her stance and enjoined upon her to come back slowly, 'let's see you paste it into the next county.'

Years of tennis playing (which, however bad for the soul, does, I admit, strengthen the thews and sinews) had given Evangeline Tewkesbury a fine physique, and Ambrose tells me that it was an inspiring sight to see her put every ounce of wrist and muscle into her shot. The only criticism which could have been made of her performance was that she missed the ball by about three inches.

It was her salvation. Evangeline Tewkesbury's was an arrogant mind, and I think there can be no question that had she succeeded at her first effort in accomplishing an outstanding drive, she would have abandoned the game on the plea that it was too easy. For this, Ambrose had shocked me by telling me, was one of the things she had said about golf when urged to take a lesson.

But she had failed, and now it was but a question of time before the golf bug ran up her leg and bit her to the bone. Suddenly Ambrose saw come into her face that strange yearning look, composite of eagerness and humility, which is the infallible first symptom.

'Let me show you,' he said, seizing his opportunity with subtle skill. And taking the club from her he waggled briefly and sent a screamer down the fairway. 'That – roughly – is the idea,' he said.

She was staring at him, in her gaze awe, admiration, respect, homage and devotion nicely blended.

'You must be terribly good at golf,' she said.

'Oh, fairish.'

'Could you teach me to play?'

'In a few lessons. Unfortunately I shall be leaving almost immediately for the Rocky Mountains, to shoot grizzly bears.'

'Oh, must you?'

'Surely it is the usual procedure for a man in my position.'

There was a silence. Her foot made arabesques on the turf.

'It seems rather tough on the grizzlies,' she said at length.

'Into each life some rain must fall.'

'Look,' said Evangeline. 'I think I see a way out.'

'There is only one way out.'

'That is the way I mean.'

Ambrose quivered from the top of his head to the soles of his sure-grip shoes, as worn by all the leading professionals.

'You mean—?'

'Yes, that's what I mean.'

'You really—?'

'Yes, really. I can't imagine what I was thinking of when I said No just now. One makes these foolish mistakes.'

Ambrose dropped the club and folded her in a long, lingering embrace.

'My mate!' he cried. 'Now,' he added, picking up the driver and placing it in her hands. 'Slow back, don't press, and keep your 'ee on the ba'.'

With the coming of dusk the blizzard which had been blowing all the afternoon had gained in force, and the trees outside the club-house swayed beneath it. The falling snow rendered the visibility poor, but the Oldest Member, standing at the smoking-room window, was able to recognize the familiar gleam of Cyril Jukes's heather-mixture plus-fours as he crossed the icebound terrace from the direction of the caddy shed, and he gave a little nod of approval. No fair weather golfer himself when still a player, he liked to see the younger generation doing its round in the teeth of November gales.

On Cyril Jukes's normally cheerful face, as he entered the room some moments later, there was the sort of look which might have been worn by a survivor of the last days of Pompeii. What had been happening to Cyril Jukes in the recent past it was impossible to say, but the dullest eye could discern that it had been plenty, and the Oldest Member regarded him sympathetically.

'Something on your mind, my boy?'

'A slight tiff with the helpmeet.'

'I am sorry. What caused it?'

'Well, you know her little brother, and you will agree with me, I think, that his long game wants polishing up.'

'Quite.'

'This can be done only by means of unremitting practice.'

'Very true.'

'So I took him out for a couple of rounds after lunch. We've just got back. We found the little woman waiting for us. She seemed rather stirred. Directing my attention to the fact that the child was bright blue and that icicles had formed on him, she said that if he expired his blood would be on my head. She then took him off to thaw him out with hot-water bottles. Life can be very difficult.'

'Very.'

'I suppose there *was* a sort of nip in the air, though I hadn't noticed it myself, but I had meant so well. Do you think that when a man's wife calls him a fat-headed sadist, she implies that married happiness is dead and the home in the melting pot?'

The Sage patted him on the shoulder.

'Courage,' he said. 'She may be a little annoyed for the moment, but the mood will pass and she will understand and forgive. Your wife is a golfer and, when calmer, cannot fail to realize how lucky she is to have married a man with the true golfing spirit. For that is what matters in this life. That is what counts. I mean the spirit that animated Horace Bewstridge, causing him to spank his loved one's mother on the eighteenth green when she interfered with his putting; the inner fire that drove Rollo Podmarsh on to finish his round, though he thought he had been poisoned, because he had a chance of breaking a hundred for the first time; the spirit which saved Agnes Flack and Sidney McMurdo, bringing them at last to peace and happiness. I think I may have mentioned Agnes Flack and Sidney McMurdo to you before. They were engaged to be married.'

'She was a large girl, wasn't she?'

'Very large. And Sidney was large, also. That was what made

the thing so satisfactory to their friends and well-wishers. Too often in this world you find the six-foot-three man teaming up with the four-foot-ten girl and the five-foot-eleven girl linking her lot with something which she would seem to have dug out of Singer's troupe of midgets: but in the union of Agnes Flack and Sidney McMurdo there was none of this discrepancy. Sidney weighed two hundred pounds and was all muscle, and Agnes weighed a hundred and sixty pounds and was all muscle, too. And, more important still, both had been assiduous golfers since childhood. Theirs was a love based on mutual respect. Sidney's habit of always getting two hundred and fifty yards from the tee fascinated Agnes, and he in his turn was enthralled by her short game, which was exceptionally accurate.'

It was in warmer weather than this (the Sage proceeded, having accepted his companion's offer of a hot toddy) that the story began which I am about to relate. The month was August, and from a cloudless sky the sun blazed down on the popular sea-shore resort of East Bampton, illuminating with its rays the beach, the pier, the boardwalk, the ice-cream stands, the hot doggeries and the simmering ocean. In the last-named, about fifty yards from shore, Agnes Flack was taking her customary cooler after the day's golf and thinking how much she loved Sidney McMurdo.

Sidney himself was not present. He was still in the city, working for the insurance company which had bespoken his services, counting the days to his vacation and thinking how much he loved Agnes Flack.

When girls are floating in warm water, dreaming of the man they adore, it sometimes happens that there comes to them a sort of exaltation of the soul which demands physical expression.

It came now to Agnes Flack. God, the way she looked at it, was in His heaven and all right with the world, and it seemed to her that something ought to be done about it. And as practically the only thing you can do in the way of physical expression in the water is to splash, she splashed. With arms and feet she churned up great fountains of foam, at the same time singing a wordless song of ecstasy.

The trouble about doing that sort of thing when swimming is that people are apt to be misled. Agnes Flack's was one of those penetrating voices which sound like the down express letting off steam at a level crossing, and in the number which she had selected for rendition there occurred a series of high notes which she held with determination and vigour. It is not surprising, therefore, that a passing stranger who was cleaving the waves in her vicinity should have got his facts twisted.

A moment later Agnes, in the middle of a high note, was surprised to find herself gripped firmly beneath the arms and towed rapidly shorewards.

Her annoyance was extreme, and it increased during the trip, most of which was made with her head under water. By the time she arrived at the beach, she had swallowed perhaps a pint and a half, and her initial impulse was to tell her assailant what she thought of his officiousness. But just as she was about to do so friendly hands, seizing her from behind, pulled her backwards and started rolling her over a barrel. And when she fought herself free the man had vanished.

Her mood was still ruffled and resentful when she stepped out of the elevator that night on her way down to dinner, for the feeling that she was full of salt water had not wholly disappeared. And it was as she was crossing the lounge with a moody frown on her brow that a voice at her side said 'Oh, hullo, there you are, what?' and she turned to see a tall, slender, willowy man with keen blue eyes and a sun-tanned face.

'Feeling all right again?' asked the handsome stranger.

Agnes, who had been about to draw herself to her full height and say 'Sir!' suddenly divined who this must be.

'Was it you—?' she began.

He raised a deprecating hand.

'Don't thank me, dear lady, don't thank me. I'm always saving people's lives, and they will try to thank me. It was nothing, nothing. Different, of course, if there had been sharks.'

Agnes was staring like a child at a saucer of ice cream. She had revised her intention of telling this man what she thought of him. His eyes, his clean-cut face, his perfect figure and his clothes had made a profound and instantaneous impression on her, giving her the sort of sensation which she had experienced on the occasion when she had done the short third at Squashy Hollow in one, a sort of dizzy feeling that life had nothing more to offer.

'Sharks get in the way and hamper a man. The time I saved the Princess della Raviogli in the Indian Ocean there were half a dozen of them, horsing about and behaving as if the place belonged to them. I had to teach one or two of them a sharp lesson with my Boy Scout pocket knife. The curse of the average shark is that if you give it the slightest encouragement it gets above itself and starts putting on airs.'

Agnes felt that she must speak, but there seemed so little that she could say.

'You're English, aren't you?' she asked.

He raised a deprecating hand.

'Call me rather a cosmopolite, dear lady. I was born in the old country and have resided there from time to time and even served my sovereign in various positions of trust such as Deputy Master of the Royal Buckhounds, but all my life I have been a rover. I flit. I move to and fro. They say of me: "Last week he was in Pernambuco, but goodness knows where he is now. China, possibly, or Africa or the North Pole." Until recently I was in Hollywood. They were doing a film of life in the jungle, where might is right and the strong man comes into his own, and they roped me in as adviser. By the way, introduce myself, what? Fosdyke is the name. Captain Jack Fosdyke.'

Agnes's emotion was now such that she was unable for a moment to recall hers. Then it came back to her.

'Mine is Flack,' she said, and the statement seemed to interest her companion.

'No, really? I've just been spending the week-end with an old boy named Flack, down at Sands Point.'

'Josiah Flack?'

'That's right. Amazing place he has. Absolute palace. They tell me he's one of the richest men in America. Rather pathetic. This lonely old man, rolling in the stuff, but with no chick or child.'

'He is my uncle. How was he?'

'Very frail. Very, very frail. Not long for this world, it seemed to me.' A sharp tremor ran through Captain Jack Fosdyke. It was as if for the first time her words had penetrated to his consciousness. 'Your *uncle*, did you say?'

'Yes.'

'Are you his only niece?'

'Yes.'

'God bless my soul!' cried Captain Jack Fosdyke with extraordinary animation. 'Here, come and have a cocktail. Come and have some dinner. Well, well, well, well, well!'

At the dinner table the spell which her companion was casting on Agnes Flack deepened in intensity. There seemed no limits to the powers of this wonder man. He met the head waiter's eye and made him wilt. He spoke with polished knowledge of food and wine, comparing the hospitality of princes of his acquaintance with that of African chiefs he had known. Between the courses he danced like something dark and slithery from the Argentine. Little wonder that ere long he had Agnes Flack fanning herself with her napkin.

A girl who could, had she seen good reason to do so, have felled an ox with a single blow, in the presence of Captain Jack Fosdyke she felt timid and fluttering. He was turning on the charm as if through the nozzle of a hose-pipe, and it was going all over her and she liked it. She was conscious of a dreamlike sensation, as if she were floating on a pink cloud over an ocean of joy. For the first time in weeks the image of Sidney McMurdo had passed completely from her mind. There was still, presumably, a McMurdo, Sidney, in the telephone book, but in the thoughts of Agnes Flack, no.

The conversation turned to sports and athleticism.

'You swim wonderfully,' she said, for that salt water had long since ceased to rankle.

'Yes, I've always been a pretty decent swimmer. I learned in the lake at Wapshott.'

'Wapshott?'

'Wapshott Castle, Wapshott-on-the-Wap, Hants., the family seat. I don't go there often nowadays – too busy – but when I do I have a good time. Plenty of ridin', shootin', fishin' and all that.'

'Are you fond of riding?'

'I like steeplechasin'. The spice of danger, don't you know, what? Ever seen the Grand National?'

'Not yet.'

'I won it a couple of times. I remember on the second occasion Lady Astor saying to me that I ought to saw off a leg and give the other fellows a chance. Lord Beaverbrook, who overheard the remark, was much amused.'

'You seem to be marvellous at everything.'

'I am.'

'Do you play golf?'

'Oh, rather. Scratch.'

'We might have a game to-morrow.'

'Not to-morrow. Lunching in Washington. A bore, but I can't get out of it. Harry insisted.'

'Harry?'

'Truman. We'll have a game when I get back. I may be able to give you a pointer or two. Bobby Jones said to me once that he would never have won the British and American Amateur and Open, if he hadn't studied my swing.'

Agnes gasped.

'You don't know Bobby Jones?'

'We're like brothers.'

'I once got his autograph.'

'Say the word, dear lady, and I'll get you a signed photograph.'

Agnes clutched at the table. She had thought for a moment that she was going to faint. And so the long evening wore on.

Mark you, I do not altogether blame Agnes Flack. Hers had been a sheltered life, and nothing like Captain Jack Fosdyke had ever happened to her before. Here was a man who, while looking like something out of a full page coloured advertisement in a slick paper magazine, seemed to have been everywhere and to know everybody.

When he took her out in the moonlight and spoke nonchalantly of Lady Astor, Lord Beaverbrook, Borneo head hunters, Mervyn Leroy and the brothers Schubert, one can appreciate her attitude and understand how inevitable it was that Sidney McMurdo should have gone right back in the betting. In accepting the addresses of Sidney McMurdo, she realized that she had fallen into the error of making her selection before walking the length of the counter.

In short, to hurry on this painful part of my story, when Sidney McMurdo eventually arrived with his suitcase and bag of clubs and was about to clasp Agnes Flack to his forty-four-inch bosom, he was surprised and distressed to observe her step back and raise a deprecating hand. A moment later she was informing him that she had made a mistake and that the photograph on her dressing-table at even date was not his but that of Captain Jack Fosdyke, to whom she was now betrothed.

This, of course, was a nice bit of news for a devoted *fiancé* to get after a four-hour journey on a hot day in a train without a dining-car, and it is not too much to say that for an instant Sidney McMurdo tottered beneath it like a preliminary bout heavyweight who has been incautious enough to place his jaw *en rapport* with the fist of a fellow member of the Truck Drivers' Union. Dimly he heard Agnes Flack saying that she would be a sister to him, and this threat, for he was a man already loaded up with sisters almost beyond capacity, brought him out of what had promised to be a lasting coma.

His eyes flashed, his torso swelled, the muscles leaped about all over him under his pullover, and with a muttered 'Is zat so?' he turned on his heel and left her, but not before he had asked for and obtained his supplanter's address. It was his intention to visit the latter and begin by picking him up by the scruff of the neck and shaking him like a rat. After that he would carry on as the inspiration of the moment dictated.

My efforts up to the present having been directed towards limning the personalities of Agnes Flack and Captain Jack Fosdyke, I have not as yet given you anything in the nature of a comprehensive character study of Sidney McMurdo. I should now reveal that he was as fiercely jealous a man as ever swung an aluminium putter. Othello might have had a slight edge on him in that respect, but it would have been a very near thing. Rob him of the girl he loved, and you roused the lion in Sidney McMurdo.

He was flexing his muscles and snorting ominously when he reached the cosy bungalow which Captain Jack Fosdyke had rented for the summer season. The Captain, who was humming one of the song hits from last year's war dance of the 'Mgubo-Mgompis and cleaning an elephant gun, looked up inquiringly as he entered, and Sidney glowered down at him, his muscles still doing the shimmy.

'Captain Fosdyke?'

'The same.'

'Pleased to meet you.'

'Naturally.'

'Could I have a word with you?'

'A thousand.'

'It is with reference to your sneaking my girl.'

'Oh, that? Are you this McMurdo bird of whom I have heard Agnes speak?'

'I am.'

'You were engaged, I understand, till I came along?'

'We were.'

'Too bad. Well, that's how it goes. Will you be seeing her shortly?'

'I may decide to confront her again.'

'Then you might tell her I've found that elephant gun I mentioned to her. She was anxious to see the notches on it.'

Sidney, who had been about to call his companion a sneaking, slinking serpent and bid him rise and put his hands up, decided that later on would do. He did not at all like this talk of notches and elephant guns.

'Are there notches on your elephant gun?'

'There are notches on all my guns, I use them in rotation. This is the one I shot the chief of the 'Mgobo-Mgumpis with.'

The chill which had begun to creep over Sidney McMurdo from the feet upwards became more marked. His clenched fists relaxed, and his muscles paused in their rhythmic dance.

'You shot him?'

'Quite.'

'Er – do you often do that sort of thing?'

'Invariably, when chaps smirch the honour of the Fosdykes. If a bally bounder smirches the honour of the Fosdykes, I shoot him like a dog.'

'Like a dog?'

'Like a dog.'

'What sort of dog?'

'Any sort of dog.'

'I see.'

There was a pause.

'Would you consider that being plugged in the eye, smirched the honour of the Fosdykes?'

'Unquestionably. I was once plugged in the eye by the chief

of the 'Mgeebo-Mgoopies. And when they buried him the little port had seldom seen a costlier funeral.'

'I see,' said Sidney McMurdo thoughtfully. 'I see. Well, goodbye. It's been nice meeting you.'

'It always is,' said Captain Jack Fosdyke. 'Drop in again. I'll show you my tommy gun.'

Sidney McMurdo had not much forehead, being one of those rugged men whose front hair finishes a scant inch or so above the eyebrows, but there was just room on it for a ruminative frown, and he was wearing this as he left the bungalow and set out for a walk along the shore. He was fully alive to the fact that in the recent interview he had cut a poorish figure, failing entirely to express himself and fulfil himself.

But how else, he asked himself, could he have acted? His was a simple nature, easily baffled by the unusual, and he frankly did not see how he could have coped with a rival who appeared to be a combination of mass murderer and United States Armoury. His customary routine of picking rivals up by the scruff of the neck and shaking them like rats plainly would not have answered here.

He walked on, brooding, and so distrait was he that anyone watching him would have given attractive odds that before long he would bump into something. This occurred after he had proceded some hundred yards, the object into which he bumped being a slender, streamlined, serpentine female who looked like one of those intense young women who used to wreck good men's lives in the silent films but seem rather to have died out since the talkies came in. She was dark and subtle and exotic, and she appeared to be weeping.

Sidney, however, who was a close observer, saw that the trouble was that she had got a fly in her eye, and to whip out his pocket handkerchief and tilt her head back and apply first aid was with him the work of an instant. She thanked him brokenly, blinking as she did so. Then, for the first time seeming to see him steadily and see him whole, she gave a little gasp, and said:

'You!'

Her eyes, which were large and dark and lustrous, like those of some inscrutable priestess of a strange old religion, focused themselves on him, as she spoke, and seemed to go through him in much the same way as a couple of red hot bullets would go through a pound of butter. He rocked back on his heels, feeling as if someone had stirred up his interior organs with an egg beater.

'I have been waiting for you – oh, so long.'

'I'm sorry,' said Sidney. 'Am I late?'

'My man!'

'I beg your pardon?'

'I love you,' explained the beautiful unknown. 'Kiss me.'

If she had studied for weeks, she could not have found a better approach to Sidney McMurdo and one more calculated to overcome any customer's sales resistance which might have been lurking in him. Something along these lines from a woman something along her lines was exactly what he had been feeling he could do with. A lover who has just got off a stuffy train to find himself discarded like a worn-out glove by the girl he has worshipped and trusted, is ripe for treatment of this kind.

His bruised spirit began to heal. He kissed her, as directed, and there started to burgeon within him the thought that Agnes Flack wasn't everybody and that it would do her no harm to have this demonstrated to her. A heartening picture flitted through his mind of himself ambling up to Agnes Flack with this spectacular number on his arm, saying to her: 'If you don't want me, it would appear that there are others who do.'

'Nice day,' he said, to help the conversation along.

'Divine. Hark to the wavelets, plashing on the shore. How they seem to fill one with a sense of the inexpressibly ineffable.'

'That's right. They do, don't they?'

'Are they singing us songs of old Greece, of Triton blowing on his wreathed horn and the sunlit loves of gods and goddesses?'

'I'm afraid I couldn't tell you,' said Sidney McMurdo. 'I'm a stranger in these parts myself.'

She sighed.

'I, too. But it is my fate to be stranger everywhere. I live a life apart; alone, aloof, solitary, separate; wrapped up in my dreams and vision. 'Tis ever so with the artist.'

'You're a painter?'

'In ink, not in oils. I depict the souls of men and women. I am Cora McGuffy Spottsworth.'

The name was new to Sidney, who seldom got much beyond the golf weeklies and the house organ of the firm for which he worked, but he gathered that she must be a writer of sorts and made a mental note to wire Brentano's for her complete output and bone it up without delay.

They walked along in silence. At the next ice cream stand he bought her a nut sundae, and she ate it with a sort of restrained emotion which suggested the presence of banked-up fires, one hand wielding the spoon, the other nestling in his like a white orchid.

Sidney McMurdo was now right under the ether. As he sipped his sarsaparilla, his soul seemed to heave and bubble like a Welsh rabbit coming to the boil. From regarding this woman merely as a sort of stooge, to be exhibited to Agnes Flack as evidence that McMurdo Preferred, even if she had seen fit to unload her holdings, was far from being a drug in the market, he had come to look upon her as a strong man's mate. So that when, having disposed of the last spoonful, she said she hoped he had not thought her abrupt just now in saying that she loved him, he replied 'Not at all, not at all,' adding that it was precisely the sort of thing he liked to hear. It amazed him that he could ever have considered a mere number-three-iron-swinging robot like Agnes Flack as a life partner.

'It needs but a glance, don't you think, to recognize one's mate?'

'Oh, sure.'

'Especially if you have met and loved before. You remember those old days in Egypt?'

'Egypt?' Sidney was a little bewildered. The town she mentioned was, he knew, in Illinois, but he had never been there.

'In Egypt, Antony.'

'The name is Sidney. McMurdo, Sidney George.'

'In your present incarnation, possibly. But once, long ago, you were Marc Antony and I was Cleopatra.'

'Of course, yes,' said Sidney. 'It all comes back to me.'

'What times those were. That night on the Nile!'

'Some party.'

'I drew Revell Carstairs in my *Furnace of Sin* from my memories of you in the old days. He was tall and broad and strong, but with the heart of a child. All these years I have been seeking for you, and now that I have found you, would you have had me hold back and mask my love from respect for outworn fetishes of convention?'

'You betcher. I mean, you betcher not.'

'What have we to do with conventions? The world would say that I have known you for a mere half-hour—'

'Twenty-five minutes,' said Sidney, who was rather a stickler for accuracy, consulting his wrist-watch.

'Or twenty-five minutes. In Egypt I was in your arms in forty seconds.'

'Quick service.'

'That was ever my way, direct and sudden and impulsive. I remember saying once to Mr Spottsworth—'

Sidney McMurdo was conscious of a quick chill, similar to that which had affected him when Captain Jack Fosdyke had spoken of elephant guns and notches. His moral code, improving after a rocky start in his Marc Antony days, had become rigid and would never allow him to be a breaker-up of homes. Besides, there was his insurance company to be considered. A scandal might mean the loss of his second vice-presidency.

'Mr Spottsworth?' he echoed, his jaw falling a little. 'Is there a Mr Spottsworth?'

'Not now. He has left me.'

'The low hound.'

'He had no option. Double pneumonia. By now, no doubt, he has been reincarnated, but probably only as a jellyfish. A jellyfish need not come between us.'

'Certainly not,' said Sidney McMurdo, speaking warmly, for he had once been stung by one, and they resumed their saunter.

Agnes Flack, meanwhile, though basking in the rays of Captain Jack Fosdyke, had by no means forgotten Sidney McMurdo. In the days that followed their painful interview, in the intervals of brushing up her fifty yards from the pin game in preparation for the Women's Singles contest which was shortly to take place, she found her thoughts dwelling on him quite a good deal. A girl who has loved, even if mistakenly, can never be indifferent to the fortunes of the man whom she once regarded as the lode star of her life. She kept wondering how he was making out, and hoped that his vacation was not being spoiled by a broken heart.

The first time she saw him, accordingly, she should have been relieved and pleased. He was escorting Cora McGuffy Spottsworth along the boardwalk, and it was abundantly obvious even from a casual glance that if his heart had ever been broken, there had been some adroit work done in the repair shop. Clark Gable could have improved his technique by watching the way he bent over Cora McGuffy Spottsworth and stroked her slender arm. He also, while bending and stroking, whispered into her shell-like ear, and you could see that what he was saying was good stuff. His whole attitude was that of a man who, recognizing that he was on a good thing, was determined to push it along.

But Agnes Flack was not relieved and pleased; she was disturbed and concerned. She was perhaps a hard judge, but Cora McGuffy Spottsworth looked to her like the sort of woman who goes about stealing the plans of forts – or, at the best, leaning back negligently on a settee and saying 'Prince, my fan.' The impression Agnes formed was of something that might be all right stepping out of a pie at a bachelor party, but not the type you could take home to meet mother.

Her first move, therefore, on encountering Sidney at the golf club one morning, was to institute a probe.

'Who,' she demanded, not beating about the bush, 'was that lady I saw you walking down the street with?'

Her tone, in which he seemed to detect the note of criticism, offended Sidney.

'That,' he replied with a touch of hauteur, 'was no lady, that was my *fiancée*.'

Agnes reeled. She had noticed that he was wearing a new tie and that his hair had been treated with Sticko, the pomade that satisfies, but she had not dreamed that matters had proceeded as far as this.

'You are engaged?'

'And how!'

'Oh, Sidney!'

He stiffened.

'That will be all of that "Oh, Sidney!" stuff,' he retorted with spirit. 'I don't see what you have to beef about. You were offered the opportunity of a merger, and when you failed to take up your option I was free, I presume, to open negotiations elsewhere. As might have been foreseen, I was snapped up the moment it got about that I was in the market.'

Agnes Flack bridled.

'I'm not jealous.'

'Then what's your kick?'

'It's just that I want to see you happy.'

'I am.'

'How can you be happy with a woman who looks like a snake with hips?'

'She has every right to look like a snake with hips. In a former incarnation she used to be Cleopatra. I,' said Sidney McMurdo, straightening his tie, 'was Antony.'

'Who told you that?'

'She did. She has all the facts.'

'She must be crazy.'

'Not at all. I admit that for a while at our first meeting some such thought did cross my mind, but the matter is readily explained. She is a novelist. You may have heard of Cora McGuffy Spottsworth?'

Agnes uttered a cry.

'What? Oh, she can't be.'

'She has documents to prove it.'

'But, Sidney, she's awful. At my school two girls were expelled because they were found with her books under their pillows. Her publisher's slogan is "Spottsworth for Blushes". You can't intend to marry a woman who notoriously has to write her love scenes on asbestos.'

'Well, what price your intending to marry a prominent international plug-ugly who thinks nothing of shooting people with elephant guns?'

'Only African chiefs.'

'African chiefs are also God's creatures.'

'Not when under the influence of trade gin, Jack says. He says you have to shoot them with elephant guns then. It means nothing more, he says, than if you drew their attention to some ruling by Emily Post. Besides, he knows Bobby Jones.'

'So does Bobby Jones's grocer. Does he play golf himself? That's the point.'

'He plays beautifully.'

'So does Cora. She expects to win the Women's Singles.'

Agnes drew herself up haughtily. She was expecting to win the Women's Singles herself.

'She does, does she?'

'Yes, she does.'

'Over my dead body.'

'That would be a mashie niblick shot,' said Sidney McMurdo thoughtfully. 'She's wonderful with her mashie niblick.'

With a powerful effort Agnes Flack choked down her choler.

'Well, I hope it will be all right,' she said.

'Of course it will be all right. I'm the luckiest man alive.'

'In any case, it's fortunate that we found out our mistake in time.'

'I'll say so. A nice thing it would have been, if all this had happened after we were married. We should have had one of those situations authors have to use a row of dots for.'

'Yes. Even if we had been married, I should have flown to Jack.'

'And I should have flown to Cora.'

'He once killed a lion with a sardine opener.'

'Cora once danced with the Duke of Windsor,' said Sidney McMurdo, and with a proud tilt of the chin, went off to give his betrothed lunch.

As a close student of the game of golf in all its phases over a considerable number of years, I should say that Women's Singles at fashionable seashore resorts nearly always follow the same general lines. The participants with a reasonable hope of bringing home the bacon seldom number more than three or four, the rest being the mere dregs of the golfing world who enter for the hell of the thing or because they know they look well in sports clothes. The preliminary rounds, accordingly, are never worth watching or describing. The rabbits eliminate each other with merry laughs and pretty squeals, and the tigresses massacre the surviving rabbits, till by the time the semi-final is reached, only grim-faced experts are left in.

It was so with the tourney this year at East Bampton. Agnes had no difficulty in murdering the four long handicap fluffies with whom she was confronted in the early stages, and entered the semi-final with the feeling that the competition proper was now about to begin.

Watching, when opportunity offered, the play of the future Mrs Sidney McMurdo, who also had won through to the penultimate round, she found herself feeling a little easier in her mind.

Cora McGuffy Spottsworth still looked to her like one of those women who lure men's souls to the shoals of sin, but there was no question that, as far as knowing what to do with a number four iron when you put it into her hands was concerned, she would make a good wife. Her apprehensions regarding Sidney's future were to a certain extent relieved.

It might be that his bride at some future date would put arsenic in his coffee or elope with the leader of a band, but before she did so, she would in all essential respects be a worthy mate. He would never have to suffer that greatest of all spiritual agonies, the misery of the husband whose wife insists on his playing with her daily because the doctor thinks she ought to have fresh air and exercise. Cora McGuffy Spottsworth might, and probably would, recline on tiger skins in the nude and expect Sidney to drink champagne out of her shoe, but she would never wear high heels on the links or say Tee-hee when she missed a putt. On the previous day, while eliminating her most recent opponent, she had done the long hole in four, and Agnes, who had just taken a rather smelly six, was impressed.

The afternoon of the semi-final was one of those heavy, baking afternoons which cause people to crawl about saying that it is not the heat they mind, but the humidity. After weeks of sunshine the weather was about to break. Thunder was in the air, and once sprightly caddies seemed to droop beneath the weight of their bags. To Agnes, who was impervious to weather conditions, this testing warmth was welcome. It might, she felt, affect her adversary's game.

Cora McGuffy Spottsworth and her antagonist drove off first, and once again Agnes was impressed by the lissom fluidity of the other's swing. Sidney, who was hovering lovingly in the offing, watched her effort with obvious approval.

'You won't want that one back, old girl,' he said, and a curious pang shot through Agnes, as if she had bitten into a bad oyster. How often had she heard him say the same thing to her! For an instant she was aware of a sorrowful sense of loss. Then her eye fell on Captain Jack Fosdyke, smoking a debonair cigarette, and the anguish abated. If Captain Jack Fosdyke was not a king among men, she told herself, she didn't know a king among men when she saw one.

When the couple ahead were out of distance, she drove off and achieved her usual faultless shot. Captain Jack Fosdyke said it reminded him of one he had made when playing a friendly round with Harry Hopkins, and they moved off.

From the moment when her adversary had driven off the first tee, Agnes Flack had realized that she had no easy task before her, but one that would test her skill to the utmost. The woman in question looked like a schoolmistress, and she hit her ball as if it had been a refractory pupil. And to increase the severity of Agnes's ordeal, she seldom failed to hit it straight.

Agnes, too, being at the top of her form, the result was that for ten holes the struggle proceeded with but slight advantage to either. At the sixth, Agnes, putting superbly, contrived to be one up, only to lose her lead on the seventh, where the schoolmistress holed out an iron shot for a birdie. They were all square at the turn, and still all square on the eleventh tee. It was as Agnes was addressing her ball here that there came a roll of thunder, and the rain which had been threatening all the afternoon began to descend in liberal streams.

It seemed to Agnes Flack that Providence was at last intervening on behalf of a good woman. She was always at her best in dirty weather. Give her a tropical deluge accompanied by thunderbolts, and other Acts of God, and she took on a new vigour. And she just had begun to be filled with a stern joy, the joy of an earnest golfer who after a gruelling struggle feels that the thing is in the bag, when she was chagrined to observe that her adversary appeared to be of precisely the same mind. So far from being discouraged by the warring elements, the school-mistress plainly welcomed the new conditions. Taking in the rain at every pore with obvious relish, she smote her ball as if it had been writing rude things about her on the blackboard, and it was as much as Agnes could do to halve the eleventh and twelfth.

All this while Captain Fosdyke had been striding round with them, chatting between the strokes of cannibals he had met and lions which had regretted meeting him, but during these last two holes a strange silence had fallen upon him. And it was as Agnes uncoiled herself on the thirteenth tee after another of her powerful drives that she was aware of him at her elbow, endeavouring to secure her attention. His coat collar was turned up, and he looked moist and unhappy.

'I say,' he said, 'what about this?'

'What?'

'This bally rain.'

'Just a Scotch mist.'

'Don't you think you had better chuck it?'

Agnes stared.

'Are you suggesting that I give up the match?'

'That's the idea.'

Agnes stared again.

'Give up my chance of getting into the final just because of a drop of rain?'

'Well, we're getting dashed wet, what? And golf's only a game, I mean, if you know what I mean.'

Agnes's eyes flashed like the lightning which had just struck a tree not far off.

'I would not dream of forfeiting the match,' she cried. 'And if you leave me now, I'll never speak to you again.'

'Oh, right ho,' said Captain Jack Fosdyke. 'Merely a suggestion.'

He turned his collar a up little higher, and the game proceeded.

Agnes was rudely shaken. Those frightful words about golf being only a game kept ringing in her head. This thing had come upon her like one of the thunderbolts which she liked to have around her when playing an important match. In the brief period of time during which she had known him, Captain Jack Fosdyke's game had appealed to her depths. He had shown himself a skilful and meritorious performer, at times brilliant. But what is golfing skill, if the golfing spirit is absent?

Then a healing thought came to her. He had but jested. In the circles in which he moved, the gay world of African chiefs and English dukes in which he had so long had his being, light-hearted badinage of this kind was no doubt *de rigueur*. To hold his place in that world, a man had to be a merry kidder, a light josher and a mad wag. It was probably because he thought she needed cheering up that he had exercised his flashing wit.

Her doubts vanished. Her faith in him was once more firm. It was as if a heavy load had rolled off her heart. Playing her second, a brassie shot, she uncorked such a snorter that a few moments later she found herself one up again.

As for Captain Jack Fosdyke, he was fully occupied with trying to keep the rain from going down the back of his neck and reminding himself that Agnes was the only niece of Josiah Flack, a man who had a deep sense of family obligations, more money than you could shake a stick at and one foot in the grave.

*   *   *

Whether or not Agnes's opponent was actually a schoolmistress, I do not know. But if she was, the juvenile education of this country is in good hands. In a crisis where a weaker woman might have wilted – one down and five to play – she remained firm and undaunted. Her hat was a frightful object, but it was still in the ring. She fought Agnes, hole after hole, with indomitable tenacity. The fourteenth and fifteenth she halved, but at the sixteenth she produced another of those inspired iron shots and the match was squared. And, going from strength to strength, she won the seventeenth with a twenty-foot putt.

'Dormy one,' she said, speaking for the first time.

It is always a mistake to chatter on the links. It disturbs the concentration. To this burst of speech I attribute the fact that the schoolmistress's tee shot at the eighteenth was so markedly inferior to its predecessors. The eighteenth was a short hole ending just outside the club-house and even rabbits seldom failed to make the green. But she fell short by some yards, and Agnes, judging the distance perfectly, was on and near the pin. The schoolmistress chipped so successfully with her second that it seemed for an instant that she was about to hole out. But the ball stopped a few inches from its destination, and Agnes, with a three-foot putt for a two, felt her heart leap up like that of the poet Wordsworth when he saw a rainbow. She had not missed more than one three-foot putt a year since her kindergarten days.

It was at this moment that there emerged from the club-house where it had been having a saucer of tea and a slice of cake, a Pekinese dog of hard-boiled aspect. It strolled on to the green, and approaching Agnes's ball subjected it to a pop-eyed scrutiny.

There is a vein of eccentricity in all Pekes. Here, one would have said, was a ball with little about it to arrest the attention of a thoughtful dog. It was just a regulation blue dot, slightly battered. Yet it was obvious immediately that it had touched a chord. The animal sniffed at it with every evidence of interest and pleasure. It patted it with its paw. It smelled it. Then, lying down, it took it in its mouth and began to chew meditatively.

To Agnes the mere spectacle of a dog on a green had been a thing of horror. Brought up from childhood to reverence the rules of Greens Committees, she had shuddered violently from head to foot. Recovering herself with a powerful effort, she advanced and said 'Shoo!' The Peke rolled its eyes sideways, inspected her, dismissed her as of no importance or enter-tainment value, and resumed its fletcherizing. Agnes advanced another step, and the schoolmistress for the second time broke her Trappist vows.

'You can't move that dog,' she said. 'It's a hazard.'

'Nonsense.'

'I beg your pardon, it is. If you get into casual water, you don't mop it up with a brush and pail, do you? Certainly you don't. You play out of it. Same thing when you get into a casual dog.'

They train these schoolmistresses to reason clearly. Agnes halted, baffled. Then her eye fell on Captain Jack Fosdyke, and she saw the way out.

'There's nothing in the rules to prevent a spectator, meeting a dog on the course, from picking it up and fondling it.'

It was the schoolmistress' turn to be baffled. She bit her lip in chagrined silence.

'Jack, dear,' said Agnes, 'pick up that dog and fondle it. And,' she added, for she was a quick-thinking girl, 'when doing so, hold its head over the hole.'

It was a behest which one might have supposed that any

knight, eager to win his lady's favour, would have leaped to fulfil. But Captain Jack Fosdyke did not leap. There was a dubious look on his handsome face, and he scratched his chin pensively.

'Just a moment,' he said. 'This is a thing you want to look at from every angle. Pekes are awfully nippy, you know. They make sudden darts at your ankles.'

'Well, you like a spice of danger.'

'Within reason, dear lady, within reason.'

'You once killed a lion with a sardine opener.'

'Ah, but I first quelled him with the power of the human eye. The trouble with Pekes is, they're so shortsighted, they can't see the human eye, so you can't quell them with it.'

'You could if you put your face right down close.'

'If,' said Captain Jack Fosdyke thoughtfully.

Agnes gasped. Already this afternoon she had had occasion to stare at this man. She now stared again.

'Are you afraid of a dog?'

He gave a light laugh.

'Afraid of dogs? That would amuse the boys at Buckingham Palace, if they could hear it. They know what a dare-devil I was in the old days when I was Deputy Master of the Royal Buckhounds. I remember one morning coming down to the kennels with my whistle and my bag of dog biscuits and finding one of the personnel in rather an edgey mood. I spoke to it soothingly – "Fido, Fido, good boy, Fido!" – but it merely bared its teeth and snarled, and I saw that it was about to spring. There wasn't a moment to lose. By a bit of luck the Bluemantle Pursuivant at Arms had happened to leave his blue mantle hanging over the back of a chair. I snatched it up and flung it over the animal's head, after which it was a simple task to secure it with stout cords and put on its muzzle. There was a good deal of comment on my adroitness. Lord Slythe and Sayle, who was present, I remember, said to Lord Knubble of Knopp, who was also present, that he hadn't seen anything so resourceful since the day when the Chancellor of the Duchy of Lancaster rang in a bad half-crown on the First Gold Stick in Waiting.'

It was the sort of story which in happier days had held Agnes Flack enthralled, but now it merely added to her depression and disillusionment. She made a last attempt to appeal to his better feelings.

'But, Jack, if you don't shift this beastly little object, I shall lose the match.'

'Well, what does that matter, dear child? A mere tiddly seaside competition.'

Agnes had heard enough. Her eyes were stony.

'You refuse? Then our engagement is at an end.'

'Oh, don't say that.'

'I do say that.'

It was plain that a struggle was proceeding in Captain Jack Fosdyke's soul, or what one may loosely call his soul. He was thinking how rich Josiah Flack was, how fond of his niece, and how frail. On the other hand, the Peke, now suspecting a plot against its well-being, had bared a small but serviceable tooth at the corner of its mouth. The whole situation was very difficult.

As he stood there at a man's cross-roads, there came out of the club-house, smoking a cigarette in a sixteen-inch holder, an expensively upholstered girl with platinum hair and vermilion finger-nails. She bent and picked the Peke up.

'My little angel would appear to be interfering with your hockey-knocking,' she said. 'Why, hello, Captain Fosdyke. You here? Come along in and give me a cocktail.'

She kissed the Peke lovingly on the top of its head and carried it into the club-house. The ball went with them.

'She's gone into the bar,' said the schoolmistress. 'You'll have to chip out from there. Difficult shot. I'd use a niblick.'

Captain Jack Fosdyke was gazing after the girl, a puzzled wrinkle on his forehead.

'I've met her before somewhere, but I can't place her. Who is she?'

'One of the idle rich,' said the schoolmistress, sniffing. Her views were Socialistic.

Captain Jack Fosdyke started.

'Idle *rich*?'

'That's Lulabelle Sprockett, the Sprockett's Superfine Sardine heiress. She's worth a hundred million in her own right.'

'In her own right? You mean she's actually got the stuff in the bank, where she can lay hands on it whenever she feels disposed? Good God!' cried Captain Jack Fosdyke. 'Bless my soul! Well, well, well, well, well!' He turned to Agnes. 'Did I hear you mention something about breaking our engagement? Right ho, dear lady, right ho. Just as you say. Nice to have known you. I shall watch your future career with considerable interest. Excuse me,' said Captain Jack Fosdyke.

There was a whirring sound, and he disappeared into the club-house.

'I concede the match,' said Agnes dully.

'Might just as well,' said the schoolmistress.

Agnes Flack stood on the eighteenth green, contemplating the ruin of her life. It was not the loss of Captain Jack Fosdyke that was making her mourn, for the scales had fallen from her eyes. He had shown himself totally lacking in the golfing spirit, and infatuation was dead. What did jar her was that she had lost Sidney McMurdo. In this dark hour all the old love had come sweeping back into her soul like a tidal wave.

Had she been mad to sever their relations?

The answer to that was 'Certainly'.

Had she, like a child breaking up a Noah's Ark with a tack hammer, deliberately sabotaged her hopes and happiness?

The reply to that was 'Quite'.

Would she ever see him again?

In the space allotted to this question she could pencil in the word 'Undoubtedly', for he was even now coming out of the locker-room entrance.

'Sidney!' she cried.

He seemed depressed. His colossal shoulders were dropping, and his eyes were those of a man who has drunk the wine of life to the lees.

'Oh, hello,' he said.

There was a silence.

'How did Mrs Spottsworth come out?' asked Agnes

'Eh? Oh, she won.'

Agnes's depression hit a new low. There was another silence.

'She has broken the engagement,' said Sidney.

The rain was still sluicing down with undiminished intensity, but it seemed to Agnes Flack, as she heard these words, that a blaze of golden sunshine had suddenly lit up the East Bampton golf course.

'She wanted to quit because of the rain,' went on Sidney, in a low, toneless voice. 'I took her by the ear and led her round, standing over her with upraised hand as she made her shots, ready to let her have a juicy one if she faltered. On one or two occasions I was obliged to do so. By these means I steered her through to victory, but she didn't like it. Having holed out on the eighteenth for a nice three, which gave her the match, she told me that I had completely changed since those days on the Nile and that she never wished to see or speak to me again in this or any other incarnation.'

Agnes was gulping like one of those peculiar fish you catch down in Florida.

'Then you are free?'

'And glad of it. What I ever saw in the woman beats me. But what good is that, when I have lost you?'

'But you haven't.'

'Pardon me. What about your Fosdyke?'

'I've just broken my engagement, too. Oh, Sidney, let's go right off and get married under an arch of niblicks before we make any more of these unfortunate mistakes. Let me tell you how that Fosdyke false alarm behaved.'

In molten words she began to relate her story, but she had not proceeded far when she was obliged to stop, for Sidney McMurdo's strong arms were about her and he was crushing her to his bosom. And when Sidney McMurdo crushed girls to his bosom, they had to save their breath for breathing purposes, inhaling and exhaling when and if they could.

Alfred Jukes and Wilberforce Bream had just holed out at the end of their match for the club championship, the latter sinking a long putt to win, and the young man sitting with the Oldest Member on the terrace overlooking the eighteenth green said that though this meant a loss to his privy purse of ten dollars, his confidence in Jukes remained unimpaired. He still considered him a better golfer than Bream.

The Sage nodded without much enthusiasm.

'You may be right,' he agreed. 'But I would not call either of them a good golfer.'

'They're both scratch.'

'True. But it is not mere technical skill that makes a man a good golfer, it is the golfing soul. These two have not the proper attitude of seriousness towards the game. Jukes once returned to the club-house in the middle of a round because there was a thunderstorm and his caddie got struck by lightning, and I have known Bream to concede a hole for the almost frivolous reason that he had sliced his ball into a hornet's nest and was reluctant to play it where it lay. This was not the Bewstridge spirit.'

'The what spirit?'

'The spirit that animated Horace Bewstridge, the finest golfer I have ever known.'

'Was he scratch?'

'Far from it. His handicap was twenty-four. But though his ball was seldom in the right place, his heart was. When I think what Horace Bewstridge went through that day he battled for the President's Cup, I am reminded of the poem, Excelsior, by the late Henry Wadsworth Longfellow, with which you are doubtless familiar.'

'I used to recite it as a child.'

'I am sorry I missed the treat,' said the Oldest Member courteously. 'Then you will recall how its hero, in his struggle to reach the heights, was laid stymie after stymie, and how in order to achieve his aim, he had to give up all idea of resting his head upon the maiden's breast, though cordially invited to do so. A tear, if you remember, stood in his bright blue eye, but with a brief "Excelsior!" he intimated that no business could result. Virtually the same thing that happened to Horace Bewstridge.'

'You know,' said the young man, 'I've always thought that Excelsior bird a bit of a fathead. I mean to say, what was there in it for him? As far as I can make out, just the walk.'

'Suppose he had been trying to win his first cup?'

'I don't recollect anything being said about any cup. Do they give cups for climbing mountains 'mid snow and ice?'

'We are getting a little muddled,' said the Oldest Member. 'You appear to be discussing the youth with the banner and the clarion voice, while I am talking about Horace Bewstridge. It may serve to clear the air and disperse the fog of misunderstanding if I tell you the latter's story. And in order that you shall miss none of the finer shades, I must begin by dwelling upon his great love for Vera Witherby.'

* * *

It was only after the thing had been going on for some time (said the Oldest Member) that I learned of this secret romance in Horace's life. As a rule, the Romeos who live about here are not backward in confiding in me when they fall in love. Indeed, I sometimes feel that I shall have to begin keeping them off with a stick. But Bewstridge was reticent. It was purely by chance that I became aware of his passion.

One rather breezy morning, I was sitting almost exactly where we are sitting now, thinking of this and that, when I observed fluttering towards me across the terrace a sheet of paper. It stopped against my foot, and I picked it up and read its contents. They ran as follows: –

MEM

O<small>LD</small> B.	Ribs. But watch eyes.
M<small>A</small> B.	Bone up on pixies. Flowers. Insects.
I.	Symp. breeziness.
A.	Concil. If poss. p., but w.o. for s.d.a.

That was all, and I studied it with close attention and, I must confess, a certain amount of alarm. There had been a number of atom-bomb spy scares in the papers recently, and it occurred to me that this might be a secret code, possibly containing information about some local atoms.

It was then that I saw Horace Bewstridge hurrying towards me. He appeared agitated.

'Have you seen a piece of paper?' he asked.

'Would this be it?'

He took it, and seemed to hesitate for a moment.

'I suppose you're wondering what it's all about?'

I admitted to a certain curiosity, and he hesitated again. Then there crept into his eyes the look which I have seen so often in the eyes of young men. I saw that he was about to confide in me. And presently out it all came, like beer from a bottle. He was in love with Vera Witherby, the niece of one Ponsford Botts, a resident in the neighbourhood.

In putting it like that, I am giving you the thing in condensed form, confining myself to the gist. Horace Bewstridge was a little long-winded about it all, going rather deeply into his emotions and speaking at some length about her eyes, which he compared to twin stars. It was several minutes before I was able to enquire how he was making out.

'Have you told your love?' I asked.

'Not yet,' said Horace Bewstridge. 'I goggle a good deal, but for the present am content to leave it at that. You see, I'm working this thing on a system. All the nibs will tell you that everything is done by propaganda nowadays, and that your first move, if you want to get anywhere, must be to rope in a *bloc* of friendly neutrals. I start, accordingly, by making myself solid with the family. I give them the old salve, get them rooting for me, and thus ensure an impressive build-up. Only then do I take direct action and edge into what you might call the *blitzkrieg*. This paper contains notes for my guidance.'

'With reference to administering the salve?'

'Exactly.'

I took the document from him, and glanced at it again.

'What,' I asked, 'does "Old B. Ribs. But watch eyes" signify?'

'Quite simple. Old Botts tells dialect stories about Irishmen named Pat and Mike, and you laugh when he prods you in the ribs. But sometimes he doesn't prod you in the ribs, merely stands there looking pop-eyed. One has to be careful about that.'

'Under the heading "Ma B.", I see you say: "Bone up on pixies." You add the words "flowers" and "insects".'

'Yes. All that is vitally important. Mrs Botts, I am sorry to say, is a trifle on the whimsy side. Perhaps you have read her books? They are three in number – *My Chums the Pixies*, *How to Talk to the Flowers*, and *Many of My Best Friends are Mosquitoes*. The programme calls for a good working knowledge of them all.'

'Who is "I", against whose name you have written the phrase: "Symp. breeziness"?'

'That is little Irwin Botts, the son of the house. He is in love with Dorothy Lamour, and not making much of a go of it. He talks to me about her, and I endeavour to be breezily sympathetic.'

'And "A"?'

'Their poodle, Alphonse. The note is to remind me to conciliate him. He is a dog of wide influence, and cannot be ignored.'

' "I poss., p., but w.o. for s.d.a."?'

'If possible, pat, but watch out for sudden dash at ankles. He is extraordinarily quick on his feet.'

I handed back the paper.

'Well,' I said, 'it all seems a little elaborate, and I should have thought better results would have been obtained by having a direct pop at the girl, but I wish you luck.'

In the days which followed, I kept a watchful eye on Horace, for his story had interested me strangely. Now and then, I would see him pacing the terrace with Ponsford Botts at his side and catch references to Pat and Mike, together with an occasional 'Begorrah', and I noted how ringing was his guffaw as the other suddenly congealed with bulging eyes.

Once, as I strolled along the road, I heard a noise like machine-gun fire and turned the corner to find him slapping little Irwin's shoulder in a breezy, elder-brotherly manner. His pockets were generally bulging with biscuits for Alphonse, and from time to time he would come and tell me how he was getting along with Mrs Botts' books. These, he confessed, called for all that he had of resolution and fortitude, but he told me that he was slowly mastering their contents and already knew a lot more about pixies than most people.

It would all have been easier, he said, if he had been in a position to be able to concentrate his whole attention upon them. But of course he had his living to earn and could not afford to neglect his office work. He held a subordinate post in the well-known firm of R. P. Crumbles Inc., purveyors of Silver Sardines (The Sardine with A Soul), and R. P. Crumbles was a hard taskmaster. And, in addition to this, he had entered for the annual handicap competition known as the President's Cup.

It was upon this latter topic, as the date of the tourney drew near, that he spoke almost as frequently and eloquently as upon the theme of his love. He had been playing golf, it appeared, for some seven years, and up till now had never come within even measurable distance of winning a trophy. Generally, he said, it was his putting that dished him. But recently, as the result of reading golf books, he had adopted a super-scientific system, and was now hoping for the best.

It was a stimulating experience to listen to his fine, frank enthusiasm. He spoke of the President's Cup as some young knight of King Arthur's Round Table might have spoken of the Holy Grail. And it was consequently with peculiar satisfaction that I noted his success in the early rounds. Step by step, he won his way into the semi-finals in his bracket, and was enabled to get triumphantly through that critical test owing to the fortunate circumstance of his opponent tripping over a passing cat on the eve of the match and spraining his ankle.

Many members of the club would, of course, have been fully competent to defeat Horace Bewstridge if they had sprained both ankles, or even broken both arms, but Mortimer Gooch, his antagonist, was not one of these. He scratched, and Horace walked over into the final.

His chances now, it seemed to me, were extremely good. According to how the semi-final in the other bracket went, he would be playing either Peter Willard, who would be as clay in his hands, or a certain Sir George Copstone, a visiting Englishman whom his employer, R. P. Crumbles, had put up for the club, and who by an odd coincidence was residing as a guest at the house of Ponsford Botts. I had watched this hand across the sea in action, and was convinced that Horace, provided he did not lose his nerve, could trim him nicely.

A meeting on the fifteenth green the afternoon before the match enabled me to convey these views to the young fellow. We were there to watch the finish of the opposition semi-final, and when Sir George Copstone had won this, I linked my arm in Horace's and told him that in my opinion the thing was in the bag.

'If Peter Willard, our most outstanding golfing cripple, can take this man to the fifteenth, your victory should be a certainty.'

'Peter was receiving thirty-eight.'

'You could give him fifty. What is this Copstone? A twenty-four like yourself, is he not?'

'Yes.'

'Then you need feel no anxiety, my boy,' I said, for when I give a pep talk I like it to be a pep talk. 'If you are not too busy to-night reading about pixies, you might be looking around your living-room for a spot to put that cup.'

He snorted devoutly, and I think he was about to burst into

one of those ecstatic monologues of his, but at this moment we reached the terrace. And, as we did so, a harsh, metallic voice called his name, and I perceived, standing at some little distance, a beetle-browed man of formidable aspect, who looked like a cartoon of Capital in a Labour paper. He was smoking a large cigar, with which he beckoned to Horace Bewstridge imperiously, and Horace, leaving my side, ambled up to him like a spaniel. From the fact that, as he ambled, he was bleating 'Oh, good evening, Mr Crumbles. Yes, Mr Crumbles. I'm coming, Mr Crumbles,' I deduced that this was the eminent sardine fancier who provided him with his weekly envelope.

Their conversation was not an extended one. R. P. Crumbles spoke rapidly and authoritatively for some moments, emphasising his remarks with swift, captain-of-industry prods at Horace's breast-bone, and then he turned on his heel and strode off in a strong, economic royalist sort of way, and Horace came back to where I stood.

Now, I had noticed once or twice during the interview that the young fellow had seemed to totter on his axis, and as he drew nearer, his pallid face, with its starting eyes and drooping jaw, told me that all was not well.

'That was my boss,' he said, in a low, faint voice.

'So I had guessed. Why did he call the conference?'

Horace Bewstridge beat his breast.

'It's about Sir George Copstone.'

'What about him!?'

Horace Bewstridge clutched his hair.

'Apparently this Copstone runs a vast system of chain stores throughout the British Isles, and old Crumbles has been fawning on him ever since his arrival in the hope of getting him to take on the Silver Sardine and propagate it over there. He says that this is a big opportunity for the dear old firm and that it behoves all of us to do our bit and push it along. So—'

'So—?'

Horace Bewstridge rent his pullover.

'So,' he whispered hoarsely, 'I've got to play Customer's Golf to-morrow and let the man win that cup.'

'Horace!' I cried.

I would have seized his hand and pressed it, but it was not there. Horace Bewstridge had left me. All that my eye encountered was a swirl of dust and his flying form disappearing in the direction of the bar. I understood and sympathized. There are moments in the life of every man when human consolation cannot avail and only two or three quick ones will meet the case.

I did not see him again until we met next afternoon on the first tee for the start of the final.

You, being a newcomer here (said the Oldest Member) may possibly have formed an erroneous impression regarding this President's Cup of which I have been speaking. Its name, I admit, is misleading, suggesting as it does the guerdon of some terrific tourney battled for by the cream of the local golfing talent. One pictures perspiring scratch men straining every nerve and history being made by amateur champions.

As a matter of fact, it is open for competition only to those whose handicap is not lower than twenty-four, and excites little interest outside the ranks of the submerged tenth who play for it. As a sporting event on our fixture list, as I often have to explain, it may be classed somewhere between the Grandmothers' Umbrella and the All day Sucker competed for by children who have not passed their seventh year.

The final, accordingly, did not attract a large gate. In fact,

I think I was the only spectator. I was thus enabled to obtain an excellent view of the contestants and to follow their play to the best advantage. And, as on the previous occasions when I had watched him perform, I found myself speculating with no little bewilderment as to how Horace's opponent had got that way.

Sir George Copstone was one of those tall, thin, bony Englishmen who seem to have been left over from the eighteen-sixties. He did not actually wear long side-whiskers of the type known as Piccadilly Weepers, nor did he really flaunt a fore-and-aft deerstalker cap of the type affected by Sherlock Holmes, but you got the illusion that this was so, and it was partly the unnerving effect of his appearance on his opponents that had facilitated his making his way into the final. But what had been the basic factor in his success was his method of play.

A deliberate man, this Copstone. Before making a shot, he would inspect his enormous bag of clubs and take out one after another, slowly, as if he were playing spillikens. Having at length made his selection, he would stand motionless beside his ball, staring at it for what seemed an eternity. Only after one had begun to give up hope that life would ever again animate the rigid limbs, would he start his stroke. He was affectionately known on our links as The Frozen Horror.

Even in normal circumstances, a sensitive, highly-strung young man like Horace Bewstridge might well have found himself hard put to it to cope with such an antagonist. And when you take into consideration the fact that he had received those special instructions from the front office, it is not surprising that he should have failed in the opening stages of the encounter to give of his best. The fourth hole found him four down, and one had the feeling that he was lucky not to be five.

At this point, however, there occurred one of those remarkable changes of fortune which are so common in golf and which make it the undisputed king of games. Teeing up at the fifty, Sir George Copstone appeared suddenly to have become afflicted with some form of shaking palsy. Where before he had stood addressing his ball like Lot's wife just after she had been turned into a pillar of salt, he now wriggled like an Ouled Nail dancer in the throes of colic. Nor did his condition improve as the match progressed. His movements took on an even freer abandon. To cut a long story short, which I am told is a thing I seldom do, he lost four holes in a row, and they came to the ninth all square.

And it was here that I observed an almost equally surprising change in the demeanour of Horace Bewstridge.

Until this moment, Horace had been going through the motions with something of the weary moodiness of a Volga boatman, his face drawn, his manner listless. But now he had become a different man. As he advanced to the ninth tee, his eyes gleamed, his ears wiggled and his lips were set. He looked like a Volga boatman who has just learned that Stalin has purged his employer.

I could see what had happened. Intoxicated with this unexpected success, he was beginning to rebel against these instructions from up top. The almost religious fervour which comes upon a twenty-four handicap man when he sees a chance of winning his first cup had him in its grip. Who, he was asking himself, was R. P. Crumbles? The man who paid him his salary and could fire him out on his ear, yes, but was money everything? Suppose he won this cup and starved in the gutter, I could almost hear him murmuring, would not that be better than losing the cup and getting his three square a day?

And when on the ninth green, by pure accident, he sank a

thirty-foot putt, I saw his lips move and I knew what he was saying to himself. It was the word 'Excelsior'.

It was as he stood gaping at the hole into which his ball had disappeared that Sir George Copstone spoke for the first time.

'Jolly good shot, what?' said Sir George, a gallant sportsman. 'Right in the old crevasse, what, what? I say, look here,' he went on, jerking his shoulders in a convulsive gesture, 'do you mind if I go and shake out the underlinen? Got a beetle or something down my back.'

'Certainly,' said Horace.

'Won't keep you long. I'll just strip off the next-the-skins and spring upon it unawares.'

He performed another complicated writhing movement, and was about to leave us, when along came R. P. Crumbles.

'How's it going?' asked R. P. Crumbles.

'Eh? What? Going? Oh, one down at the turn.'

'He is?'

'No, I am,' said Sir George. 'He, in sharp contradistinction, is one up. Sank a dashed fine putt on this green. Thirty feet, if an inch. Well, excuse me, I'll just buzz off and bash this beetle.'

He hastened away, twitching in every limb, and R. P. Crumbles turned to Horace. His face was suffused.

'Do I get no co-operation, Bewstridge?' he demanded. 'What the devil do you mean by being one up? And what's all this nonsense about thirty-foot putts? How dare you sink thirty-foot putts?'

I could have told him that Horace was in no way responsible for what had occurred and that the thing must be looked on as an Act of God, but I hesitated to wound the young man's feelings, and R. P. Crumbles continued.

'Thirty-foot putts, indeed! Have you forgotten what I told you?'

Horace Bewstridge met his accusing glare without a tremor. His face was like granite. His eyes shone with a strange light.

'I have not forgotten the inter-office memo. to which you refer,' he said, in a firm, quiet voice. 'But I am ignoring it. I intend to trim the pants off this stranger in our midst.'

'You do, and see what happens.'

'I don't care what happens.'

'Bewstridge,' said R. P. Crumbles, 'nine more holes remain to be played. During these nine holes, think well. I shall be waiting on the eighteenth to see the finish. I shall hope to find,' he added significantly, 'that the match has ended before then.'

He walked away, and I think I have never seen the back of any head look more sinister. Horace, however, merely waved his putter defiantly, as if it had been a banner with a strange device and the other an old man recommending him not to try a pass.

'Nuts to you, R. P. Crumbles!' he cried, with a strange dignity. 'Fire me, if you will. This is the only chance I shall ever have of winning a cup, and I'm going to do it.'

I stood for a moment motionless. This revelation of the nobility of this young man's soul had stunned me. Then I hurried to where he stood, and gripped his hand. I was still shaking it, when an arch contralto voice spoke behind us.

'Good afternoon, Mr Bewstridge.'

Mrs Botts was in our midst. She was accompanied by her husband, Ponsford, her son Irwin, and her dog, Alphonse.

'How is the match going?' asked Mrs Botts.

Horace explained the position of affairs.

'We shall all be on the eighteenth green, to see the finish,' said Mrs Botts. 'But you really must not beat Sir George. That would be very naughty. Where is Sir George?'

As she spoke, Sir George Copstone appeared, looking quite his old self again.

'Bashed him!' he said. 'Whopping big chap. Put up the dickens of a struggle. But I settled him in the end. He'll think twice before he tackles a Sussex Copstone again.'

Mrs Botts uttered a girlish scream.

'Somebody attacked you, Sir George?'

'I should say so. Whacking great brute of a beetle. But I fixed him.'

'You killed a beetle?'

'Well, stunned him, at any rate. Technical knockout.'

'But, Sir George, don't you remember what Coleridge said – He prayeth best who loveth best all things both great and small?'

'Not beetles?'

'Of course. Some of my closest chums are beetles.'

The other seemed amazed.

'This friend of yours, this Coleridge, really says – he positively asserts that we ought to love beetles?'

'Of course.'

'Even when they get under the vest and start doing buck and wing dances along the spine?'

'Of course.'

'Sounds a bit of a silly ass to me. Not the sort of chap one would care to know. Well, come on, Bewstridge, let's be moving, what? I say,' went on Sir George, as they passed out of earshot, 'do you know that old geezer? Potty, what? Over in England, we'd have her in a padded cell before she could say "Pip, pip". Beetles, egad! Coleridge, forsooth! And do you know what she said to me this morning? Told me to be careful where I stepped on the front lawn, because it was full of pixies. Can't stand that husband of hers, either. Always talking rot about Irishmen. And what price the son and heir? There's a young blister for you. And as for that flea storage depot she calls a dog... Well, I'll tell you. If I'd known what I was letting myself in for, staying at her house, I'd have gone to a hotel. Carry on, Bewstridge. It's your honour.'

It was perhaps the exhilaration due to hearing these frank criticisms of a quartette whom he had never liked, though he had striven to love them for Vera Witherby's sake, that lent zip to Horace's drive from the tenth tee. Normally, he was a man who alternated between a weak slice and a robust hook, but on this occasion his ball looked neither to right nor left. He pasted it straight down the middle, and with such vehemence that he had no difficulty in winning the hole and putting himself two up.

But now the tide of fortune began to change again. His recent victory over the beetle had put Sir George Copstone right back into the old mid-season form. Once more he had become the formidable Frozen Horror whose deliberate methods of play had caused three stout men to succumb before his onslaught in the preliminary rounds. With infinite caution, like one suspecting a trap of some kind, he selected clubs from his bulging bag; with unremitting concentration he addressed and struck his ball. And for a while there took place as stern a struggle as I have ever witnessed on the links.

But gradually Sir George secured the upper hand. Little by little he recovered the ground he had lost. He kept turning in steady sevens, and came a time when Horace began to take nines. The strain had uncovered his weak spot. His putting touch had left him.

I could see what was wrong, of course. He was being much too scientific. He was remembering the illustrated plates in the golf books and trying to make the club head move from Spot A. through Line B. to ball C. and that is always a fatal thing for a high handicap man to do. I have talked to a great many of our most successful high handicap men, and they all assured me that the only way in which it was possible to obtain results was to shut the eyes, breathe a short prayer and loose off into the unknown.

Still, there it was, and there was nothing that could be done about it. Horace went on studying the line and taking the Bobby Jones stance and all the rest of it, and gradually, as I say, Sir George recovered the ground he had lost. One down on the thirteenth, he squared the match at the fifteenth, and it was only by holing out a fortunate brassie shot to win on the seventeenth that Horace was enabled to avoid defeat by two and one. As it was, they came to the eighteenth on level terms, and everything, therefore, depended on what Fate held in store for them there.

I had a melancholy feeling that the odds were all in favour of the older man. At the time of which I am speaking, the eighteenth was not the long hole which we are looking at as we sit here, but that short, tricky one which is now the ninth – the one where you stand at the foot of the hill and pop the ball up vertically with a mashie, trusting that you will not overdrive and run across the green into the deep chasm on the other side. At such a hole, a cautious, calculating player like Sir George Copstone inevitably has the advantage over a younger and more ardent antagonist, who is apt to put too much beef behind his tee shot.

My fear, however, that Horace would fall into this error was not fulfilled. His ball soared in a perfect arc, and one could see at a glance that it must have dropped very near the pin. Sir George's effort, though sound and scholarly, was not in the same class, and there could be no doubt that on reaching the summit we should find that he was away. And so it proved. The first thing I saw as I arrived, was a group consisting of Ponsford Botts, little Irwin Botts and the poodle, Alphonse; the second, Horace's ball lying some two feet from the flag; the third, that of his opponent at least six feet beyond it.

Sir George, a fighter to the last, putting to within a few inches of the hole, and I heard Horace draw a deep breath.

'This for it,' he said. And, as he spoke, there was a rapid pattering of feet, and what looked like a bundle of black cotton-wool swooped past him, seized the ball in its slavering jaws and bore it away. At this crucial moment, with Horace Bewstridge's fortunes swaying in the balance, the poodle Alphonse had got the party spirit.

The shocked 'Hoy!' that sprang from my lips must have sounded to the animal like the Voice of Conscience, for he started visibly and dropped the ball. I had at least prevented him from going to the last awful extreme of carrying it down into the abyss.

But the spot where he had dropped it, was on the very edge of the green, and Horace Bewstridge stood motionless, with ashen face. Once before, in the course of this match, he had sunk a putt of this length, but he was doubting if that sort of thing happened twice in a lifetime. He would have to concentrate, concentrate. With knitted brow, he knelt down to study the line. And, as he did so, Alphonse began to bark.

Horace rose. Almost as clearly as if he had given them verbal utterance, I could read the thoughts that were passing through his mind.

This dog, he was saying to himself, was the apple of Irwin Botts' eye. It was also the apple of Ponsford Botts' eye. To seek it out and kick it in the slats, therefore, would be to shoot that system of his to pieces beyond repair. Irwin Botts would look at him askance. Ponsford Botts would look at him askance. And if they looked at him askance, Vera Witherby would look at him askance, too, for they were presumably the apples of her eye, just as Alphonse was the apple of theirs.

On the other hand, he could not putt with a noise like that going on.

He made his decision. If he should lose Vera Witherby, it would be most unfortunate, but not so unfortunate as losing the President's Cup. Horace Bewstridge, as I have said, was a golfer.

The next moment, the barking had broken off in a sharp yelp, and Alphonse was descending into the chasm like a falling star. Horace returned to his ball, and resumed his study of the line.

The Bottses, Irwin and Ponsford, had been stunned witnesses of the assault. They now gave tongue simultaneously.

'Hey!' cried Irwin Botts.

'Hi!' cried Ponsford Botts.

Horace frowned meditatively at the hole. Even apart from the length of it, it was a difficult shot. He would have to allow for the undulations of the green. There was a nasty little slope there to the right. That must be taken into consideration. There was also, further on, a nasty little slope to the left. The thing called for profound thought, and for some reason he found himself unable to give his whole mind to the problem.

Then he saw what the trouble was. Irwin Botts was standing beside him, shouting 'Hey!' in his left ear, and Ponsford Botts was standing on the other side, shouting 'Hi!' in his right ear. It was this that was affecting his concentration.

He gazed at them, momentarily at a loss. How, he asked himself, would Bobby Jones have handled a situation like this?

The answer came in a flash. He would have taken Irwin Botts by the scruff of his neck, led him to the brink of the chasm and kicked him into it. He would then have come back for Ponsford Botts.

Horace did this, and resumed the scrutiny of the line. And at this moment, accompanied by a pretty, soulful-looking girl in whom I recognized Vera Witherby, R. P. Crumbles came on to the green. As his eye fell on Horace, his face darkened. He asked Sir George Copstone how the match stood.

'I should have thought,' he said, chewing his cigar ominously, 'that it would have been over long before this. I had supposed that you would have won on about the fifteenth or sixteenth.'

'It is a point verging very decidedly on the moot,' replied Sir George, 'if I'm going to win on the eighteenth. He's got this for it, and I expect him to sink it, now that there's nothing to distract his mind. He was being a bit bothered a moment ago,' he explained, 'by Botts senior, Botts junior and the Botts dog. But he has just kicked them all into the chasm, and can now give his whole attention to the game. Capable young feller, that. Just holed out a two hundred yard brassie shot. Judged it to a nicety.'

I heard Vera Witherby draw in her breath sharply. R. P. Crumbles, switching his cigar from one side of his mouth to the other, strode across to where Horace was bending over his ball, and spoke rapidly and forcefully.

It was a dangerous thing to do, and one against which his best friends would have advised him. There was no 'Yes, Mr Crumbles', 'No, Mr Crumbles' about Horace Bewstridge now. I saw him straighten him with a testy frown. The next moment, he had attached himself to the scruff of the other's neck and was adding him to the contents of the chasm.

This done, he returned, took another look at the hole with his head on one side, and seemed satisfied. He rose, and addressed his ball. He was drawing the club head back, when a sudden scream rent the air. Glancing over his shoulder, exasperated, he saw that their little group had been joined by Mrs Botts. She was bending over the edge of the chasm, endeavouring to establish communication with its inmates. Muffled voices rose from the depths.

'Ponsford!'

'Wah, wah, wah.'

'Mr Crumbles!'

'Wah, wah, wah.'

'Irwin!'

'Wah, wah, wah.'

'Alphonse!'

'Woof, woof, woof.'

Mrs Botts bent still further forward, one hand resting on the turf, the other cupped to her ear.

'What? What did you say? I can't hear. What are you doing down there? What? I can't hear. What is Mr Crumbles doing down there? Why has he got his foot in Irwin's eye? Irwin, take your eye away from Mr Crumbles' foot immediately. What? I can't hear. Tell whom he is fired, Mr Crumbles? I can't hear. Why is Alphonse biting Mr Crumbles in the leg? What? I can't hear. I wish you would speak plainly. Your mouth's full of what? Ham? Oh, sand? Why is your mouth full of sand? Why is Alphonse now biting Irwin? Skin whom, Mr Crumbles? What? I can't hear. You've swallowed your cigar? Why? What? I can't hear.'

It seemed to Horace Bewstridge, that this sort of thing, unless firmly checked at the source, might go on indefinitely. And to attempt to concentrate while it did, was hopeless. Clicking his tongue in annoyance at these incessant interruptions, he stepped across to where Mrs Botts crouched. There was a sound like a pistol shot. Mrs Botts joined the others. Horace came back, rubbing his hand, studied the line again and took his stance.

'Mr Bewstridge!'

The words, spoken in his left ear just as he was shooting, were little more than a whisper, but they affected Horace as if an ammunition dump had exploded beneath him. Until this moment, he had evidently been unaware of the presence of the girl he loved, and this unexpected announcement of it caused him to putt rather strongly.

His club descended with a convulsive jerk, and the ball, as if feeling that now that all that scientific nonsense was over, it knew where it was, started off for the hole at forty miles an hour in a dead straight line. There were slopes to the right. There were slopes to the left. It ignored them. Sizzling over the turf, it struck the back of the cup, soared into the air like a rocket, came down, soared up again, fell once more bounced and rebounded and finally, after rattling round and round for perhaps a quarter of a minute, rested safe at journey's end. The struggle for the President's Cup was over.

'Nice work,' said Sir George Copstone. 'Your match, what?'

Horace was gazing at Vera Witherby.

'You spoke?' he said.

She blushed in pretty confusion.

'It was nothing. I only wanted to thank you.'

'Thank me?'

'For what you did to Aunt Lavender.'

'Me, too,' said Sir George Copstone, who had joined them. 'Precisely what the woman needed. Should be a turning point in her life. That'll take her mind off pixies for a bit. *And* beetles.'

Horace stared at the girl. He had thought to see her shrink from him in loathing. Instead of which, she was looking at him with something in her eyes which, if he was not very much mistaken, was the love light.

'Vera ... Do you mean ... ?'

Her eyes must have given him his answer, for he sprang forward and clasped her to his bosom, using the interlocking grip. She nestled in his arms.

'I misjudged you, Horace,' she whispered. 'I thought you were a sap. I mistrusted anyone who could be as fond as you seemed to be of Aunt Lavender, Uncle Ponsford, little Irwin and Alphonse. And I had always yearned for one of those engagements where my man, like Romeo, would run fearful risks to come near me, and I would have to communicate with him by means of notes in hollow trees.'

'Romantic,' explained Sir George. 'Many girls are.'

Into the ecstasy of Horace Bewstridge's mood there crept a chilling thought. He had won her love. He had won the President's Cup. But, unless he had quite misinterpreted the recent exchange of remarks between Mrs Botts and R. P. Crumbles at the chasm side, he had lost his job and so far from being able to support a wife, would now presumably have to starve in the gutter.

He explained this, and Sir George Copstone pooh-poohed vehemently.

'Starve in the gutter? Never heard such bally rot. What do you want to go starving in gutters for? Join me, what? Come over to England, I mean to say, and accept a prominent position in my chain of dashed stores. Name your own salary, of course.'

Horace reeled.

'You don't mean that?'

'Of course I mean it. What do you think I meant? What other possible construction could you have put on my words?'

'But you don't know what I can do.'

Sir George stared.

'Not know what you can do? Why, I've seen you in action, dash it. If what you have just done isn't enough to give a discerning man an idea of your capabilities, I'd like to know what is. Ever since I went to stay at that house, I've wanted to find someone capable of kicking that dog, kicking that boy, kicking old Botts and giving Ma Botts a juicy one right on the good old spot. I'm not merely grateful to you, my dear chap, profoundly grateful, I'm overcome with admiration. Enormously impressed, I am. Never saw anything so adroit. What I need in my business is a man who thinks on his feet and does it now. Ginger up some of my branch managers a bit. Of course, you must join me, dear old thing, and don't forget about making the salary big. And now that's settled, how about trickling off to the bar and having a few? Yoicks!'

'Yoicks!' said Horace.

'Yoicks!' said Vera Witherby.

'Tallo-ho!' said Sir George.

'Tallo-ho!' said Horace.

'Tally-ho!' said Vera Witherby.

'Tally-bally-ho!' said Sir George, driving the thing home beyond any possibility of misunderstanding. 'Come on, let's go.'

The Oldest Member, who had been in a reverie, came out of it abruptly and began to speak with the practised ease of a raconteur who does not require a cue to start him off on a story.

When William Bates came to me that afternoon with his tragic story (said the Oldest Member, as smoothly as if we had been discussing William Bates, whoever he might be, for hours), I felt no surprise that he should have selected me as a confident. I have been sitting on the terrace of this golf club long enough to know that that is what I am there for. Everybody with a bit of bad news always brings it to me.

'I say,' said William Bates.

This William was a substantial young man constructed rather on the lines of a lorry, and as a rule he shared that vehicle's placid and unruffled outlook on life. He lived mainly on chops and beer, and few things were able to disturb him. Yet, as he stood before me now, I could see that he was all of a twitter, as far as a fourteen-stone-six man full of beer and chops can be all of a twitter.

'I say,' said William. 'You know Rodney?'

'Your brother-in-law, Rodney Spelvin?'

'Yes. I believe he's gone cuckoo.'

'What gives you that impression?'

'Well, look. Listen to this. We were playing our usual four-some this morning, Rodney and Anastatia and me and Jane, a bob a corner, nip and tuck all the way around, and at the eighteenth Jane and I were lying dead in four and Rodney had a simple chip to reach the green in three. You get the set-up?'

I said I got the set-up.

'Well, knowing my sister Anastatia's uncanny ability to hole out from anywhere within fifteen yards of the pin, I naturally thought the thing was in the bag for them. I said as much to Jane. "Jane," I said, "be ready with the stiff upper lip. They've dished us." And I had already started to feel in my pocket for my bob, when I suddenly saw that Rodney was picking up his ball.'

'Picking up his ball?'

'And what do you think his explanation was? His explanation was that in order to make his shot he would have had to crush a daisy. "I couldn't crush a daisy," he said. "The pixies would never forgive me." What do you make of it?'

I knew what I made of it, but I had not the heart to tell him. I passed it off by saying that Rodney was one of those genial clowns who will do anything for a laugh and, William being a simple soul, my efforts to soothe him were successful. But his story had left me uneasy and apprehensive. It seemed to me only too certain that Rodney Spelvin was in for another attack of poetry.

I have generally found, as I have gone through the world, that people are tolerant and ready to forgive, and in our little community it was never held against Rodney Spelvin that he had once been a poet and a very virulent one, too; the sort of man who would produce a slim volume of verse bound in squashy mauve leather at the drop of the hat, mostly on the subject of sunsets and pixies. He had said good-bye to all that directly he took up golf and announced his betrothal to William's sister Anastatia.

It was golf and the love of a good woman that saved Rodney Spelvin. The moment he had bought his bag of clubs and signed up Anastatia Bates as a partner for life's medal round, he was a different man. He now wrote mystery thrillers, and with such success that he and Anastatia and their child Timothy were enabled to live like fighting cocks. It was impossible not to be thrilled by Rodney Spelvin, and so skilful was the technique which he had developed that he was soon able to push out his couple of thousand words of wholesome blood-stained fiction each morning before breakfast, leaving the rest of the day for the normal fifty-four holes of golf.

At golf, too, he made steady progress. His wife, a scratch player who had once won the Ladies' Championship, guided him with loving care, and it was not long before he became a skilful twenty-one and was regarded in several knowledgeable quarters as a man to keep your eye on for the Rabbits Umbrella, a local competition open to those with a handicap of eighteen or over.

But smooth though the putting green of Anastatia Spelvin's happiness was to the casual glance, there lurked on it, I knew, a secret worm-cast. She could never forget that the man she loved was a man with a past. Deep down in her soul there was always the corroding fear lest at any moment a particularly fine sunset or the sight of a rose in bud might undo all the work she had done, sending Rodney hot-foot once more to his Thesaurus and rhyming dictionary. It was for this reason that she always hurried him indoors when the sun began to go down and refused to have rose trees in her garden. She was in the same position as a wife who has married a once heavy drinker and, though tolerably certain that he has reformed, nevertheless feels it prudent to tear out the whisky advertisements before giving him his *Tatler*.

And now, after seven years, the blow was about to fall. Or so I felt justified in supposing. And I could see that Anastatia thought the same. There was a drawn look on her face, and she was watching her husband closely. Once when I was dining at her house and a tactless guest spoke of the June moon, she changed the subject hurriedly, but not before I had seen Rodney Spelvin start and throw his head up like a war horse at the sound of the bugle. He recovered himself quickly, but for an instant he had looked like a man who has suddenly awaked to the fact that 'June' rhymes with 'moon' and feels that steps of some sort ought to be taken.

A week later suspicion became certainty. I had strolled over to William's cottage after dinner, as I often did, and I found him and Anastatia in the morning-room. At a glance I could see that something was wrong. William was practising distrait swings with a number three iron, a moody frown on his face, while Anastatia in what seemed to me a feverish way sat knitting a sweater for her little nephew, Braid Bates, the son of William and Jane, at the moment away from home undergoing intensive instruction from a leading professional in preparation for the forthcoming contest for the Children's Cup. Both William and Jane rightly felt that the child could not start getting the competition spirit too soon.

Anastatia was looking pale, and William would have been, too, no doubt, if it had been possible for him to look pale. Years of incessant golf in all weathers had converted his cheeks into a substance resembling red leather.

'Lovely evening,' I said.

'Beautiful,' replied Anastatia wildly.

'Good weather for the crops.'

'Splendid,' gasped Anastatia.

'And where is Rodney?'

Anastatia quivered all over and dropped a stitch. 'He's out, I think,' she said in a strange, strangled voice.

William's frown deepened. A plain, blunt man, he dislikes evasions.

'He is not out,' he said curtly. 'He is at his home, writing poetry. Much better to tell him,' he added to Anastatia, who had uttered a wordless sound of protest. 'You can't keep the thing dark, and he will be able to handle it. He has white whiskers. A fellow with white whiskers is bound to be able to handle things better than a couple of birds like us who haven't white whiskers. Stands to reason.'

I assured them that they could rely on my secrecy and discretion and that I would do anything that lay in the power of myself and my whiskers to assist them in their distress.

'So Rodney is writing poetry?' I said. 'I feared that this might happen. Yes, I think I may say I saw it coming. About pixies, I suppose?'

Anastatia gave a quick sob and William a quick snort.

'About pixies, you suppose, do you?' he cried. 'Well, you're wrong. If pixies were all the trouble, I wouldn't have a word to say. Let Rodney Spelvin come in at the door and tell me he has written a poem about pixies, and I will clasp him in my arms. Yes,' said William, 'to my bosom. The thing has gone far, far beyond the pixie stage. Do you know where Rodney is at this moment? Up in the nursery, bending over his son Timothy's cot, gathering material for a poem about the unfortunate little rat when asleep. Some boloney, no doubt, about how he hugs his teddy bear and dreams of angels. Yes, that is what he is doing, writing poetry about Timothy. Horrible whimsical stuff that ... Well, when I tell you that he refers to him throughout as "Timothy Bobbin", you will appreciate what we are up against.'

I am not a weak man, but I confess that I shuddered.

'Timothy Bobbin?'

'Timothy by golly Bobbin. No less.'

I shuddered again. This was worse than I had feared And yet, when you examined it, how inevitable it was. The poetry virus always seeks out the weak spot. Rodney Spelvin was a devoted father. It had long been his practice to converse with his offspring in baby talk, though hitherto always in prose. It was only to be expected that when he found verse welling up in him, the object on which he would decant it would be his unfortunate son.

'What it comes to,' said William, 'is that he is wantonly laying up a lifetime of shame and misery for the wretched little moppet. In the years to come, when he is playing in the National Amateur, the papers will print photographs of him with captions underneath explaining that he is the Timothy Bobbin of the well-known poems—'

'Rodney says he expects soon to have sufficient material for a slim volume,' put in Anastatia in a low voice.

'– and he will be put clean off his stroke. Misery, desolation and despair,' said William. 'That is the programme, as I see it.'

'Are these poems so very raw?'

'Read these and judge for yourself. I swiped them off his desk.'

The documents which he thrust upon me appeared to be in the nature of experimental drafts, intended at a later stage to be developed more fully; what one might perhaps describe as practice swings.

The first ran:

Timothy Bobbin has a puppy,
A dear little puppy that goes Bow-wow. . . .

Beneath this were the words:

Woa! Wait a minute!

followed, as though the writer had realized in time that this
'uppy' rhyming scheme was going to present difficulties, by some
scattered notes: –

Safer to change to rabbit?
(Habit . . . Grab it . . . Stab it . . . Babbitt)

Rabbit looks tough, too. How about canary?
(Airy, dairy, fairy, hairy, Mary, contrary, vary)

Note: Canaries go tweet-tweet.
(Beat, seat, feet, heat, meet, neat, repeat, sheet, complete,
discreet).

Yes, canary looks like goods.
Timothy Bobbin has a canary.

Gosh, this is pie.
Timothy Bobbin has a canary.
As regards its sex opinions vary.
If it just goes tweet-tweet,
We shall call it Pete,
But if it lays an egg, we shall switch to Mary.

(Query: Sex motif too strongly stressed)

That was all about canaries. The next was on a different
theme:

Timothy Bobbin has ten little toes.
He takes them out walking wherever he goes.
And if Timothy gets a cold in the head,
His ten little toes stay with him in bed.

William saw me wince, and asked if that was the toes one. I said it was and hurried on to the third and last.

It ran:

Timothy
      Bobbin
           Goes
                Hoppity
                    Hoppity
                        Hoppity
                            Hoppity
                                Hop.

With this Rodney appeared to have been dissatisfied, for beneath it he had written the word

Reminiscent?

as though he feared that he might have been forestalled by some other poet, and there was a suggestion in the margin that instead of going Hoppity-hoppity-hop his hero might go Boppity-Boppity-bop. The alternative seemed to me equally melancholy, and it was with a grave face that I handed the papers back to William.

'Bad,' I said gravely.

'Bad is right.'

'Has this been going on long?'

'For days the fountain pen has hardly been out of his hand.'

I put the question which had been uppermost in my mind from the first.

'Has it affected his golf?'

'He says he is going to give up golf.'

'What! But the Rabbits Umbrella?'

'He intends to scratch.'

There seemed to be nothing more to be said. I left them. I wanted to be alone, to give this sad affair my undivided attention. As I made for the door, I saw that Anastatia had buried her face in her hands, while William, with brotherly solicitude, stood scratching the top of her head with the number three iron, no doubt in a well-meant effort to comfort and console.

For several days I brooded tensely on the problem, but it was all too soon borne in upon me that William had over-estimated the results-producing qualities of white whiskers. I think I may say with all modesty that mine are as white as the next man's, but they got me nowhere. If I had been a clean-shaven juvenile in the early twenties, I could not have made less progress towards a satisfactory settlement.

It was all very well, I felt rather bitterly at times, for William to tell me to 'handle it', but what could I do? What can any man do when he is confronted by these great natural forces? For years, it was evident, poetry had been banking up inside Rodney Spelvin, accumulating like steam in a boiler on the safety valve of which someone is sitting. And now that the explosion had come, its violence was such as to defy all ordinary methods of treatment. Does one argue with an erupting crater? Does one reason with a waterspout? When William in his airy way told me to 'handle it', it was as if someone had said to the young man who bore 'mid snow and ice the banner with the strange device Excelsior – 'Block that avalanche'.

I could see only one gleam of light in the whole murky affair. Rodney Spelvin had not given up golf. Yielding to his wife's prayers, he had entered for the competition for the Rabbits Umbrella, and had shown good form in the early rounds. Three of the local cripples had fallen victims to his prowess, leaving him a popular semi-finalist. It might be, then, that golf would work a cure.

It was as I was taking an afternoon nap a few days later that I was aroused by a sharp prod in the ribs and saw William's wife Jane standing beside me.

'Well?' she was saying.

I blinked, and sat up.

'Ah, Jane,' I said.

'Sleeping at a time like this,' she exclaimed, and I saw that she was regarding me censoriously. If Jane Bates has a fault, it is that she does not readily make allowances.

'But perhaps you are just taking a well-earned rest after doping out the scheme of a lifetime?'

I could not deceive her.

'I am sorry. No.'

'No scheme?'

'None.'

Jane Bates's face, like that of her husband, had been much worked upon by an open-air life, so she did not pale. But her nose twitched with sudden emotion and she looked as if she had foozled a short putt for hole and match in an important contest. I saw her glance questioningly at my whiskers.

'Yes,' I said, interpreting her look, 'I know they are white, but I repeat: No scheme. I have no more ideas than a rabbit; indeed not so many.'

'But William said you would handle the thing.'

'It can't be handled.'

'It must be. Anastatia is going into a decline. Have you seen Timothy lately?'

'I saw him yesterday in the woods with his father. He was plucking a bluebell.'

'No, he wasn't.'

'He certainly had the air of one who is plucking a bluebell.'

'Well, he wasn't. He was talking into it. He said it was a fairy telephone and he was calling up the Fairy Queen to invite her to a party on his teddy bear's birthday. Rodney stood by, taking notes, and that evening wrote a poem about it.'

'Does Timothy often do that sort of thing?'

'All the time. The child has become a ham. He never ceases putting on an act. He can't eat his breakfast cereal without looking out of the corner of his eye to see how it's going with the audience. And when he says his prayers at night his eyes are ostensibly closed, but all the while he is peering through his fingers and counting the house. And that's not the worst of it. A wife and mother can put up with having an infant ham in the home, constantly popping out at her and being cute, provided that she is able to pay the household bills, but now Rodney says he is going to give up writing thrillers and devote himself entirely to poetry.'

'But his contracts?'

'He says he doesn't give a darn for any contracts. He says he wants to get away from it all and give his soul a chance. The way he talks about his soul and the raw deal it has had all these years, you would think it had been doing a stretch in Wormwood Scrubs. He says he is fed up with bloodstains and that the mere thought of bodies in the library with daggers of Oriental design in their backs make him sick. He broke the news to his agent on the telephone last night, and I could hear the man's screams as plainly as if he had been in the next room.'

'But is he going to stop eating?'

'Practically. So is Anastatia. He says they can get along quite nicely on wholesome and inexpensive vegetables. He thinks it will help his poetry. He says look at Rabindranath Tagore. Never wrapped himself around a T-bone steak in his life, and look where he fetched up. All done on rice, he said, with an occasional draft of cold water from the spring. I tell you my heart bleeds for Anastatia. A lunatic husband and a son who talks into blue-bells, and she'll have to cope with them on Brussels sprouts. She certainly drew the short straw when she married that bard.'

She paused in order to snort, and suddenly, without warning, as so often happens, the solution came to me.

'Jane!' I said, 'I believe I see the way out.'

'You do?'

There flashed into her face a look which I had only once seen there before, on the occasion when the opponent who had fought her all the way to the twentieth hole in the final of the Ladies' Championship of the club was stung by a wasp while making the crucial putt. She kissed me between the whiskers and was good enough to say that she had known all along that I had it in me.

'When do you expect your son Braid back?'

'Some time to-morrow afternoon.'

'When he arrives, send him to me. I will outline the position of affairs to him, and I think we can be safe in assuming that he will immediately take over.'

'I don't understand.'

'You know what Braid is like. He has no reticences.'

I spoke feelingly. Braid Bates was one of those frank, un-inhibited children who are not afraid to speak their minds, and there had been certain passages between us in the not distant past in the course of which I had learned more about my personal appearance from two minutes of his conversation than I could have done from years of introspective study. At the time, I confess, I had been chagrined and had tried fruitlessly to get at him with a niblick, but now I found myself approving whole-heartedly of this trait in his character.

'Reflect. What will Braid's reaction be to the news that these poems are being written about Timothy? He will be revolted, and will say so, not mincing his words. Briefly, he will kid the pants off the young Spelvin, and it should not be long before the latter, instead of gloating obscenely, will be writhing in an agony of shame at the mention of Timothy Bobbin and begging Rodney to lay off. And surely even a poet cannot be deaf to the pleadings of the child he loves. Leave it to Braid. He will put everything right.'

Jane had grasped it now, and her face was aglow with the light of mother love.

'Why, of course!' she cried, clasping her hands in a sort of ecstasy. 'I ought to have thought of it myself. People may say what they like about my sweet Braid, but they can't deny that he is the rudest child this side of the Atlantic Ocean. I'll send him to you the moment he clocks in.'

Braid Bates at that time was a young plug-ugly of some nine summers, in appearance a miniature edition of William and in soul and temperament a combination of Dead End Kid and army mule; a freckled, hard-boiled character with a sardonic eye and a mouth which, when not occupied in eating, had a cynical twist to it. He spoke little as a general thing, but when he did speak seldom failed to find a chink in the armour. The impact of such a personality on little Timothy must, I felt, be tremendous, and I was confident that we could not have placed the child in better hands.

I lost no time in showing him the poem about the Fairy Queen and the bluebell. He read it in silence, and when he had finished drew a deep breath.

'Is Timothy Bobbin Timothy?'

'He is.'

'This poem's all about Timothy?'

'Precisely.'

'Will it be printed in a book?'

'In a slim volume, yes. Together with others of the same type.'

I could see that he was deeply stirred, and felt that I had sown the good seed.

'You will probably have quite a good deal to say about this to Timothy at one time and another,' I said. 'Don't be afraid to speak out for fear of wounding his feelings. Remind yourself that it is all for his good. The expression "cruel to be kind" occurs to one.'

His manner, as I spoke, seemed absent, as if he were turning over in his mind a selection of good things to be said to his little cousin when they met, and shortly afterwards he left me, so moved that on my offering him a ginger ale and a slice of cake he appeared not to have heard me. I retired to rest that night with the gratifying feeling that I had done my day's good deed, and was on the verge of falling asleep when the telephone bell rang.

It was Jane Bates. Her voice was agitated.

'You and your schemes!' she said.

'I beg your pardon?'

'Do you know what has happened?'

'What?'

'William is writing poetry.'

It seemed to me that I could not have heard her correctly.

"William?'

'William.'

'You mean Rodney—'

'I don't mean Rodney. Let me tell you in a few simple words what has happened. Braid returned from your house like one in a dream.'

'Yes, I thought he seemed impressed.'

'Please do not interrupt. It makes it difficult for me to control myself, and I have already bitten a semi-circle out of the mouth-piece. Like one in a dream, I was saying. For the rest of the evening he sat apart, brooding and not answering when spoken to. At bedtime he came out of the silence. And how!'

'And what?'

'I said "And how!" He announced that that poem of Rodney's about the Fairy Queen was the snappiest thing he had ever read and he didn't see why, if Rodney could write poems about Timothy, William couldn't write poems about *him*. And when we told him not to talk nonsense, he delivered his ultimatum. He said that if William did not immediately come through, he would remove his name from the list of entrants for the Children's Cup. What did you say?'

'I said nothing. I was gasping.'

'You may well gasp. In fact, it will be all right with me if you choke. It was you who started all this. Of course, he had got us cold. It has been our dearest wish that he should win the Children's Cup, and we have spent money lavishly to have his short game polished up. Naturally, when he put it like that, we had no alternative. I kissed William, shook him by the hand, tied a wet towel around his head, gave him pencil and paper and locked him up in the morning-room with lots of hot coffee. When I asked him just now how he was making out, he said that he had had no inspiration so far but would keep on swinging. His voice sounded very hollow. I can picture the poor darling's agony. The only thing he has ever written before in his life was a stiff letter to the Greens Committee beefing about the new bunker on the fifth, and that took him four days and left him as limp as a rag.'

She then turned the conversation to what she described as my mischief-making meddling, and I thought it advisable to hang up.

A thing I have noticed frequently in the course of a long life, and it is one that makes for optimism, is that tragedy, while of course rife in this world of ours, is seldom universal. To give an instance of what I mean, while the barometer of William and Jane Bates pointed to 'Further Outlook Unsettled', with Anastatia Spelvin the weather conditions showed signs of improvement.

That William and his wife were in the depths there could be no question. I did not meet Jane, for after the trend of her telephone conversation I felt it more prudent not to, but I saw William a couple of times at luncheon at the club. He looked weary and haggard and was sticking cheese straws in his hair. I heard him ask the waiter if he knew any good rhymes, and when the waiter said 'To what?', William replied 'To anything'. He refused a second chop, and sighed a good deal.

Anastatia, on the other hand, whom I overtook on my way to the links to watch the final of the Rabbits Umbrella a few days later, I found her old cheerful self again. Rodney was one of the competitors in the struggle which was about to begin, and she took a rosy view of his chances. His opponent was Joe Stocker, and it appeared that Joe was suffering from one of his bouts of hay fever.

'Surely,' she said, 'Rodney can trim a man with hay fever? Of course, Mr Stocker is trying Sneezo, the sovereign remedy, but, after all, what is Sneezo?'

'A mere palliative.'

'They say he broke a large vase yesterday during one of his paroxysms. It flew across the room and was dashed to pieces against the wall.'

'That sounds promising.'

'Do you know,' said Anastatia, and I saw that her eyes were shining, 'I can't help feeling that if all goes well Rodney may turn the corner.'

'You mean that his better self will gain the upper hand, making him once again the Rodney we knew and loved?'

'Exactly. If he wins his final, I think he will be a changed man.'

I saw what she meant. A man who has won his first trophy, be it only a scarlet umbrella, has no room in his mind for anything but the improving of his game so that he can as soon as possible win another trophy. A Rodney Spelvin with the Rabbits Umbrella under his belt would have little leisure or inclination for writing poetry. Golf had been his salvation once. It might prove to be so again.

'You didn't watch the preliminary rounds, did you?' Anastatia went on. 'Well, at first Rodney was listless. The game plainly bored him. He had taken a note-book out with him, and he kept stopping to jot down ideas. And then suddenly, half-way through the semi-final, he seemed to change. His lips tightened. His face grew set. And on the tenth a particularly significant incident occurred. He was shaping for a brassy shot, when a wee little blue butterfly fluttered down and settled on his ball. And instead of faltering he clenched his teeth and swung at it with every ounce of weight and muscle. It had to make a quick jump to save its life. I have seldom seen a butterfly move more nippily. Don't you think that was promising?'

'Highly promising. And this brighter state of things continued?'

'All through the semi-final. The butterfly came back on the seventeenth and seemed about to settle on his ball again. But it took a look at his face and moved off. I feel so happy.'

I patted her on the shoulder, and we made our way to the first tee, where Rodney was spinning a coin for Joe Stocker to call. And presently Joe, having won the honour, drove off.

A word about this Stocker. A famous amateur wrestler in his youth, and now in middle age completely muscle bound, he made up for what he lacked in finesse by bringing to the links the rugged strength and directness of purpose which in other days had enabled him to pin one and all to the mat: and it had been well said of him as a golfer that you never knew what he was going to do next. It might be one thing, or it might be another. All you could say with certainty was that he would be in there, trying. I have seen him do the long fifteenth in two, and I have seen him do the short second in thirty-seven.

To-day he made history immediately by holing out his opening drive. It is true that he holed it out on the sixteenth green, which lies some three hundred yards away and a good deal to the left of the first tee, but he holed it out, and a gasp went up from the spectators who had assembled to watch the match. If this was what Joseph Stocker did on the first, they said to one another, the imagination reeled stunned at the prospect of the heights to which he might soar in the course of eighteen holes.

But golf is an uncertain game. Taking a line through that majestic opening drive, one would have supposed that Joe Stocker's tee shot at the second would have beaned a lady, too far off to be identified, who was working in her garden about a quarter of a mile to the south-west. I had, indeed, shouted a warning 'Fore!'

So far from doing this, however, it took him in a classical curve straight for the pin, and he had no difficulty in shooting a pretty three. And as Rodney had the misfortune to sink a ball in the lake, they came to the third all square.

The third, fourth and fifth they halved. Rodney won the sixth, Stocker the seventh. At the eighth I fancied that Rodney was about to take the lead again, for his opponent's third had left his ball entangled in a bush of considerable size, from which it seemed that it could be removed only with a pair of tweezers.

But it was at moments like this that you caught Joseph Stocker at his best. In some of the more scientific aspects of the game he might be forced to yield the palm to more skilful performers, but when it came to a straight issue of muscle and the will to win he stood alone. Here was where he could use his niblick, and Joe Stocker, armed with his niblick, was like King Arthur wielding his sword Excalibur. The next instant the ball, the bush, a last year's bird's nest and a family of caterpillars which had taken out squatter's rights were hurtling toward the green, and shortly after that, Rodney was one down again.

And as they halved the ninth, it was in this unpleasant position that he came to the turn. Here Stocker, a chivalrous antagonist, courteously suggested a quick one at the bar before proceeding, and we repaired thither.

All through these nine gruelling holes, with their dramatic

mutations of fortune, I had been watching Rodney carefully, and I had been well pleased with what I saw. There could be no doubt whatever that Anastatia had been right and that the game had gripped this backslider with all its old force. Here was no poet, pausing between shots to enter stray thoughts in a note-book, but something that looked like a Scotch pro in the last round of the National Open. What he had said to his caddy on the occasion of the lad cracking a nut just as he was putting had been music to my ears. It was plain that the stern struggle had brought out all that was best in Rodney Spelvin.

It seemed to me, too, an excellent sign that he was all impatience to renew the contest. He asked Stocker with some brusqueness if he proposed to spend the rest of the day in the bar, and Stocker hastily drained his second ginger ale and Sneezo and we went out.

As we were making our way to the tenth tee, little Timothy suddenly appeared from nowhere, gambolling up in an arch way like a miniature chorus-boy, and I saw at once what Jane had meant when she had spoken of him putting on an act. There was a sort of ghastly sprightliness about the child. He exuded whimsicality at every pore.

'Daddee,' he called, and Rodney looked round a little irritably, it seemed to me, like one interrupted while thinking of higher things.

'Daddee, I've made friends with such a nice beetle.'

It was a remark which a few days earlier would have had Rodney reaching for his note-book with a gleaming eye, but now he was plainly distrait. There was an absent look on his face, and watching him swing his driver one was reminded of a tiger of the jungle lashing its tail.

'Quite,' was all he said.

'It's green. I call it Mister Green Beetle.'

This idiotic statement – good, one would have thought, for at least a couple of stanzas – seemed to arouse little or no enthusiasm in Rodney. He merely nodded curtly and said 'Yes, yes, very sensible'.

'Run away and have a long talk with it,' he added.

'What about?'

'Why – er – other beetles.'

'Do you think Mister Green Beetle has some dear little brothers and sisters, Daddee?'

'Extremely likely. Good-bye. No doubt we shall meet later.'

'I wonder if the Fairy Queen uses beetles as horses, Daddee?'

'Very possibly, very possibly. Go and make inquiries. And you,' said Rodney, addressing his cowering caddy, 'if I hear one more hiccough out of you while I am shooting – just one – I shall give you two minutes to put your affairs in order and then I shall act. Come on, Stocker, come on, come on, come on. You have the honour.'

He looked at his opponent sourly, like one with a grievance, and I knew what was in his mind. He was wondering where this hay fever of Stocker's was, of which he had heard so much.

I could not blame him. A finalist in a golf tournament, playing against an antagonist who has been widely publicized as a victim to hay fever, is entitled to expect that the latter will give at least occasional evidence of his infirmity, and so far Joseph Stocker had done nothing of the kind. From the start of the proceedings he had failed to foozle a single shot owing to a sudden sneeze, and what Rodney was feeling was that while this could not perhaps actually be described as sharp practice, it was sailing very near the wind.

The fact of the matter was that the inventor of Sneezo

knew his stuff. A quick-working and harmless specific highly recommended by the medical fraternity and containing no deleterious drugs, it brought instant relief. Joe Stocker had been lowering it by the pailful since breakfast, and it was standing him in good stead. I have fairly keen ears, but up to now I had not heard him even sniffle. He played his shots dry-eyed and without convulsions, and whatever holes Rodney had won he had had to win by sheer unassisted merit.

There was no suggestion of the hay fever patient as he drove off now. He smote his ball firmly and truly, and it would unquestionably have travelled several hundred yards had it not chanced to strike the ladies' tee box and ricocheted into the rough. Encouraged by this, Rodney played a nice straight one down the middle and was able to square the match again.

A ding-dong struggle ensued, for both men were now on their mettle. First one would win a hole, then the other: and then, to increase the dramatic suspense, they would halve a couple. They arrived at the eighteenth all square.

The eighteenth was at that time one of those longish up-hill holes which present few difficulties if you can keep your drive straight, and it seemed after both men had driven that the issue would be settled on the green. But golf, as I said before, is an uncertain game. Rodney played a nice second to within fifty yards of the green, but Stocker, pressing, topped badly and with his next missed the globe altogether, tying himself in the process into a knot from which for an instant I thought it would be impossible to unravel him.

But he contrived to straighten himself out, and was collecting his faculties for another effort, when little Timothy came trotting up. He had a posy of wild flowers in his hand.

'Smell my pretty flowers, Mr Stocker,' he chirped. And with

an arch gesture he thrust the blooms beneath Joseph Stocker's
nose.

A hoarse cry sprang from the other's lips, and he recoiled as
if the bouquet had contained a snake.

'Hey, look out for my hay fever!' he cried, and already I saw
that he was beginning to heave and writhe. Under a direct frontal
attack like this even Sneezo loses its power to protect.

'Don't bother the gentleman now, dear,' said Rodney mildly.
A glance at his face told me that he was saying to himself that
this was something like family teamwork. 'Run along and wait
for Daddy on the green.'

Little Timothy skipped off, and once more Stocker addressed
his ball. It was plain that it was going to be a close thing. A
sneeze of vast proportions was evidently coming to a head within
him like some great tidal wave, and if he meant to forestall it he
would have to cut his customary deliberate waggle to something
short and sharp like George Duncan's. And I could see that he
appreciated this.

But quickly though he waggled, he did not waggle quickly
enough. The explosion came just as the club head descended on
the ball.

The result was one of the most magnificent shots I have ever
witnessed. It was as if the whole soul and essence of Joseph
Stocker, poured into that colossal sneeze, had gone to the making
of it. Straight and true, as if fired out of a gun, the ball flew up
the hill and disappeared over the edge of the green.

It was with a thoughtful air that Rodney Spelvin prepared to
play his chip shot. He had obviously been badly shaken by the
miracle which he had just observed. But Anastatia had trained
him well, and he made no mistake. He, too, was on the green

and, as far as one could judge, very near the pin. Even supposing that Stocker was lying dead, he would still be in the enviable position of playing four as against the other's five. And he was a very accurate putter.

Only when we arrived on the green were we able to appreciate the full drama of the situation. Stocker's ball was nowhere to be seen, and it seemed for a moment as if it must have been snatched up to heaven. Then a careful search discovered it nestling in the hole.

'Ah,' said Joe Stocker, well satisfied. 'Thought for a moment I had missed it.'

There was good stuff in Rodney Spelvin. The best he could hope for now was to take his opponent on the nineteenth, but he did not quail. His ball was lying some four feet from the hole, never at any time an easy shot but at the crisis of a hard fought match calculated to unman the stoutest, and he addressed it with a quiet fortitude which I liked to see.

Slowly he drew his club back, and brought it down. And as he did so, a clear childish voice broke the silence.

'Daddee!'

And Rodney, starting as if a red-hot iron had been placed against the bent seat of his knickerbockers, sent the ball scudding yards past the hole. Joseph Stocker was the winner of that year's Rabbits Umbrella.

Rodney Spelvin straightened himself. His face was pale and drawn.

'Daddee, are daisies little bits of the stars that have been chipped off by the angels?'

A deep sigh shook Rodney Spelvin. I saw his eyes. They were alight with a hideous menace. Quickly and silently, like an

African leopard stalking its prey, he advanced on the child. An instant later the stillness was disturbed by a series of reports like pistol shots.

I looked at Anastatia. There was distress on her face, but mingled with the distress a sort of ecstasy. She mourned as a mother, but rejoiced as a wife.

Rodney Spelvin was himself again.

That night little Braid Bates, addressing his father, said:

'How's that poem coming along?'

William cast a hunted look at his helpmeet, and Jane took things in hand in her firm, capable way.

'That,' she said, 'will be all of that. Daddy isn't going to write any poem, and we shall want you out on the practice tee at seven sharp to-morrow, my lad.'

'But Uncle Rodney writes poems to Timothy.'

'No, he doesn't. Not now.'

'But...'

Jane regarded him with quiet intentness.

'Does Mother's little chickabiddy want his nose pushed sideways?' she said. 'Very well, then.'

A marriage was being solemnized in the church that stands about a full spoon shot from the club-house. The ceremony had nearly reached its conclusion. As the officiating clergyman, coming to the nub of the thing, addressed the young man in the cutaway coat and spongebag trousers, there reigned throughout the sacred edifice a tense silence, such as prevails upon a race-course just before the shout goes up, 'They're off!'

'Wilt thou,' he said, '– hup – Smallwood, take this – hup – Celia to be thy wedded wife?'

A sudden gleam came into the other's horn-rimmed spectacled eyes.

'Say, listen,' he began. 'Lemme tell you what to—'

He stopped, a blush mantling his face.

'I will,' he said.

A few moments later, the organ was pealing forth 'The Voice that breathed o'er Eden'. The happy couple entered the vestry. The Oldest Member, who had been among those in the ringside pews, walked back to the club-house with the friend who was spending the week-end with him.

The friend seemed puzzled.

'Tell me,' he said. 'Am I wrong, or did the bridegroom at one point in the proceedings start to *ad lib* with some stuff that was not on the routine?'

'He did, indeed,' replied the Oldest Member. 'He was about to advise the minister what to do for his hiccoughs. I find the fact that he succeeded in checking himself very gratifying. It seems to show that his cure may be considered permanent.'

'His cure?'

'Until very recently Smallwood Bessemer was a confirmed adviser.'

'Bad, that.'

'Yes. I always advise people never to give advice. Mind you, one can find excuses for the young fellow. For many years he had been a columnist on one of the morning papers, and to columnists, accustomed day after day to set the world right on every conceivable subject, the giving of advice becomes a habit. It is an occupational risk. But if I had known young Bessemer better, I would have warned him that he was in danger of alienating Celia Todd, his betrothed, who was a girl of proud and independent spirit.

Unfortunately, he was not a member of our little community. He lived in the city, merely coming here for occasional weekends. At the time when my story begins, I had met him only twice, when he arrived to spend his summer vacation. And it was not long before, as I had feared would be the case, I found that all was not well between him and Celia Todd.

The first intimation I had of this (the Sage proceeded) was when she called at my cottage accompanied by her Pekinese, Pirbright, to whom she was greatly attached, and unburdened her soul to me. Sinking listlessly into a chair, she sat silent for some moments. Then, as if waking from a reverie, she spoke abruptly.

'Do you think,' she said, 'that true love can exist between a woman and a man, if the woman feels more and more every day that she wants to hit the man over the head with a brick?'

I was disturbed. I like to see the young folks happy. And my hope that she might merely be stating a hypothetical case vanished as she continued.

'Take me and Smallwood, for instance. I have to clench my fists sometimes till the knuckles stand out white under the strain, in order to stop myself from beaning him. This habit of his of scattering advice on every side like a sower going forth sowing is getting me down. It has begun to sap my reason. Only this morning, to show you what I mean, we were walking along the road and we met that wolfhound of Agnes Flack's, and it said something to Pirbright about the situation in China that made him hot under the collar. The little angel was just rolling up his sleeves and starting in to mix it, when I snatched him away. And Smallwood said I shouldn't have done it. I should have let them fight it out, he said, so that they could get it out of their systems, after which a beautiful friendship would have resulted. I told him he was the sort of human fiend who ought to be eating peanuts in the front row at a bull fight, and we parted on rather distant terms.'

'The clouds will clear away.'

'I wonder,' said Celia. 'I have a feeling that one of these days he will go too far, and something will crack.'

In the light of this conversation, what happened at the dance becomes intelligible. Every Saturday night we have a dance at the club-house, at which all the younger set assembles. Celia was there, escorted by Smallwood Bessemer, their differences having apparently been smoothed over, and for a while all seems to have gone well. Bessemer was an awkward and clumsy dancer, but the girl's love enabled her to endure the way in which he jumped on and off her feet. When the music stopped, she started straightening out her toes without the slightest doubt in her mind that he was a king among men.

And then suddenly he turned to her with a kindly smile.

'I'd like to give you a bit of advice,' he said. 'What's wrong with your dancing is that you give a sort of jump at the turn, like a trout leaping at a fly. Now, the way to cure this is very simple. Try to imagine that the ceiling is very low and made of very thin glass, and that your head just touches it and you mustn't break it. You've dropped your engagement ring,' he said, as something small and hard struck him on the side of the face.

'No, I haven't,' said Celia. 'I threw it at you.'

And she strode haughtily out on to the terrace. And Small-wood Bessemer, having watched her disappear, went to the bar to get a quick one.

There was only one man in the bar, and yet it looked well filled. This was because Sidney McMurdo, its occupant, is one of those vast, muscled individuals who bulge in every direction. He was sitting slumped in a chair, scowling beneath beetling brows, his whole aspect that of one whose soul has just got the sleeve across the windpipe.

Sidney was not in any sense an intimate of Smallwood Bessemer. They had met for the first time on the previous after-noon, when Bessemer had advised Sidney always to cool off slowly after playing golf, as otherwise he might contract pneu-monia and cease to be with us, and Sidney, who is a second vice-president of a large insurance company, had taken advantage of this all-flesh-is-as-grass note which had been introduced into the conversation to try to sell Bessemer his firm's all-accident policy.

No business had resulted, but the episode had served to make them acquainted, and they now split a bottle. The influence of his share on Sidney McMurdo was mellowing enough to make him confidential.

'I've just had a hell of a row with my *fiancée*,' he said.

'I've just had a hell of a row with *my fiancée*,' said Smallwood Bessemer, struck by the coincidence.

'She told me I ought to putt off the right foot. I said I was darned well going to keep right along putting off the left foot, as I had been taught at my mother's knee. She then broke off the engagement.'

Smallwood Bessemer was not a golfer, but manlike he sympathized with the male, and he was in a mood to be impatient of exhibitions of temperament in women.

'Women,' he said, 'are all alike. They need to be brought to heel. You have to teach them where they get off and show them that they can't go about the place casting away a good man's love as if it were a used tube of toothpaste. Let me give you a bit of advice. Don't sit brooding in bars. Do as I intend to do. Go out and start making vigorous passes at some other girl.'

'To make her jealous?'

'Exactly.'

'So that she will come legging it back, pleading to be forgiven?'

'Precisely.'

Sidney brightened.

'That sounds pretty good to me. Because I mean to say there's always the chance that the other girl will let you kiss her, and then you're that much ahead of the game.'

'Quite,' said Smallwood Bessemer.

He returned to the dance room, glad to have been able to be of assistance to a fellow man in his hour of distress. Celia was nowhere to be seen, and he presumed that she was still cooling off on the terrace. He saw Sidney, who had stayed behind for a moment to finish the bottle, flash past in a purposeful way, and then he looked about him to decide who should be his assistant in the little psychological experiment which he proposed to undertake. His eyes fell on Agnes Flack, sitting in a corner, rapping her substantial foot on the floor.

Have you met Agnes Flack? You don't remember? Then you have not, for once seen she is not forgotten. She is our female club champion, a position which she owes not only to her skill at golf but to her remarkable physique. She is a fine, large, handsome girl, built rather on the lines of Pop-Eye the sailor, and Smallwood Bessemer, who was on the slender side, had always admired her.

He caught her eye, and she smiled brightly. He went over to where she sat, and presently they were out on the floor. He saw Celia appear at the French windows and stand looking in, and intensified the silent passion of his dancing, trying to convey the idea of being something South American, which ought to be chained up and muzzled in the interests of pure womanhood. Celia sniffed with a violence that caused the lights to flicker, and an hour or so later Smallwood Bessemer went home, well pleased with the start he had made.

He was climbing into bed, feeling that all would soon be well once more, when the telephone rang and Sidney McMurdo's voice boomed over the wire.

'Hoy!' said Sidney.

'Yes?' said Bessemer.

'You know that advice you gave me?'

'You took it, I hope?'

'Yes,' said Sidney. 'And a rather unfortunate thing has

occurred. How it happened, I can't say, but I've gone and got engaged.'

'Too bad,' said Bessemer sympathetically. 'There was always that risk, of course. The danger on these occasions is that one may overdo the thing and become too fascinating. I ought to have warned you to hold yourself in. Who is the girl?'

'A frightful pie-faced little squirt named Celia Todd,' said Sidney and hung up with a hollow groan.

To say that this information stunned Smallwood Bessemer would scarcely be to overstate the facts. For some moments after the line had gone dead, he sat motionless, his soul seething within him like a welsh rabbit at the height of its fever. He burned with rage and resentment, and all the manhood in him called to him to make a virile gesture and show Celia Todd who was who and what was what.

An idea struck him. He called up Agnes Flack.

'Miss Flack?'

'Hello?'

'Sorry to disturb you at this hour, but will you marry me?'

'Certainly. Who is that?'

'Smallwood Bessemer.'

'I don't get the second name.'

'Bessemer. B. for banana, e for erysipelas—'

'Oh, Bessemer? Yes, delighted. Good night, Mr Bessemer.'

'Good night, Miss Flack.'

Sometimes it happens that after a restorative sleep a man finds that his views on what seemed in the small hours a pretty good idea have undergone a change. It was so with Bessemer. He woke next morning oppressed by a nebulous feeling that in some way, which for the moment eluded his memory, he had made rather a chump of himself overnight. And then, as he was brushing his teeth, he was able to put his finger on the seat of the trouble. Like a tidal wave, the events of the previous evening came flooding back into his mind, and he groaned in spirit.

Why in this dark hour he should have thought of me, I cannot say, for we were the merest acquaintances. But he must have felt that I was the sort of man who would lend a sympathetic ear, for he called me up on the telephone and explained the situation, begging me to step round and see Agnes and sound her regarding her views on the matter. An hour later, I was able to put him abreast.

'She says she loves you devotedly.'

'But how can she? I scarcely know the girl.'

'That is what she says. No doubt you are one of those men who give a woman a single glance and – bing! – all is over.'

There was a silence at the other end of the wire. When he spoke again, there was an anxious tremor in his voice.

'What would you say chances were,' he asked, 'for explaining that it was all a little joke, at which I had expected that no one would laugh more heartily than herself?'

'Virtually nil. As a matter of fact, that point happened to come up, and she stated specifically that if there was any rannygazoo – if, in other words, it should prove that you had been pulling her leg and trying to make her the plaything of an idle moment – she would know what to do about it.'

'Know what to do about it.'

'That was the expression she employed.'

'Know what to do about it,' repeated Smallwood Bessemer thoughtfully. ''Myes. I see what you mean. Know what to do about it. Yes. But why on earth does this ghastly girl love me? She must be cuckoo.'

'For your intellect, she tells me. She says she finds you a refreshing change after her late *fiancé*, Sidney McMurdo.'

'Was she engaged to Sidney McMurdo?'

'Yes.'

'H'm!' said Bessemer.

He told me subsequently that his first action after he had hung up was to go to his cupboard and take from it a bottle of tonic port which he kept handy in case he required a restorative or stimulant. He had fallen into the habit of drinking a little of this whenever he felt low, and Reason told him that he was never going to feel lower than he did at that moment. To dash off a glass and fill another was with him the work of an instant.

Generally, the effect of this tonic port was to send the blood coursing through his veins like liquid fire and make him feel that he was walking on the tip of his toes with his hat on the side of his head. But now its magic seemed to have failed. Spiritually, he remained a total loss.

Nor, I think, can we be surprised at this. It is not every day that a young fellow loses the girl he worships and finds that he has accumulated another whom he not only does not love but knows that he can never love. Smallwood Bessemer respected Agnes Flack. He would always feel for her that impersonal admiration which is inspired by anything very large, like the Empire State Building or the Grand Canyon of Arizona. But the thought of being married to her frankly appalled him.

And in addition to this there was the Sidney McMurdo angle.

Smallwood Bessemer, as I say, did not know Sidney McMurdo well. But he knew him well enough to be aware that his reactions on finding that another man had become engaged to his temporarily ex-*fiancée* would be of a marked nature. And as the picture rose before his eyes of that vast frame of his and those almost varicose muscles that rippled like dangerous snakes beneath his pullover, his soul sickened and he had to have a third glass of tonic port.

It was while he was draining it that Sidney McMurdo came lumbering over the threshold, and so vivid was the impression he created of being eight foot high and broad in proportion that Smallwood Bessemer nearly swooned. Recovering himself, he greeted him with almost effusive cordiality.

'Come in, McMurdo, come in,' he cried buoyantly. 'Just the fellow I wanted to see. I wonder, McMurdo, if you remember what you were saying to me the other day about the advisability of my taking out an all-accident insurance with your firm? I have been thinking it over, and am strongly inclined to do so.'

'It's the sensible thing,' said Sidney McMurdo. 'A man ought to look to the future.'

'Precisely.'

'You never know when you may not get badly smashed up.'

'Never. Shall we go round to your place and get a form?'

'I have one with me.'

'Then I will sign it at once,' said Bessemer.

And he had just done so and had written out a cheque for the first year's premium, when the telephone bell rang.

'Yoo-hoo, darling,' bellowed a voice genially, and he recognized it as Agnes Flack's. A quick glance out of the corner of his eye told him that his companion had recognized it, too. Sidney McMurdo had stiffened. His face was flushed. He sat clenching and unclenching his hands. When Agnes Flack spoke on the telephone, there was never any need for extensions to enable the bystander to follow her remarks.

Smallwood Bessemer swallowed once or twice.

'Oh, good morning, Miss Flack,' he said formally.

'What do you mean – Miss Flack? Call me Aggie. Listen, I'm at the club-house. Come on out. I want to give you a golf lesson.'

'Very well.'

'You mean "Very well, darling".'

'Er – yes. Er – very well, darling.'

'Right,' said Agnes Flack.

Smallwood Bessemer hung up the receiver, and turned to find his companion scrutinizing him narrowly. Sidney McMurdo had turned a rather pretty mauve, and his eyes had an incandescent appearance. It seemed to Bessemer that with a few minor changes he could have stepped straight into the Book of Revelations and no questions asked.

'That was Agnes Flack!' said McMurdo hoarsely.

'Er – yes,' said Bessemer. 'Yes, I believe it was.'

'She called you "darling".'

'Er – yes. Yes, I believe she did.'

'You called her "darling".'

'Er – yes. That's right. She seemed to wish it.'

'Why?' asked Sidney McMurdo, who was one of those simple, direct men who like to come straight to the point.

'I've been meaning to tell you about that,' said Smallwood Bessemer. 'We're engaged. It happened last night after the dance.'

Sidney McMurdo gave a hitch to his shoulder muscles, which were leaping about under his pullover like adagio dancers. His scrutiny, already narrow, became narrower.

'So it was all a vile plot, was it?'

'No, no.'

'Of course it was a vile plot,' said Sidney McMurdo petulantly, breaking off a corner of the mantelpiece and shredding it through his fingers. 'You gave me that advice about going out and making passes purely in order that you should be left free to steal Agnes from me. If that wasn't a vile plot, then I don't know a vile plot when I see one. Well, well, we must see what we can do about it.'

It was the fact that Smallwood Bessemer at this moment sprang nimbly behind the table that temporarily eased the strain of the situation. For as Sidney McMurdo started to remove the obstacle, his eye fell on the insurance policy. He stopped as if spellbound, staring at it, his lower jaw sagging.

Bessemer, scanning him anxiously, could read what was passing through his mind. Sidney McMurdo was a lover, but he was also a second vice-president of the Jersey City and All Points West Mutual and Co-operative Life and Accident Insurance Company, an organization which had an almost morbid distaste for parting with its money. If as the result of any impulsive action on his part the Co. were compelled to pay over a large sum to Smallwood Bessemer almost before they had trousered his first cheque, there would be harsh words and raised eyebrows. He might even be stripped of his second vice-president's desk in the middle of a hollow square. And next to Agnes Flack and his steel-shafted driver, he loved his second vice-presidency more than anything in the world.

For what seemed an eternity, Smallwood Bessemer gazed at a strong man wrestling with himself. Then the crisis passed. Sidney McMurdo flung himself into a chair, and sat moodily gnashing his teeth.

'Well,' said Bessemer, feeling like Shadrach, Meshach and Abednego, 'I suppose I must be leaving you. I am having my first golf lesson.'

Sidney McMurdo started.

'Your *first* golf lesson? Haven't you ever played?'

'Not yet.'

A hollow groan escaped Sidney McMurdo.

'To think of my Agnes marrying a man who doesn't know the difference between a brassie and a niblick!'

'Well, if it comes to that,' retorted Bessemer, with some spirit, 'what price my Celia marrying a man who doesn't know the difference between Edna St Vincent Millay and Bugs Baer?'

Sidney McMurdo stared.

'Your Celia? You weren't engaged to that Todd pipsqueak?'

'She is not a pipsqueak.'

'She is, too, a pipsqueak, and I can prove it. She reads poetry.'

'Naturally. I have made it my loving task to train her eager mind to appreciate all that is best and most beautiful.'

'She says I've got to do it, too.'

'It will be the making of you. And now,' said Smallwood Bessemer, 'I really must be going.'

'Just a moment,' said Sidney McMurdo. He reached out and took the insurance policy, studying it intently for a while. But it was as he feared. It covered everything. 'All right,' he said sombrely, 'pop off.'

I suppose there is nothing (proceeded the Oldest Member) more painful to the man of sensibility than the spectacle of tangled hearts. Here were four hearts as tangled as spaghetti, and I grieved for them. The female members of the quartette did not confide in me, but I was in constant demand by both McMurdo and Bessemer, and it is not too much to say that these men were passing through the furnace. Indeed, I cannot say which moved me the more – Bessemer's analysis of his emotions when jerked out of bed at daybreak by a telephone call from Agnes, summoning him to the links before breakfast, or McMurdo's description of how it felt to read W. H. Auden. Suffice it that each wrung my heart to the uttermost.

And so the matter stood at the opening of the contest for the Ladies' Vase.

This was one of our handicap events, embracing in its comprehensive scope almost the entire female personnel of the club, from the fire-breathing tigresses to the rabbits who had taken up golf because it gave them an opportunity of appearing in sports clothes. It was expected to be a gift once more for Agnes Flack, though she would be playing from scratch and several of the contestants were receiving as much as forty-eight. She had won the Vase the last two years, and if she scooped it in again, it would become her permanent possession. I mention this to show you what the competition meant to her.

For a while, all proceeded according to the form book. Playing in her usual bold, resolute style, she blasted her opponents off the links one by one, and came safely through into the final without disarranging her hair.

But as the tournament progressed, it became evident that a platinum blonde of the name of Julia Prebble, receiving twenty-seven, had been grossly under-handicapped. Whether through some natural skill at concealing the merits of her game, or because she was engaged to a member of the handicapping committee, one cannot tell, but she had, as I say, contrived to scrounge a twenty-seven when ten would have been more suitable. The result was that she passed into the final bracket with consummate ease, and the betting among the wilder spirits was that for the first time in three years Agnes Flack's mantelpiece would have to be looking about it for some other ornament than the handsome silver vase presented by the club for the annual competition among its female members.

And when at the end of the first half of the thirty-six hole final Agnes was two down after a gruelling struggle, it seemed as though their prognostications were about to be fulfilled.

It was in the cool of a lovely summer evening that play was resumed. I had been asked to referee the match, and I was crossing the terrace on my way to the first tee when I encountered Smallwood Bessemer. And we were pausing to exchange a word or two, when Sidney McMurdo came along.

To my surprise, for I had supposed relations between the two men to be strained, Bessemer waved a cordial hand.

'Hyah, Sidney,' he called.

'Hyah, Smallwood,' replied the other.

'Did you get that tonic?'

'Yes. Good stuff, you think?'

'You can't beat it,' said Bessemer, and Sidney McMurdo passed along towards the first tee.

I was astonished.

'You seem on excellent terms with McMurdo,' I said.

'Oh, yes,' said Bessemer. 'He drops in at my place a good deal. We smoke a pipe and roast each other's girls. It draws us very close together. I was able to do him a good turn this morning. He was very anxious to watch the match, and Celia wanted him to go into town to fetch a specialist for her Peke, who is off colour to-day. I told him to give it a shot of that tonic port I drink. Put it right in no time. Well, I'll be seeing you.'

'You are not coming round?'

'I may look in toward the finish. What do you think of Agnes's chances?'

'Well, she has been battling nobly against heavy odds, but—'

'The trouble with Agnes is that she believes all she reads in the golf books. If she would only listen to me ... Ah, well,' said Smallwood Bessemer, and moved off.

It did not take me long after I had reached the first tee to see that Agnes Flack was not blind to the possibility of being deprived of her Vase. Her lips were tight, and there was a furrow in her forehead. I endeavoured to ease her tension with a kindly word or two.

'Lovely evening,' I said.

'It will be,' she replied, directing a somewhat acid glance at her antagonist, who was straightening the tie of the member of the handicapping committee to whom she was betrothed, 'if I can trim that ginger-headed Delilah and foil the criminal skull-duggery of a bunch of yes-men who ought to be blushing themselves purple. Twenty-seven, forsooth!'

Her warmth was not unjustified. After watching the morning's round, I, too, felt that that twenty-seven handicap of Julia Prebble's had been dictated by the voice of love rather than by a rigid sense of justice. I changed the subject.

'Bessemer is not watching the match, he tells me.'

'I wouldn't let him. He makes me nervous.'

'Indeed?'

'Yes. I started teaching him golf a little while ago, and now he's started teaching *me*. He knows it all.'

'He is a columnist,' I reminded her.

'At lunch to-day he said he was going to skim through Alex Morrison's book again, because he had a feeling that Alex hadn't got the right angle on the game.'

I shuddered strongly, and at this moment Julia Prebble detached herself from her loved one, and the contest began.

* * *

I confess that, as I watched the opening stages of the play, I found a change taking place in my attitude towards Agnes Flack. I had always respected her, as one must respect any woman capable of pasting a ball two hundred and forty yards, but it was only now that respect burgeoned into something like affection. The way she hitched up her sleeves and started to wipe off her opponent's lead invited sympathy and support.

At the outset, she was assisted by the fact that success had rendered Julia Prebble a little over-confident. She did not concentrate. The eye which should have been riveted on her ball had a tendency to smirk sideways at her affianced, causing her to top, with the result that only three holes had been played before the match was all square again.

However, as was inevitable, these reverses had the effect of tightening up Julia Prebble's game. Her mouth hardened, and she showed a disposition to bite at the man she loved, whom she appeared to consider responsible. On the fifth, she told him not to stand in front of her, on the sixth not to stand behind her, on the seventh she asked him not to move while she was putting. On the eighth she suggested that if he had really got St Vitus Dance he ought to go and put himself in the hands of some good doctor. On the ninth she formally broke off the engagement.

Naturally, all this helped her a good deal, and at the tenth she recovered the lead she had lost. Agnes drew level at the eleventh, and after that things settled down to the grim struggle which one generally sees in finals. A casual observer would have said that it was anybody's game.

But the strain of battling against that handicap was telling on Agnes Flack. Once or twice, her iron resolution seemed to waver. And on the seventeenth Nature took its toll. She missed a short putt for the half, and they came to the eighteenth tee with Julia Prebble dormy one.

The eighteenth hole takes you over the water. A sort of small lake lies just beyond that tee, spanned by a rustic bridge. Across the bridge I now beheld Smallwood Bessemer approaching.

'How's it going?' he asked, as he came to where I stood.

I told him the state of the game, and he shook his head.

'Looks bad,' he said. 'I'm sorry. I don't like Agnes Flack, and never shall, but one has one's human feelings. It will cut her to the heart to lose that Vase. And when you reflect that if she had only let me come along, she would have been all right, it all seems such a pity, doesn't it? I could have given her a pointer from time to time, which would have made all the difference. But she doesn't seem to want my advice. Prefers to trust to Alex Morrison. Sad. Very sad. Ah,' said Smallwood Bessemer, 'She didn't relax.'

He was alluding to Julia Prebble, who had just driven off. Her ball had cleared the water nicely, but it was plain to the seeing eye that it had a nasty slice on it. It came to rest in a patch of rough at the side of the fairway, and I saw her look sharply round, as if instinctively about to tell her betrothed that she wished he wouldn't shuffle his feet just as she was shooting. But he was not there. He had withdrawn to the club-house, where, I was informed later, he drank six Scotches in quick succession, subsequently crying on the barman's shoulder and telling him what was wrong with women.

In the demeanour of Agnes Flack, as she teed up, there was something that reminded me of Boadicea about to get in amongst a Roman legion. She looked dominant and conquering. I knew what she was thinking. Even if her opponent recovered from the moral shock of a drive like that, she could scarcely be down in less than six, and this was a hole which she, Agnes, always did in four. This meant that the match would go to the thirty-seventh, in which case she was confident that her stamina and the will to win would see her through.

She measured her distance. She waggled. Slowly and forcefully she swung back. And her club was just descending in a perfect arc, when Smallwood Bessemer spoke.

'Hey!' he said.

In the tense silence the word rang out like the crack of a gun. It affected Agnes Flack visibly. For the first time since she had been a slip of a child, she lifted her head in the middle of a stroke, and the ball, badly topped, trickled over the turf, gathered momentum as it reached the edge of the tee, bounded towards the water, hesitated on the brink for an instant like a timid diver on a cold morning and then plunged in.

'Too bad,' said Julia Prebble.

Agnes Flack did not reply. She was breathing heavily through her nostrils. She turned to Smallwood Bessemer.

'You were saying something?' she asked.

'I was only going to remind you to relax,' said Smallwood Bessemer. 'Alex Morrison lays great stress on the importance of pointing the chin and rolling the feet. To my mind, however, the whole secret of golf consists in relaxing. At the top of the swing the muscles should be—'

'My niblick, please,' said Agnes Flack to her caddie.

She took the club, poised it for an instant as if judging its heft, then began to move forward swiftly and stealthily, like a tigress of the jungle.

Until that moment, I had always looked on Smallwood Bessemer as purely the man of intellect, what you would describe as the thoughtful, reflective type. But he now showed that he could, if the occasion demanded it, be the man of action. I do not think I have ever seen anything move quicker than the manner in which he dived head-foremost into the thick clump of bushes which borders the eighteenth tee. One moment, he was there; the next, he had vanished. Eels could have taken his correspondence course.

It was a move of the highest strategic quality. Strong woman though Agnes Flack was, she was afraid of spiders. For an instant, she stood looking wistfully at the bushes: then, hurling her niblick into them, she burst into tears and tottered into the arms of Sidney McMurdo, who came up at this juncture. He had been following the match at a cautious distance.

'Oh, Sidney!' she sobbed.

'There, there,' said Sidney McMurdo.

He folded her in his embrace, and they walked off together. From her passionate gestures, I could gather that she was explaining what had occurred and was urging him to plunge into the undergrowth and break Smallwood Bessemer's neck, and the apologetic way in which he waved his hands told me that he was making clear his obligations to the Jersey City and All Points West Mutual and Co-operative Life and Accident Insurance Co.

Presently, they were lost in the gathering dusk, and I called to Bessemer and informed him that the All Clear had been blown.

'She's gone?' he said.

'She has been gone some moments.'

'Are you sure?'

'Quite sure.'

There was a silence.

'No,' said Bessemer. 'It may be a trap. I think I'll stick on here a while.'

I shrugged my shoulder and left him.

*   *   *

The shades of night were falling fast before Smallwood Bessemer, weighing the pros and cons, felt justified in emerging from his lair. As he started to cross the bridge that spans the water, it was almost dark. He leaned on the rail, giving himself up to thought.

The sweet was mingled with the bitter in his meditations. He could see that the future held much that must inevitably be distasteful to a man who liked a quiet life. As long as he remained in the neighbourhood, he would be compelled to exercise ceaseless vigilance and would have to hold himself in readiness, should the occasion arise, to pick up his feet and run like a rabbit.

This was not so good. On the other hand, it seemed reasonable to infer from Agnes Flack's manner during the recent episode that their engagement was at an end. A substantial bit of velvet.

Against this, however, must be set the fact that he had lost Celia Todd. There was no getting away from that, and it was this thought that caused him to moan softly as he gazed at the dark water beneath him. And he was still moaning, when there came to his ears the sound of a footstep. A woman's form loomed up in the dusk. She was crossing the bridge towards him. And then suddenly a cry rent the air.

Smallwood Bessemer was to discover shortly that he had placed an erroneous interpretation upon this cry, which had really been one of agitation and alarm. To his sensitive ear it had sounded like the animal yowl of an angry woman sighting her prey, and he had concluded that this must be Agnes Flack, returned to the chase. Acting upon this assumption, he stood not on the order of going but immediately soared over the rail and plunged into the water below. Rising quickly to the surface and clutching out for support, he found himself grasping some-thing wet and furry.

For an instant, he was at a loss to decide what this could be. It had some of the properties of a sponge and some of a damp hearthrug. Then it bit him in the fleshy part of the thumb and he identified it as Celia Todd's Pekinese, Pirbright. In happier days he had been bitten from once to three times a week by this animal, and he recognized its technique.

The discovery removed a great weight from his mind. If Pirbright came, he reasoned, could Celia Todd be far behind. He saw that it must be she, and not Agnes Flack, who stood on the bridge. Greatly relieved, he sloshed to the shore, endeavour-ing as best he might to elude the creature's snapping jaws.

In this he was not wholly successful. Twice more he had to endure nips, and juicy ones. But the physical anguish soon passed away as he came to land and found himself gazing into Celia's eyes. They were large and round, and shone with an adoring light.

'Oh, Smallwood!' she cried. 'Thank heaven you were there! If you had not acted so promptly, the poor little mite would have been drowned.'

'It was nothing,' protested Bessemer modestly.

'Nothing? To have the reckless courage to plunge in like that? It was the sort of thing people get expensive medals for.'

'Just presence of mind,' said Bessemer. 'Some fellows have it, some haven't. How did it happen?'

She caught her breath.

'It was Sidney McMurdo's doing.'

'Sidney McMurdo's?'

'Yes. Pirbright was not well to-day, and I told him to fetch the vet. And he talked me into trying some sort of tonic port, which he said was highly recommended. We gave Pirbright a saucer full, and he seemed to enjoy it. And then he suddenly uttered a piercing bark and ran up the side of the wall. Finally he dashed out of the house. When he returned, his manner was lethargic, and I thought a walk would do him good. And as he came on to the bridge, he staggered and fell. He must have had some form of vertigo.'

Smallwood Bessemer scrutinized the animal. The visibility was not good, but he was able to discern in its bearing all the symptoms of an advanced hangover.

'Well, I broke off the engagement right away,' proceeded Celia Todd. 'I can respect a practical joker. I can admire a man who is cruel to animals. But I cannot pass as fit for human consumption a blend of the two. The mixture is too rich.'

Bessemer started.

'You are not going to marry Sidney McMurdo?'

'I am not.'

'What an extraordinary coincidence. I am not going to marry Agnes Flack.'

'You aren't?'

'No. So it almost looks—'

'Yes, doesn't it?'

'I mean, both of us being at a loose end, as it were . . .'

'Exactly.'

'Celia!'

'Smallwood!'

Hand in hand they made their way across the bridge. Celia uttered a sudden cry causing the dog Pirbright to wince as if somebody had driven a red hot spike into his head.

'I haven't told you the worst,' she said. 'He had the effrontery to assert that you had advised the tonic port.'

'The low blister!'

'I knew it could not be true. Your advice is always so good. You remember telling me I ought to have let Pirbright fight Agnes Flack's wolfhound? Well, you were quite right. He met it when he dashed out of the house after drinking that tonic port, and cleaned it up in under a minute. They are now the best of friends. After this, I shall always take your advice and ask for more.'

Smallwood Bessemer mused. Once again he was weighing the pros and cons. It was his habit of giving advice that had freed him from Agnes Flack. On the other hand, if it had not been for his habit of giving advice, Agnes Flack would never, so to speak, have arisen.

'Do you know,' he said, 'I doubt if I shall be doing much advising from now on. I think I shall ask the paper to release me from my columnist contract. I have a feeling that I shall be happier doing something like the Society News or the Children's Corner.'

The day was so fair, the breeze so gentle, the sky so blue and the sun so sunny, that Lord Emsworth, that vague and woollen-headed peer who liked fine weather, should have been gay and carefree, especially as he was looking at flowers, a thing which always gave him pleasure. But on his face, as he poked it over the hedge beyond which the flowers lay, a close observer would have noted a peevish frown. He was thinking of his younger son Freddie.

Coming to America to attend the wedding of one of his nieces to a local millionaire of the name of Tipton Plimsoll, Lord Emsworth had found himself, in the matter of board and lodging, confronted with a difficult choice. The British Government, notoriously slow men with a dollar, having refused to allow him to take out of England a sum sufficient to enable him to live in a New York hotel, he could become the guest of the bridegroom's aunt, who was acting as M.C. of the nuptials, or he could dig in with Freddie in the Long Island suburb where the latter had made his home. Warned by his spies that Miss Plimsoll maintained in her establishment no fewer than six Pekinese dogs, a breed of animal which always made straight for his ankles, he had decided on Freddie and was conscious now of having done the wrong thing. Pekes chew the body, but Freddie seared the soul.

The flowers grew in the garden of a large white house at the end of the road, and Lord Emsworth had been goggling at them for some forty minutes, for he was a man who liked to take his time over these things, when his reverie was interrupted by the tooting of a horn and the sound of a discordant voice singing 'Buttons and Bows'. Freddie's car drew up, with Freddie at the wheel.

'Oh, there you are, guv'nor,' said Freddie.

'Yes,' said Lord Emsworth, who was. 'I was looking at the flowers. A nice display. An attractive garden.'

'Where every prospect pleases and only man is vile,' said Freddie austerely. 'Keep away from the owner of that joint, guv'nor. He lowers the tone of the neighbourhood.'

'Indeed? Why is that?'

'Not one of the better element. His wife's away, and he throws parties. I've forgotten his name...Griggs or Follansbee or something...but we call him the Timber Wolf. He's something in the lumber business.'

'And he throws parties?'

'Repeatedly. You might say incessantly. Entertains blondes in droves. All wrong. My wife's away, but do you find me festooned in blondes? No. I pine for her return. Well, I must be oozing along. I'm late.'

'You are off somewhere?'

Freddie clicked his tongue.

'I told you yesterday, guv'nor, and I told you twice this morning, that I was giving a prospect lunch to-day at the golf club. I explained that I couldn't ask you to join us at the trough, because I shall be handing this bird a sales talk throughout the meal. You'll find your rations laid out on a tray. A cold collation to-day, because it's Thursday and on Thursdays the domestic staff downs tools.'

He drove on, all briskness and efficiency, and Lord Emsworth tut-tutted an irritable tut-tut.

There, he was telling himself, you had in a nutshell what made Freddie such a nerve-rasping companion. He threw his weight about. He behaved as if he were the Spirit of Modern Commerce. He was like something out of one of those advertisements which show the employee who has taken the correspondence course in Confidence and Self-Reliance looking his boss in the eye and making him wilt.

Freddie worked for Donaldson's Inc., dealers in dog biscuits of Long Island City, and had been doing so now for three years. And in those three years some miracle had transformed him from a vapid young London lizard into a go-getter, a live wire and a man who thought on his feet and did it now. Every night since Lord Emsworth had come to enjoy his hospitality, if enjoy is the word, he had spoken lyrically and at length of his success in promoting the interests of Donaldson's Dog Joy ('Get Your Dog Thinking The Donaldson Way'), making no secret of his view that it had been a lucky day for the dear old firm when it had put him on the payroll. As a salesman he was good, a fellow who cooked with gas and did not spare himself, and he admitted it.

All of which might have been music to Lord Emsworth's ears, for a younger son earning his living in America is unquestionably a vast improvement on a younger son messing about and getting into debt in England, had it not been for one circumstance. He could not rid himself of a growing conviction that after years of regarding this child of his as a drone and a wastrel, the child was now regarding him as one. A world's worker himself, Freddie eyed with scorn one who, like Lord Emsworth, neither toiled nor spun. He patronized Lord Emsworth. He had never actually called Lord Emsworth a spiv, but he made it plain that it was in this category that he had mentally pencilled in the author of his being. And if there is one thing that pierces the armour of an English father of the upper classes, it is to be looked down on by his younger son. Little wonder that Lord Emsworth, as he toddled along the road, was gritting his teeth. A weaker man would have gnashed them.

His gloom was not lightened by the sight of the cold collation which leered at him on his return to the house. There was the tray of which Freddie had spoken, and on it a plate on which, like corpses after a battle, lay a slice of vermilion ham, a slice of sepia corned beef, a circle of mauve liverwurst and, of all revolting things, a large green pickle. It seemed to Lord Emsworth that Freddie's domestic staff was temperamentally incapable of distinguishing between the needs of an old gentleman who had to be careful what he ate and those of a flock of buzzards taking pot luck in the Florida Everglades.

For some moments he stood gaping at this unpleasant picture in still life; then there stole into his mind the thought that there might be eggs in the ice-box. He went thither and tested his theory and it was proved correct.

'Ha!' said Lord Emsworth. He remembered how he had frequently scrambled eggs at school.

But his school days lay half a century behind him, and time in its march robs us of our boyhood gifts. Since the era when he had worn Eton collars and ink spots on his face, he had lost the knack, and it all too speedily became apparent that Operation

Eggs was not going to be the walkover he had anticipated. Came a moment when he would have been hard put to it to say whether he was scrambling the eggs or the eggs were scrambling him. And he had paused to clarify his thoughts on this point, when there was a ring at the front door bell. Deeply incrusted in yolk, he shuffled off to answer the summons.

A girl was standing in the porch. He inspected her through his pince-nez with the vacant stare on which the female members of his family had so often commented adversely. She seemed to him, as he drank her slowly in, a nice sort of girl. A man with a great many nieces who were always bursting in on him and bally-ragging him when he wanted to read his pig book, he had come to fear and distrust the younger members of the opposite sex, but this one's looks he liked immediately. About her there was none of that haughty beauty and stormy emotion in which his nieces specialized. She was small and friendly and companionable.

'Good morning,' he said.

'Good morning. Would you like a richly bound encyclopædia of Sport?'

'Not in the least,' said Lord Emsworth cordially. 'Can you scramble eggs?'

'Why, sure.'

'Then come in,' said Lord Emsworth. 'Come in. And if you will excuse me leaving you, I will go and change my clothes.'

Women are admittedly wonderful. It did not take Lord Emsworth long to remove his best suit, which he had been wearing in deference to the wishes of Freddie, who was a purist on dress, and don the older and shabbier one which made him look like a minor employee in some shady firm of private detectives, but, brief though the interval had been, the girl had succeeded in bringing order out of chaos. Not only had she quelled what had threatened to become an ugly revolt among the eggs, but she had found bacon and coffee and produced toast. What was virtually a banquet was set out in the living-room, and Lord Emsworth was about to square his elbows and have at it, when he detected an omission.

'Where is your plate?' he asked.

'Mine?' The girl seemed surprised. 'Am I in on this?'

'Most certainly.'

'That's mighty nice of you. I'm starving.'

'These eggs, said Lord Emsworth some moments later, speaking thickly through a mouthful of them, 'are delicious. Salt?'

'Thanks.'

'Pepper? Mustard? Tell me,' said Lord Emsworth, for it was a matter that had been perplexing him a good deal, 'why do you go about the countryside offering people richly bound encyclopædias of Sport? Deuced civil of you, of course,' he added hastily, lest she might think that he was criticizing, 'but why do you?'

'I'm selling them.'

'Selling them?'

'Yes.'

A bright light shone upon Lord Emsworth. It had been well said of him that he had an I.Q. some thirty points lower than that of a not too agile-minded jelly-fish, but he had grasped her point. She was selling them.

'Of course, yes. Quite. I see what you mean. You're *selling* them.'

'That's right. They set you back five dollars and I get forty per cent. Only I don't.'

'Why not?'

'Because people won't buy them.'

'No?'

'No, sir.'

'Don't people want richly bound encyclopædias of Sport?'

'If they do, they keep it from me.'

'Dear, dear.' Lord Emsworth swallowed a piece of bacon emotionally. His heart was bleeding for this poor child. 'That must be trying for you.'

'It is.'

'But why do you have to sell the bally things?'

'Well, it's like this. I'm going to have a baby.'

'Good God!'

'Oh, not immediately. Next January. Well, that sort of thing costs money. Am I right or wrong?'

'Right, most decidedly,' said Lord Emsworth, who had never been a young mother himself but knew the ropes. 'I remember my poor wife complaining of the expense when my son Frederick was born. "Oh dear, oh dear, oh dear," I remember her saying. She was alive at the time,' explained Lord Emsworth.

'Ed. works in a garage.'

'Does he? I don't think I have met him. Who is Ed.?'

'My husband.'

'Oh, your husband? You mean your husband. Works in a garage, does he?'

'That's right. And the take-home pay doesn't leave much over for extras.'

'Like babies?'

'Like babies. So I got this job. I didn't tell Ed., of course. He'd have a fit.'

'He is subject to fits?'

'He wants me to lie down and rest.'

'I think he's right.'

'Oh, he's right, all right, but how can I? I've got to hustle out and sell richly bound encyclopædias.'

'Of Sport?'

'Of Sport. And it's tough going. You do become discouraged. Besides getting blisters on the feet. I wish you could see my feet right now.'

On the point of saying that he would be delighted, Lord Emsworth paused. He had had a bright idea and it had taken his breath away. This always happened when he had bright ideas. He had had one in the Spring of 1921 and another in the Summer of 1933, and those had taken his breath away, too.

'I will sell your richly bound encyclopædias of Sport,' he said.

'You?'

The bright idea which had taken Lord Emsworth's breath away was that if he went out and sold richly bound encyclopædias of Sport, admitted by all the cognoscenti to be very difficult to dispose of, it would rid him once and for all of the inferiority complex which so oppressed him when in the society of his son Freddie. The brassiest of young men cannot pull that Spirit of Modern Commerce stuff on a father if the father is practically a Spirit of Modern Commerce himself.

'Precisely,' he said.

'But you couldn't.'

Lord Emsworth bridled. A wave of confidence and self-reliance was surging through him.

'Who says I couldn't? My son Frederick sells things, and I resent the suggestion that I am incapable of doing anything that Frederick can do.' He wondered if it would be possible to explain to her what a turnip-headed young ass Frederick was, then gave up the attempt as hopeless. 'Leave this to me,' he said. 'Lie down on that sofa and get a nice rest.'

'But—'

'Don't argue,' said Lord Emsworth dangerously, becoming the dominant male. 'Lie down on that sofa.'

Two minutes later, he was making his way down the road, still awash with that wave of confidence and self-reliance. His objective was the large white house where the flowers were. He was remembering what Freddie had said about its owner. The man, according to Freddie, threw parties and entertained blondes in his wife's absence. And while we may look askance from the moral standpoint at one who does this, we have to admit that it suggests the possession of sporting blood. That reckless, raffish type probably buys its encyclopædias of Sport by the gross.

But one of the things that make life so difficult is that waves of confidence and self-reliance do not last. They surge, but they recede, leaving us with dubious minds and cooling feet. Lord Emsworth had started out in uplifted mood, but as he reached the gate of the white house the glow began to fade.

It was not that he had forgotten the technique of the thing. Freddie had explained it too often for him to do that. You rapped on the door. You said 'I wonder if I could interest you in a good dog biscuit?' And then by sheer personal magnetism you cast a spell on the householder so that he became wax in your hands. All perfectly simple and straightforward. And yet, having opened the gate and advanced a few feet into the driveway, Lord Emsworth paused. He removed his pince-nez, polished them, replaced them on his nose, blinked, swallowed once or twice and ran a finger over his chin. The first fine frenzy had abated. He was feeling like a nervous man who in an impulsive moment has volunteered to go over Niagara Falls in a barrel.

He was still standing in the driveway, letting 'I dare not' wait upon 'I would', as cats do in adages, when the air became full of tooting horns and grinding brakes and screaming voices.

'God bless my soul,' said Lord Emsworth, coming out of his coma.

The car which had so nearly caused a vacancy in the House of Lords was bursting with blondes. There was a blonde at the wheel, another at her side, further blondes in the rear seats and on the lap of the blonde beside the blonde at the wheel a blonde Pekinese dog. They were all shouting, and the Pekinese dog was hurling abuse in Chinese.

'God bless my soul,' said Lord Emsworth. 'I beg your pardon. I really must apologize. I was plunged in thought.'

'Oh, was that what you were plunged in?' said the blonde at the wheel, mollified by his suavity. Speak civilly to blondes, and they will speak civilly to you.

'I was thinking of dog biscuits. Of dog biscuits. Of ... er ... in short ... dog biscuits. I wonder,' said Lord Emsworth, striking while the iron was hot, 'if I could interest you in a good dog biscuit?'

The blonde at the wheel weighed the question.

'Not me,' she said. 'I never touch 'em.'

'Nor me,' said a blonde at the back. 'Doctor's orders.'

'And if you're thinking of making a quick sale to Eisenhower here,' said the blonde beside the driver, kissing the Pekinese on the tip of its nose, a feat of daring at which Lord Emsworth marvelled, 'he only eats chicken.'

Lord Emsworth corrected himself.

'When I said dog biscuit,' he explained, 'I meant a richly bound encyclopædia of Sport.'

The blondes exchanged glances.

'Look,' said the one at the wheel. 'If you don't know the difference between a dog biscuit and a richly bound encyclopædia of Sport, seems to me you'd be doing better in some other line of business.'

'Much better,' said the blonde beside her.

'A whole lot better,' agreed the blonde at the back.

'No future in it, the way you're going,' said the blonde at the wheel, summing up. 'That's the first thing you want to get straight on, the difference between dog biscuits and richly bound encyclopædias of Sport. It's a thing that's cropping up all the time. There is a difference. I couldn't explain it to you offhand, but you go off into a corner somewheres and mull it over quietly and you'll find it'll suddenly come to you.'

'Like a flash,' said the blonde at the back.

'Like a stroke of lightning or sump'n,' assented the blonde at the wheel. 'You'll be amazed how you ever came to mix them up. Well, good-bye. Been nice seeing you.'

The car moved on toward the house, and Lord Emsworth, closing his burning ears to the happy laughter proceeding from its interior, tottered out into the road. His spirit was broken. It was his intention to return home and stay there. And he had started on his way when there came stealing into his mind a disturbing thought.

That girl. That nice young Mrs Ed. who was going to have a fit in January . . . or, rather, a baby. (It was her husband, he recalled, who had the fits). She was staking everything on his salesmanship. Could he fail her? Could he betray her simple trust?

The obvious answer was 'Yes, certainly', but the inherited chivalry of a long line of ancestors, all of whom had been noted for doing the square thing by damsels in distress, caused Lord

Emsworth to shrink from making it. In the old days when knighthood was in flower and somebody was needed to rescue a suffering female from a dragon or a two-headed giant, the cry was always 'Let Emsworth do it!', and the Emsworth of the period had donned his suit of mail, stropped his sword, parked his chewing gum under the round table and snapped into it. A pretty state of things if the twentieth century holder of the name were to allow himself to be intimidated by blondes.

Blushing hotly, Lord Emsworth turned and made for the gate again.

In the living-room of the white house, cool in the shade of the tree which stood outside its window, there had begun to burgeon one of those regrettable neo-Babylonian orgies which are so frequent when blondes and men who are something in the lumber business get together. Cocktails were circulating, and the blonde who had been at the wheel of the car was being the life and soul of the party with her imitation of the man outside who had been unable to get himself straightened out in the matter of dog biscuits and richly bound encyclopædias. Her 'Lord Emsworth' was a nice bit of impressionistic work, clever but not flattering.

She was giving a second encore when her performance was interrupted by a shrill yapping from without, and the blonde who had sat beside her knitted her brow in motherly concern.

'Somebody's teasing Eisenhower,' she said.

'Probably found a cat,' said the timber wolf. 'Tell me more. What sort of a character was this character?'

'Tall,' said a blonde.

'Old,' said another blonde.

'Skinny,' said a third blonde.

And a fourth blonde added that he had worn pince-nez.

A sudden gravity fell upon the timber wolf. He was remembering that on several occasions these last few days he had seen just such a man peering over his hedge in a furtive and menacing manner, like Sherlock Holmes on the trail. This very morning he had seen him. He had been standing there outside the hedge, motionless . . . watching . . . watching . . .

The fly in the ointment of men who throw parties for blondes when their wives are away, the thing that acts as a skeleton at the feast and induces goose pimples when the revelry is at its height, is the fact that they can never wholly dismiss the possibility that these wives, though they ought to be ashamed of themselves for entertaining unworthy suspicions, may have engaged firms of private detectives to detect them privately and report on their activities. It was this thought that now came whistling like an east wind through the mind of the timber wolf, whose name, just to keep the record straight, was not Griggs or Follansbee but Spenlow (George).

And as he quivered beneath its impact, one of his guests, who had hitherto taken no part in the conversation, spoke as follows:

'Oo, look! Eisenhower's got him up a tree!'

And George Spenlow, following her pointing finger, saw that she was correct. There the fellow was, roosting in the branches and adjusting his pince-nez as if the better to view the scene within. He quivered like a jelly and stared at Lord Emsworth. Lord Emsworth stared at him. Their eyes met.

Much has been written of the language of the eyes, but except between lovers it is never a very satisfactory medium of communication. George Spenlow, trying to read the message in Lord Emsworth's, completely missed the gist.

What Lord Emsworth was trying to convey with the language

of the eye was an apology for behaviour which at first sight, he admitted, might seem a little odd. He had rapped on the door, he was endeavouring to explain, but, unable to attract attention to his presence, had worked his way round the house to where he heard voices, not a thought on his mind except a passionate desire to sell richly bound encyclopædias of Sport, and suddenly something had exploded like a land mine on the ground beside him and, looking down, he had perceived a Pekinese dog advancing on him with bared teeth. This had left him no option but to climb the tree to avoid its slavering jaws. 'Oh, for the wings of a dove!' he had said to himself, and had got moving. He concluded his remarks by smiling a conciliatory smile.

It pierced George Spenlow like a dagger. It seemed to him that this private investigator, elated at having caught him with the goods, was gloating evilly.

He gulped.

'You girls stay here,' he said hoarsely. 'I'll go talk to this fellow.'

He climbed through the window, scooped up the Pekinese, restored it to its proprietress and addressed Lord Emsworth in a quavering voice.

'Now listen,' he said.

These men high up in the lumber business are quick thinkers. George Spenlow had seen the way.

'Now listen,' said George Spenlow.

He had taken Lord Emsworth affectionately by the arm and was walking him up and down the lawn. He was a stout, pink, globular man, so like Lord Emsworth's pig, Empress of Blandings, in appearance that the latter felt a wave of homesickness.

'Now listen,' said George Spenlow. 'I think you and I can get together.'

Lord Emsworth, to show that his heart was in the right place, smiled another conciliatory smile.

'Yes, yes, I know,' said George Spenlow, wincing. 'But I think we can. I'll put my cards on the table. I know all about it. My wife. She gets ideas into her head. She imagines things.'

Lord Emsworth, though fogged, was able to understand this.

'My late wife was like that,' he said.

'All women are like that,' said George Spenlow. 'It's something to do with the bone structure of their heads. They let their imagination run away with them. They entertain unworthy suspicions.'

Here again Lord Emsworth was able to follow him. He said he had noticed the same thing in his sister Constance, and George Spenlow began to feel encouraged.

'Sure. Sisters, wives, late wives . . . they're all the same, and it doesn't do to let them get away with it. So here's what. What you tell her is that you found me enjoying a quiet home afternoon with a few old college friends . . . Wait, wait,' said George Spenlow urgently. 'Wait while I finish.'

He had observed his guest shake his head. This was because a mosquito had just bitten Lord Emsworth on the ear, but he had no means of divining this. Shakes of the head are as hard to interpret as the language of the eyes.

'Wait while I finish,' said George Spenlow. 'Hear what I was going to say. You're a man of the world. You want to take the broad, sensible outlook. You want to study the situation from every angle and find out what there is in it for you. Now then how much?'

'You mean how many?'

'Eh?'

'How many would you like?'

'How many what?'

'Richly bound encyclopædias of Sport.'

'Oh yes, yes, yes,' said George Spenlow, enlightened 'Oh, sure, sure, sure, sure, sure. I didn't get you for a moment. About how many would you suggest? Fifty?'

Lord Emsworth shook his head again – petulantly, it seemed to George Spenlow. The mosquito had returned.

'Well, naturally,' proceeded George Spenlow, 'when I said fifty, I meant a hundred. I think that's a nice round number.'

'Very nice,' agreed Lord Emsworth. 'Or would you care for a gross?'

'A gross might be better.'

'You can give them to your friends.'

'That's right. On their birthdays.'

'Or at Christmas.'

'Of course. So difficult to think of a suitable Christmas present.'

'Extraordinarily difficult.'

'Shall we say five hundred dollars on account?'

'That would be capital.'

'And remember,' said George Spenlow, with all the emphasis at his disposal. 'Old college friends.'

A passer-by, watching Lord Emsworth as he returned some twenty minutes later to Freddie's dream house down the road, would have said to himself that there went an old gentleman who had found the blue bird, and he would have been right. Lord Emsworth, as he fingered the crisp roll of bills in his trouser pocket, was not actually saying 'Whooppee!', but it was a very near thing. He was feeling as if a great burden had been removed from his shoulders.

The girl was asleep when he reached the house. Gently, without disturbing her slumbers, Lord Emsworth reached for her bag and deposited the five hundred dollars in it. Then he tiptoed out and set a course for the golf club. He wanted to find his son Freddie.

'Ah,' Frederick,' he would say. 'So you sell dog biscuits, do you? Pooh! Anyone can sell dog biscuits. Give me something tougher, like richly bound encyclopædias of Sport. Now, I strolled out just now and sold a gross at the first house I visited. So don't talk to me about dog biscuits. In fact, don't talk to me at all, because I am sick of the sound of your voice And STOP THAT SINGING!!'

Yes, when Freddie began singing 'Buttons and Bows', that would be the moment to strike.

The story of Conky Biddle's great love begins at about six-forty-five on an evening in June in the Marylebone district of London. He had spent the day at Lord's cricket ground watching a cricket match, and driving away at close of play had been held up in a traffic jam. And held up alongside his taxi was a car with a girl at the wheel. And he had just lit a cigarette and was thinking of this and that, when he heard her say:

'Cricket is not a game. It is a mere shallow excuse for walking in your sleep.'

It was at this point that love wound its silken fetters about Conky. He leaped like a jumping bean and the cigarette fell from his nerveless fingers. If a girl who talked like that was not his dream girl, he didn't know a dream girl when he heard one.

You couldn't exactly say that he fell in love at first sight, for owing to the fact that in between him and her, obscuring the visibility, there was sitting a robust blighter in blue flannel with a pin stripe, he couldn't see her. All he had to go on was her voice, but that was ample. It was a charming voice with an American intonation. She was probably, he thought, an American angel who had stepped down from Heaven for a short breather in London.

'If I see another cricket game five thousand years from now,' she said, 'that'll be soon enough.'

Her companion plainly disapproved of these cracks. He said in a stiff, sniffy sort of way that she had not seen cricket at its best that afternoon, play having been greatly interfered with by rain.

'A merciful dispensation,' said the girl. 'Cricket with hardly any cricket going on is a lot better than cricket where the nuisance persists uninterrupted. In my opinion the ideal contest would be one where it rained all day and the rival teams stayed home doing their crossword puzzles.'

The traffic jam then broke up and the car shot forward like a B.29, leaving the taxi nowhere.

The reason why this girl's words had made so deep an impression on the young Biddle was that of all things in existence, with the possible exception of slugs and his uncle Everard, Lord Plumpton, he disliked cricket most. As a boy he had been compelled to play it, and grown to man's estate he was compelled to watch it. And if there was one spectacle that saddened him more than another in a world where the man of sensibility is always being saddened by spectacles, it was that of human beings, the heirs of the ages, waddling about in pads and shouting 'How's that, umpire?'

He had to watch cricket because Lord Plumpton told him to, and he was dependent on the other for his three squares a day. Lord Plumpton was a man who knew the batting averages of every first-class cricketer back to the days when they used to play in top hats and whiskers, and recited them to Conky after dinner. He liked to show Conky with the assistance of an apple (or, in winter, of an orange) how Bodger of Kent got the fingerspin which enabled him to make the ball dip and turn late on a sticky wicket. And frequently when Conky was walking along the street with him and working up to touching him for a tenner, he would break off the conversation at its most crucial point in order to demonstrate with his umbrella how Codger of Sussex made his late cut through the slips.

It was to the home of this outstanding louse, where he had a small bedroom on an upper floor, that Conky was now on his way. Arriving at journey's end, he found a good deal of stir and bustle going on, with doctors coming downstairs with black bags and parlourmaids going upstairs with basins of gruel, and learned from the butler that Lord Plumpton had sprained his ankle.

'No, really?' said Conky, well pleased, for if his uncle had possessed as many ankles as a centipede he would thoroughly have approved of him spraining them all. 'I suppose I had better go up and view the remains.'

He proceeded to the star bedroom and found his uncle propped up with pillows, throwing gruel at the parlourmaid. It was plain that he was in no elfin mood. He was looking like a mass murderer, though his face lacked the genial expression which you often see in mass murderers, and he glared at Conky with the sort of wild regret which sweeps over an irritable man when he sees a loved one approaching his sick bed and realizes that he has used up all the gruel.

'What ho, Uncle Everard,' said Conky. 'The story going the round of the clubs is that you have bust a joint of sorts. What happened?'

Lord Plumpton scowled darkly. He looked now like a mass murderer whose stomach ulcers are paining him.

'I'll tell you what happened. You remember I had to leave you at Lord's to attend a committee meeting at my club. Well, as I was walking back from the club, there were some children playing cricket in the street and one of them skied the ball towards extra cover, so naturally I ran out into the road to catch it. I judged it to a nicety and had just caught it when a homicidal lunatic of a girl came blinding along at ninety miles an hour in her car and knocked me base over apex. One of these days,' said Lord Plumpton, licking his lips, 'I hope to meet that girl again, preferably down a dark alley. I shall skin her very slowly with a blunt knife, dip her in boiling oil, sever her limb from limb, assemble those limbs on the pavement and dance on them.'

'And rightly,' said Conky. 'These girls who bust your ankles and prevent you going to Lord's to-morrow need a sharp lesson.'

'What do you mean, prevent me going to Lord's to-morrow? Do you think a mere sprained ankle will stop me going to a cricket match? I shall be there, with you at my side. And now,' said Lord Plumpton, wearying of these exchanges, 'go to hell!'

Conky did not go to hell, but he went downstairs and out on to the front steps to get a breath of air. He was feeling low and depressed. He had been so certain that he would be able to get to-morrow off. He had turned to go in again when he heard a noise of brakes as a car drew up behind him.

'Excuse me,' said a voice. 'Could I see Lord Plumpton?'

Simple words, but their effect on Conky as he recognized that silvery voice was to make him quiver from stay-combed hair to shoe sole. He uttered a whinnying cry which, as he swivelled round and for the first time was privileged to see her face, became a gasp. The voice had been the voice of an angel. The face measured up to the voice.

Seeing him, she too gasped. This was apt to be the reaction of the other sex on first beholding Conky Biddle, for though his I.Q. was low his outer crust was rather sensational. He was, indeed, a dazzlingly good-looking young man, who out-Caryed Grant and began where Gregory Peck left off.

'I say,' he said, going to the car and placing a foot on the running-board, 'Don't look now, but did I by chance hear you expressing a wish to meet my uncle, Lord Plumpton?'

'That's right. I recently flattened him out with my car, and I was planning to give him some flowers.'

'I wouldn't,' said Conky. 'I really wouldn't. I say this as a friend. Time, the great healer, will have to pull up its socks and spit on its hands quite a bit before it becomes safe for you to enter the presence.'

'I see. Then I'll take the blooms around the corner and have them delivered by a messenger boy. How's that, umpire?'

Corky winced. It was as though he had heard this divine creature sully her lips with something out of a modern historical novel.

'Good God!' he said. 'Where did you pick up that obscene expression?'

'From your uncle. He was chanting it at the top of his voice when I rammed him. A mental case, I imagine. What does it mean?'

'It's what you say at cricket.'

'Cricket!' The girl shuddered strongly. 'Shall I tell you what I think of cricket?'

'I have already heard your views. Your car got stuck abaft my taxi in a traffic block this evening. I was here, if you follow what I mean, and you were there, a few feet to the nor'-nor'-east, so I was able to drink in what you were saying about cricket. Would you mind if I thanked you with tears in my eyes?'

'Not at all. But don't you like cricket? I thought all English-men loved it.'

'Not this Englishman. It gives me the pip.'

'Me, too. I ought never to have gone near that Lord's place. But in a moment of weakness I let myself be talked into it by my *fiancé*.'

Conky reeled.

'Oh, my sainted aunt! Have you got a *fiancé*?'

'Not now.'

Conky stopped reeling.

'Was he the bloke you were talking to in the car?'

'That's right. Eustace Davenport-Simms. I think he plays for Essex or Sussex or somewhere. My views were too subversive for him, so after kidding back and forth for a while we decided to cancel the order for the wedding cake.'

'I thought he seemed a bit sniffy.'

'He got sniffier.'

'Very sensible of you not to marry a cricketer.'

'So I felt.'

'The upshot, then, when all the smoke has blown away, is that you are once more in circulation?'

'Yes.'

'Well, that's fine,' said Conky. A sudden thought struck him. 'I say, would you object if I pressed your little hand?'

'Some other time, I think.'

'Any time that suits you.'

'You see, I have to hie me back to my hotel and dress. I'm late already, and my father screams like a famished hyæna if he's kept waiting for his rations.'

And with a rapid thrust of her shapely foot she set the machinery in motion and vanished round the corner on two wheels, leaving Conky staring after her with a growing feeling of desolation. He had just realized that he was unaware of her name, address and telephone number and had had what was probably his last glimpse of her. If the expression 'Ships that pass in the night' had been familiar to him, he would certainly have uttered it, using clenched teeth for the purpose.

It was a Conky with heart bowed down and a general feeling of having been passed through the wringer who accompanied his uncle to Lord's next morning. The thought that a Grade A soulmate had come into his life and buzzed out again, leaving no clue to her identity or whereabouts, was a singularly bitter one. Lord Plumpton on the journey to the Mecca of cricket spoke well and easily of the visit of the Australian team of 1921, but Conky proved a distrait listener; so distrait that Lord Plumpton prodded him irascibly in the ribs and called him an infernal goggle-eyed fathead, which of course he was.

He was still in a sort of trance when they took their seats in the pavilion, but here it was less noticeable, for everybody else was in a sort of trance. The somnambulists out in the field tottered to and fro, and the spectators lay back and let their eyes go glassy. For perhaps an hour nothing happened except that Hodger of Middlesex, waking like Abou ben Adhem from a deep dream of peace, flicked his bat at a rising ball and edged it into the hands of a sleeper dozing in what is technically known as the gully. Then Lord Plumpton, who had been silent except for an occasional 'Nice! Nice!' sat up with a sudden jerk and an explosive 'Well, I'm dashed!' and glared sideways at the three shilling seats which adjoined the pavilion. And Conky, following his gaze, felt his heart execute four separate buck and wing steps and come to rest quivering like a jelly in a high wind.

'Well, I'm dashed!' said Lord Plumpton, continuing to direct at the three shilling seats the kind of look usually associated with human fiends in mystery stories. 'There's that blasted girl!'

It was not a description which Conky himself would have applied to the divinest of her sex, nor one which he enjoyed hearing applied to her, and for a moment he was in two minds as to whether to haul off and sock his relative on the beezer. Wiser counsels prevailed, and he said:

'Yes, there she spouts.'

Lord Plumpton seemed surprised.

'You know her?'

'Just slightly. She ran into me last night.'

'Into you, too? Good gad, the female's a public menace. If she's allowed to remain at large, the population of London will be decimated. I've a good mind to go over and tell her what I think of her.'

'But your uncle, ankle.'

'What the devil are you gibbering about?'

'I mean your ankle, uncle. You mustn't walk about on it. How would it be if I popped over and acquainted her with your displeasure?'

Lord Plumpton considered.

'Yes, that's not a bad idea. A surprisingly good idea, in fact, considering what a nitwit you are. But pitch it strong.'

'Oh, I will,' said Conky.

He rose and hurried off, and Lord Plumpton fell into conversation with the barely animate spectator on his left. They were soon deep in an argument as to whether it was at square leg or at extra cover that D. C. L. Wodger of Gloucestershire had fielded in 1904.

If the girl had looked like the better class of angel in the uncertain light of last night, she looked more than ever so in the reasonably bright sunshine of to-day. She was one of those lissom girls of medium height. Her eyes and hair were a browny hazel. The general effect was of a seraph who ate lots of yeast.

'Oh, hullo,' said Conky, lowering himself into a seat beside her. 'We meet again, what?'

She seemed surprised and startled. In her manner, as she gazed at his clean-cut face and then into his frank blue eyes, there was something that might almost be described as fluttering.

'You!' she cried. 'What are you doing here?'

'Just watching cricket.'

'But you told me last night that cricket gave you the pip, which I imagine is something roughly equivalent to the megrims or the heeby-jeebies.'

'Quite. But, you see, it's like this. My uncle is crazy about the ghastly game and I'm dependent on him, so when he says "Come along and watch cricket", I have to come along and watch it like a lynx.'

The girl frowned. It was as if she had been hurt and disappointed.

'Why are you dependent on your uncle? Why don't you get a job?'

Conky hastened to defend himself.

'I do get a job. I get dozens of jobs. But I lose them all. The trouble is, you see, that I'm not very bright.'

'No?'

'Not very. That's why they call me Conky.'

'Do they call you Conky?'

'Invariably. What started it was an observation one of the masters at school happened to drop one day. He said, addressing me – "To attempt to drive information into your head, Biddle, is no easy task, for Providence, mysterious in its workings, has given you instead of the more customary human brain a skull full of concrete." So after that everyone called me Conky.'

'I see. What sort of jobs have you tried?'

'Practically everything except Chancellor of the Duchy of Lancaster.'

'And you get fired every time?'

'Every time.'

'I'm sorry.'

'It's dashed white of you to be sorry, but as a matter of fact it's all right.'

'How do you mean it's all right?'

Conky hesitated. Then he reflected that if you couldn't confide in an angel in human shape, who could you confide in? He glanced about him. Except for themselves, the three shilling tier of seats was almost empty.

'Well, you'll keep it under your hat, won't you, because it's supposed to be very hush-hush at the moment. I am on the eve of making a stupendous fortune. You know sea water?'

'The stuff that props the ship up when you come over from New York?'

'That's right. Well, you probably aren't aware of it, but it's full of gold, and I'm in with a fellow who's got a secret process for scooping it out. I saw his advertisement in the paper saying that if you dashed along and brassed up quick you could get in on an invention of vast possibilities, so I dashed along and brassed up. He was a nice chap and let me into the thing without a murmur.'

Bloke of the name of MacSporran. I happened to have scraped up ten quid, so I put that in and he tells me that at a conservative estimate I shall get back about two hundred and fifty thousand. I call that a nice profit.'

'Very nice.'

'Yes, it's all very convenient. And when I say that, I'm not thinking so much of the jolliness of having all that splosh in the old sock, I am alluding more to the difference this has made in what you might call my matrimonial plans. If I want to get married, I mean. What I'm driving at,' said Conky, giving her a melting look, 'is that I am now in a position, when I meet the girl I love, to put the binge on a practical basis.'

'I see.'

'In fact,' said Conky, edging a little closer, 'I might almost start making my plans at once.'

'That's the spirit. Father's slogan is "Do it now", and he's a tycoon.'

'I thought a tycoon was a sort of storm.'

'No, a millionaire.'

'Is your father a millionaire?'

'Yes, and more pouring in all the time.'

'Oh?'

A sudden chill had come over Conky's dashing mood. The one thing he had always vowed he would never do was marry for money. For years his six uncles and seven aunts had been urging him to cash in on his looks and grab something opulent. They had paraded heiresses before him in droves, but he had been firm. He had his principles.

Of course, in the present case it was different. He loved this girl with every fibre of his being. But all the same . . . No, he told himself, better wait till his bank balance was actually bulging.

With a strong effort he changed the conversation.

'Well, as I was saying,' he said, 'I hope to clean up shortly on an impressive scale, and when I do I'll never watch another cricket match as long as I live. Arising from which, what on earth are you doing here, holding the views on cricket which you do?'

A slight shadow of disappointment seemed to pass over the girl's face. It was as if she had been expecting the talk to develop along different lines.

'Oh, I came for a purpose.'

'Eh? What purpose?'

She directed his attention to the rows of living corpses in the pavilion. Lord Plumpton and his friend, having settled the Wodger question, were leaning back with their hats over their eyes. It was difficult to realize that life still animated those rigid limbs.

'When I was here yesterday, I was greatly struck by the spectacle of those stiffs over there. I wondered if it was possible to stir them up into some sort of activity.'

'I doubt it.'

'I'm a little dubious myself. They're like fish on a slab or a Wednesday matinee audience. Still, I thought I would try. Yesterday, of course I hadn't elastic and ammo with me.'

'Elastic? Ammo?'

Conky stared. From the recesses of her costume she had produced a piece of stout elastic and a wad of tin foil. She placed the tin foil on the elastic and then between her teeth. Then, turning, she took careful aim at Lord Plumpton.

For a sighting shot it was an admirable effort. Conky, following the projectile with a rapt gaze, saw his uncle start and put a hand to his ear. There seemed little reason to doubt that he had caught it amidships.

'Good Lord!' he cried. 'Here, after you with that elastic. I used to do that at school, and many was the fine head I secured. I wonder if the old skill still lingers.'

It was some minutes later that Lord Plumpton turned to the friend beside him.

'Wasps very plentiful this year,' he said.

The friend blinked drowsily.

'Watts?'

'Wasps.'

'There was A. R. K. Watts who used to play for Sussex. Ark we used to call him.'

'Not Watts. Wasps.'

'Wasps?'

'Wasps.'

'What about them?'

'They seem very plentiful. One stung me in the ear just now. And now one of them has knocked off my hat. Most extra-ordinary.'

A man in a walrus moustache who had played for Surrey in 1911 came along, and Lord Plumpton greeted him cordially.

'Hullo, Freddie.'

'Hullo.'

'Good game.'

'Very. Exciting.'

'Wasps are a nuisance, though.'

'Wasps?'

'Wasps.'

'What wasps?'

'I don't know their names. The wasps around here.'

'No wasps around here.'

'Yes.'

'Not in the pavilion at Lord's. You can't get in unless you're a member.'

'Well, one has just knocked off my hat. And look, there goes Jimmy's hat.'

The walrus shook his head. He stooped and picked up a piece of tin foil.

'Someone's shooting this stuff at you. Used to do it myself a long time ago. Ah yes,' he said, peering about him, 'I see where the stuff's coming from. That girl over there in the three shilling seats with your nephew. If you look closely, you'll see she's drawing a bead on you now.

Lord Plumpton looked, started and stiffened.

'That girl again! Is one to be beset by her through all eternity? Send for the attendants! Rouse the attendants and give them their divisional orders. Instruct the attendants to arrest her immediately and bring her to the committee room.

And so it came about that just as Conky was adjusting the elastic to his lips a short while later and preparing to loose off, a heavy hand fell on his shoulder, and there was a stern-faced man in the uniform of a Marylebone Cricket Club attendant. And simultaneously another heavy hand fell on the girl's shoulder, and there was another stern-faced man in the uniform of another Marylebone Cricket Club attendant.

It was a fair cop.

The committee room of the Marylebone Cricket Club is a sombre and impressive apartment. Photographs of bygone cricketers, many of them with long beards, gaze down from the walls – accusingly, or so it seems to the man whose conscience is not as clear as it might be. Only a man with an exceptionally clear conscience can enter this holy of holies without feeling that he is about to be stripped of his M.C.C. tie and formally ticketed as a social leper.

This is particularly so when, as in the present instance the President himself is seated at his desk. It was at Lord Plumpton's request that he was there now. It had seemed to Lord Plumpton that a case of this magnitude could be dealt with adequately only at the very highest levels.

He mentioned this in his opening speech for the prosecution.

'I demand,' said Lord Plumpton, 'the most exemplary punishment for an outrage unparalleled in the annals of the Marylebone Cricket Club, the dear old club we all love so well, if you know what I mean.' Here he paused as if intending to bare his head, but realizing that he had not got his hat on continued, 'I mean to say, taking pot-shots at members with a series of slabs of tin foil, dash it! If that isn't a nice bit of box fruit, what is? Bad enough, if you see what I'm driving at, to take pot-shots at even the *cannaille*, as they call them in France, who squash in in the free seats, but when it comes to pot-shotting members in the pavilion, I mean where are we? Personally I would advocate skinning the girl, but if you consider that too extreme I am prepared to settle for twenty years in solitary confinement. A menace to the community, that's what this girl is. Bustling about in her car and knocking people endways with one hand and flicking their hats off with the other, if you follow my drift. She reminds me of . . . who was that woman in the Bible whose work was always so raw? . . . Delilah? . . . No . . . It's on the tip of my tongue . . . Ah yes, Jezebel. She's a modern streamlined Jezebel, dash her insides.'

'Uncle Everard,' said Conky, 'you are speaking of the woman I love.'

The girl gave a little gasp.

'No, really?' she said.

'Absolutely,' said Conky. 'I had intended to mention it earlier. I don't know your name...'

'Clarissa. Clarissa Binstead.'

'How many s's?'

'Three, if you count the Binstead.'

'Clarissa, I love you. Will you be my wife?'

'Sure,' said the girl. 'I was hoping you'd suggest it. And what all the fuss is about is more than I can understand. Why when we go to a ball game in America, we throw pop bottles.'

There was a silence.

'Are you an American, madam?' said the President.

'One hundred per cent. Oh, say, can you see...No, I never can remember how it goes after that. I could whistle it for you.'

The President had drawn Lord Plumpton aside. His face was grave and anxious.

'My dear Everard,' he said in an urgent undertone, 'we must proceed carefully here, very carefully. I had no notion this girl was American. Somebody should have informed me. The last thing we want is an international incident, particularly at a moment when we are hoping, if all goes well, to get into America's ribs for a bit of the stuff. I can fully appreciate your wounded feelings...'

'And how about my wounded topper?'

'The club will buy you a new hat, and then, my dear fellow, I would strongly urge that we consider the matter closed.'

'You mean not skin her?'

'No.'

'Not slap her into the cooler for twenty years?'

'No. There might be very unfortunate repercussions.'

'Oh, all right,' said Lord Plumpton sullenly. 'Oh, very well. But,' he proceeded on a brighter note, 'there is one thing I can do, and that is disinherit this frightful object here. Hoy!' he said to Conky.

'Hullo?' said Conky.

'You are no longer a nephew of mine.'

'Well, that's a bit of goose,' said Conky.

As he came out of the committee room, he was informed by an attendant that a gentleman wished to speak to him on the telephone. Excusing himself to Clarissa and bidding her wait for him downstairs, Conky went to the instrument, listened for a few moments, then reeled away, his eyes bulging and his jaw a-droop. He found Clarissa at the spot agreed upon.

'Hullo, there,' said Conky. 'I say, you remember me asking you to be my wife?'

'Yes.'

'You said you would.'

'Yes.'

'Well, the words that spring to the lips are "*Will* you?" Because I'm afraid the whole thing's off. That was MacSporran on the 'phone. He said he'd made a miscalculation, and my tenner won't be enough to start that sea water scheme going. He said he would need another thirty thousand pounds and could I raise it? I said No, and he said "Too bad, too bad". And I said: "Do I get my tenner back?", and he said: "No, you don't get your tenner back." So there you are. I can't marry you.'

Clarissa wrinkled her forehead.

'I don't see it. Father's got it in gobs. He will provide.'

'Not for me, he won't. I always swore I'd never marry a girl for her money.'

'You aren't marrying me for my money. You're marrying me because we're soulmates.'

'That's true. Still, you appear to have a most ghastly lot of the stuff, and I haven't a bean.'

'Suppose you had a job?'

'Oh, if I had a job.'

'That's all right, then. Father runs a gigantic business and he can always find room for another Vice-President.'

'Vice-President?'

'Yes.'

'But I don't know enough to be a Vice-President.'

'It's practically impossible not to know enough to be a Vice-President. All you would have to do would be to attend conferences and say "Yes" when Father made a suggestion.'

'What, in front of a whole lot of people?'

'Well, at least you could nod.'

'Oh yes, I could nod.'

'Then that's settled. Kiss me.'

Their lips met long and lingeringly. Conky came out of the clinch with sparkling eyes and a heightened colour. He raised a hand to heaven.

'How's that, umpire?' he cried.

'Jolly good show, sir,' said Clarissa.

I

To a man like myself, accustomed to making his mid-day meal off bread and cheese and a pint of bitter, it was very pleasant to be sitting in the grill-room of the best restaurant in London, surrounded by exiled Grand Dukes, chorus girls and the better type of millionaire, and realizing that it wasn't going to cost me a penny. I beamed at Ukridge, my host, and across the table with its snowy napery and shining silver he beamed back at me. He reminded me of a genial old eighteenth century Squire in the coloured supplement of a Christmas number presiding over a dinner to the tenantry.

'Don't spare the cavaire, Corky,' he urged cordially.

I said I wouldn't.

'Eat your fill of the whitebait.'

I said I would.

'And when the porterhouse steak comes along, wade into it with your head down and your elbows out at right angles.'

I had already been planning to do this. A man in the dream-like position of sharing lunch at an expensive restaurant with a Stanley Featherstonehaugh Ukridge who has announced his intention of paying the score does not stint himself. His impulse is to get his while the conditions prevail. Only when the cigars arrived and the founder of the feast, ignoring the lesser breeds, selected a couple that looked like young torpedoes did I feel impelled to speak a word of warning.

'I suppose you know those cost about ten bob apiece?'

'A bagatelle, laddie. If I find them a cool, fragrant and refreshing smoke, I shall probably order a few boxes.'

I drew at my torpedo in a daze. During the past week or two rumours had been reaching me that S. F. Ukridge, that battered football of Fate, was mysteriously in funds. Men spoke of having met him and having had the half-crowns which they automatically produced waved away with a careless gesture and an amused laugh. But I had not foreseen opulence like this.

'Have you got a job?' I asked. I knew that his aunt, the well-known novelist Miss Julia Ukridge, was always trying to induce him to accept employment, and it seemed to me that she must have secured for him some post which carried with it access to the till.

Ukridge shook his head. 'Better than that, old horse. I have at last succeeded in amassing a bit of working capital, and I am on the eve of making a stupendous fortune. What at, you ask? That, laddie, it is too early to say. I shall look about me. But I'll tell you one thing. I shall not become master of ceremonies at an East End boxing joint, which was the walk in life which I was contemplating until quite recently. When did I see you last?'

'Three weeks ago. You touched me for a half a crown.'

'Rest assured that you will be repaid a thousandfold. I feed such sums to the birds. Three weeks ago, eh? My story begins about then. It was shortly after that that I met the man in the pub who offered me the position of announcer and master of ceremonies at the Mammoth Palace of Pugilism in Bottleton East.'

'What made him do that?'

'He seemed impressed by my voice. I had just been having a political argument with a deaf Communist at the other end of the bar, and he said he had been looking for a man with a good, carrying voice. He told me that there was an unexpected vacancy, owing to the late incumbent having passed out with cirrhosis of the liver, and said the job was mine, if I cared to take it. Of course, I jumped at it. I had been looking out for something with a future.'

'There was a future in it, you felt?'

'A very bright future. Think it out for yourself. Although the patrons of an institution like that are mostly costermongers and jellied-eel sellers, mingled with these there is a solid body of the intelligentsia of the racing world – trainers, jockeys, stable lads, touts and what not. They all fawn on the master of ceremonies, and it would, I anticipated, be but a question of time before some inside tip was whispered in my ear, enabling me to clean up on an impressive scale. And so I thanked the man profusely and stood him drinks, and it was only after he had about six that he revealed where the catch lay. Quite casually, in the middle of the love feast, he said how much he was looking forward to seeing me standing in the ring in my soup-and-fish.'

Ukridge paused dramatically, gazing at me through the pince-nez which he had fastened to his ears, as always, with ginger-beer wire.

'Soup-and-fish, Corky.'

'That upset you?'

'The words were like a slosh on the third waistcoat button.'

'You mean you hadn't got dress clothes?'

'Exactly. Some months previously, when I was living with my aunt, she had bought me a suit, but I had long since sold it to

defray living expenses. And the man went on to make it sicken-
ingly clear that a master of ceremonies at the Bottleton East
Mammoth Palace of Pugilism simply could not get by without
what the French call the *grande tenue*. One can see, of course,
why this is so. An M.C. must impress. He must diffuse a glam-
our. Costermongers and jellied-eel merchants like to look on him
as a being from another and more rarefied world, and faultless
evening dress, preferably with a diamond solitaire in the shirt
front, is indispensable.

'So that was that. A stunning blow, you will agree. Many
fellows would have fallen crushed beneath it. But not me, Corky.
Who was it said: "You can't keep a good man down"?'

'Jonah, taunting the whale.'

'Well, that was what I said to myself. Quickly pulling myself
together, I thought the whole thing out, and I saw that all was
not lost. A tie, a celluloid collar, a celluloid dickey and a diamond
solitaire – you can get them for threepence, if you know where
to go – were within my means. The only problem now was
securing the actual suit.' He paused, puffing at his cigar.

II

Next day (Ukridge went on) I called upon George Tupper at the
Foreign Office, full of the will to win. For the purchase of a
secondhand suit of dress clothes it seemed to me that a fiver
should be ample, and if you catch old Tuppy in a good mood,
on a morning when mysterious veiled women haven't been
pinching his draft treaties, you can often work him for a fiver.

But the happy ending was not to be. Tuppy was away on
holiday. In my opinion, Corky, these pampered bureaucrats take

too many holidays and I don't like it. As one of the people of England, I pay George Tupper his salary, and I expect service.

Still, there it was. I came away and went round to your rooms, only to find that you had locked up all your effects. I wouldn't let this cold, suspicious frame of mind grow upon me, Corky. It's bad for the character.

Well, after that, there was nothing left for me to do but go to The Cedars, Wimbledon Common, and endeavour to get into my aunt's ribs. It was not a task to which I looked forward with a great deal of relish, for we were on distant terms at the time. In fact, when kicking me out of the house, she had firmly stated that she never wished to see my ugly face again.

I did not expect to be effusively welcomed, nor was I. I found her on the point of departure for the Riviera. The car was actually at the door when I arrived, and Oakshott, the butler, was assisting her to enter. On seeing me, she sniffed with a sound like someone tearing a sheet of calico. But she did not actually bat me over the head with her umbrella, so I got in, too, and we drove off.

My first move, of course, was to give her the old oil.

'Well, Aunt Julia,' I began, 'you're looking fine.'

She said I was looking terrible, and asked what I wanted.

'Merely to see you, Aunt Julia. Simply to assure myself that you continue in good health. A nephew's natural anxiety. Still, if you do happen to have a suit of dress clothes on you—'

'Why do you want dress clothes? What has become of the suit I bought you?'

'It is a long and sad story.'

'I suppose you sold it.'

'Certainly not. If you think that of me—'

'I do.'

'In that case, I have nothing more to say.'

'Then you had better get out. Tell Wilson to stop the car.'

I had no intention of telling Wilson to stop the car until I had reasoned and pleaded. I did so all the way to the station, but without avail.

'Ah, well,' I said, at length abandoning the fruitless discussion. We were standing on the platform by that time. 'Then shall we compound for a fiver, just to keep the books straight?'

Her metallic snort told me that the suggestion had not gone well.

'I would not dream of giving you money. I know you, Stanley. The first thing you would do would be to go and gamble with it.'

And so saying, she got into the train, not even pausing to bestow a farewell kiss, and I stood there shaking in every limb. A boy with a wheeled vehicle tried to interest me in buns, sandwiches and nut chocolate, but I scarcely heard him. Absorbed and distrait, I was examining from every angle the colossal idea which had just leaped into my mind. It was that word 'gamble' that had done it. It is often that way with me. The merest hint is enough.

One of the most interesting phenomena of this modern life of ours, Corky, is the tendency of owners of large houses to convert them for the night, or for as many nights as they can manage without being raided, into gambling joints. They buy half a dozen shemmy shoes, some cards and a few roulette wheels and send out word to the sporting element that the doings are on, and the latter come surging round in shoals. With the customary rake-off for the house the profits are enormous.

Why, then, I was asking myself, should I not, during my aunt's absence, throw The Cedars, Wimbledon Common, open to the pleasure-seeking and scoop in a vast fortune?

I could detect no flaws in the scheme. Always cautious and prudent, I tried hard to find some, but without success.

Once or twice in most lifetimes projects present themselves which the dullest and most naked eye can spot at sight as pure goose, and this was one of them. It was that almost unheard-of-rarity, a good thing with no strings attached to it.

Of course, before the venture could become a going concern, there were certain preliminaries that had to be seen to. It would, for instance, be necessary to square Oakshott, who had been left in charge of the premises, and even to cut him in as a partner. For it was he who would have to supply from his savings the capital required for the initial outlay.

Shemmy shoes cost money. So do cards. And you cannot obtain a roulette wheel by mere charm of manner. Obviously, someone would have to do a bit of digging down, and – I, being, as I have shown, a trifle strapped at the moment – everything seemed to point to this butler. But I felt confident that I should be able to make him see that here was his big chance. I had run into him at race meetings once or twice on his afternoon off and knew him to be well equipped with sporting blood. A butler, but one of the boys.

I found Oakshott in his pantry. Dismissing with a gesture the housemaid who was sitting on his knee, I unfolded my proposition. And a few moments later, Corky, you could have knocked me down with a feather! That blighted butler would have none of it. Instead of dancing round in circles on the tips of his toes, strewing roses from his bowler hat and crying 'My benefactor!' he pursed his ruddy lips and dished out an unequivocal refusal to co-operate.

I stared at the man, aghast. Then, thinking that he must have failed to grasp the true inwardness of the thing, with all its infinite promise of money for pickles, I went over it all again, speaking slowly and distinctly. But once more all that sprang to his lips was the raspberry.

'Certainly not, sir,' he said with cold rebuke, staring at me like an archdeacon who has found a choirboy sucking acid drops during divine service. 'Would you have me betray a position of trust?'

I said that that was the idea in a nutshell, and he said I had surprised and shocked him. He then put on his coat, which he had removed in order to cuddle the housemaid, and showed me to the door.

Well, Corky, old horse, you have often seen me totter beneath the buffets of Fate, only to come up smiling again after a brief interval for rest and recuperation. If you were asked to describe me in a word, the adjective you would probably employ is 'resilient', and you would be right. I am resilient.

But on this occasion I am not ashamed to confess that I felt like throwing in the towel and turning my face to the wall, so terrific had been the blow. I wonder if you have ever been slapped in the eye with a wet fish? I was once, during a religious argument with a fishmonger down Bethnal Green way, and the sensation was almost identical.

I had been so confident that I had wealth within my grasp. That was what stunned the soul and numbed the faculties. It had never so much as occurred to me to associate Oakshott with scruples. It was as if I had had in my possession the winning ticket in the Irish Sweep and the promoters had refused to brass up on the ground that they disapproved of lotteries.

III

I left that butler's presence a broken man, and for some days went about in a sort of dream. Then I rallied sufficiently to be able to turn my thoughts, if only languidly, to the practical issues of life. I started to try to make arrangements for floating a loan in connection with the purchase of that suit of dress clothes.

But I was not my old self. Twice, from sheer inertia, I allowed good prospects to duck down side streets and escape untouched. And when one morning I ran across Looney Coote in Piccadilly, and said: 'Hullo, Looney, old man, you're looking fine, can you lend me five?' and he affected to believe that I meant five bob and paid off accordingly, I just trousered the money listlessly. How little it all seemed to matter!

You remember Looney Coote, who was at school with us? As crazy a bimbo as ever went through life one jump ahead of the Lunacy Commissioners, but rich beyond dreams of avarice. If he has lingered in your memory at all, it is probably as the bloke with the loudest laugh and the widest grin of your acquaintance. He should have been certified ten years ago, but nobody can say he isn't sunny.

This morning, however, a cloud was on his brow. He appeared to be brooding on something.

'I'll swear it wasn't straight,' I heard him utter. 'Do you think it could have been straight?'

'What, Looney, old man?' I asked. Five bob isn't much, but one has to be civil.

'This game I've been telling you about.'

He hadn't been telling me about any game, I said, and he seemed surprised.

'Haven't I? I thought I had. I've been telling everybody. I went to one of those gambling places last night and got skinned, and, on thinking it over, I'm convinced the game was not on the level.'

The thought of someone as rich as Looney going to gambling places in which I was not financially interested caused the old wound, as you may well imagine, to start throbbing afresh. He asked me what I was snorting about, and I said I wasn't snorting, I was groaning hollowly.

'Where was this?' I asked.

'Down Wimbledon way. One of those big houses on the Common.'

Corky, there are times when I have a feeling that I must be clairvoyant. As he spoke these words, I did not merely suspect that he was alluding to the Auntery. I knew.

I clutched his sleeve. 'This house? What was it called?'

'One of those fatheaded names they have out in those parts. The Beeches, or The Weeping Willows, or something.'

'The Cedars?'

'That's right. You know it, do you? Well, I've practically decided to give that nest of crooks a sharp lesson. I'm going—'

I left him. I wanted to be alone, to think; to ponder, Corky; to turn this ghastly thing over in my mind and examine it in pitiless detail ... And the more I turned it over and examined it, the more did I recoil in horror from the dark pit into which I was peering. If there is one thing that gives your clean-living, clean-thinking man the pip, it is being compelled to realize to what depths human nature can sink, if it spits on its hands and really gets down to it.

For it was only too revoltingly obvious what had happened. That fiend in butler's shape had done the dirty on me. He stood definitely revealed as a twister of the first order. From the very moment I had started outlining my proposition, he must have resolved to swipe the fruits of my vision and broad outlook. No doubt he had begun putting matters in train directly I left him.

To go and confront him was with me the work of an instant. Well, not exactly an instant, because it's a long way to Wimbledon and a cab was not within my means. This time he was in my aunt's bedroom, having apparently decided to move in there for the duration. I found him reclining in an armchair, smoking a cigar and totting up figures on a sheet of paper, and it was not long before I saw that the fourpence which the journey had cost me was going to be money chucked away.

The idea I had had was that on beholding me the man would quail. But he didn't. I suppose a man like that doesn't quail. Quailing, after all, is the result of conscience doing its stuff, and no doubt his conscience had packed up and handed in its portfolio during his early boyhood. When I towered over him with folded arms and said 'Serpent!' he merely said 'Sir?' and took another suck at the cigar. It made it rather difficult to know what to say next.

However, I got down to it, accusing him roundly of having sneaked my big idea and chiselled me out of my legitimate earnings, and he admitted the charge with a complacent smirk. He even – though with your pure mind, Corky, you will find this hard to believe – thanked me for putting him on to a good thing. Finally, with incredible effrontery, he offered me a fiver in full settlement of all claims, saying that one of these days soft-heartedness would be his ruin.

First, of course, I took a pop at coercing him into a partnership by threatening to inform my aunt, but he waved this away airily by saying that he knew a few things about me, too. And that cinched that, because there was a pretty good chance that he did. Then, laddie, I began to speak my mind.

I am a pretty eloquent chap, when stirred, and I can't remember leaving out much. Waving away his degrading bribe, I called him names which I had heard second mates use to able-bodied seamen, and others which the able-bodied seamen had used in describing the second mates later on in the privacy of the foc's'le. Then, turning on my heel, I strode out, pausing at the door to add something which a trimmer had once said to the barman of a Montevideo bar in my presence when the latter had refused to serve him on the ground that he had already had enough. And as I slammed the door, I was filled with a glow of exaltation. It seemed to me that in a difficult situation I had borne myself well.

I don't know, Corky, if you have ever done the fine, dignified thing, refusing to accept money because it was tainted and there wasn't enough of it, but I have always noticed on these occasions that there comes a time when the glow of exaltation begins to ebb. Reason returns to its throne, and you find yourself wondering whether in doing the fine, dignified thing you have not behaved like a silly ass.

With me this happened as I was about half-way through a restorative beer at a pub in Jermyn Street. For it was at that moment that the Bottleton East bloke came in and said he had been looking for me everywhere. What he had to tell me was that I must make my decision about that M.C. job within the next twenty-four hours, as the authorities could not hold it open any longer. And the thought that I had deliberately rejected the fiver which would have placed a secondhand suit of dress clothes within my grasp seemed to gash me like a knife.

I assured him that I would let him know next day without fail, and went out, to pace the streets and ponder.

The whole thing was extraordinarily difficult and complex. On the one hand, pride forbade me to crawl back to that inky-souled butler and tell him that I would accept his grimy money after all. And yet, on the other hand ...

You see, with old Tuppy out of town I hardly knew where to turn for the ready, and it was imperative that I obtain employment at an early date. And, apart from that, what the bloke had said about watching me standing in the ring in my soup-and-fish had inflamed my imagination. I could see myself dominating that vast audience with upraised hand and, silence secured, informing it that the next item on the programme would be a four-round bout between Porky Jones of Bermondsey and Slugger Smith of the New Cut, or whoever it might be, and I confess that I found the picture intoxicating. The thought of being the cynosure of all eyes, my lightest word greeted with respectful whistles, moved me proudly. Vanity, of course, but is any of us free from it?

That night I set out once more for The Cedars. I was fully alive to the fact that the pride of the Ukridges was going to get one of the worst wallops it had ever sustained, but there are moments when pride has to take the short end.

IV

It was fortunate that I had gone prepared to have my *amour propre* put through the wringer, for the first thing that happened was that I was refused admittance at the front door because I was not dressed. It was Oakshott himself who inflicted this indignity upon me, bidding me curtly to go round to the back and wait for him in his pantry. He added that he would be glad if I did it quick, as the guests would be arriving shortly. He seemed to think that the sight of what he evidently looked on as a Forgotten Man would distress them.

So I went to the pantry and waited, and presently I could hear cars driving up and merry voices calling to one another and all the other indications of a big night; sounds which, as you may imagine, were like acid to the soul. It must have been nearly an hour before Oakshott condescended to show up, and when he did his manner was curt and forbidding.

'Well?' he said. I tried to think that he had said: 'Well, sir?' but I knew he hadn't. It was only too plain from the very outset that the butler side of him was in complete abeyance. It was more like being granted an audience by a successful company promoter.

I got down to the *res* immediately, informing him – for there is never any sense in wasting time on these occasions – that I had been thinking things over and had decided to take that fiver of his. Whereupon he informed me that he had been thinking it over and had decided not to ruddy well let me have it. There was a nasty glint in his eye, as he spoke, which I didn't like. In the course of a long career I have seen men who wore that indefinable air of not intending to part with fivers, but never one in whom it was so well-marked.

'Your manner this morning was extremely offensive,' he said.

I sank the pride of the Ukridges another notch, and urged him not to allow mere surface manner to influence him. Had he, I asked, never heard of the gruff exterior that covers the heart of gold?

'You called me a —'

'I could not deny it.'

'And a —'

Again I was forced to admit that this was substantially correct.

'And just as you were about to leave you turned at the door and called me a — — —'

I saw that something must be done to check this train of thought.

'Did I hurt your feelings, Oakshott?' I said sympathetically. 'Did I wound you, Oakshott, old pal? It was quite unintentional. If you had been watching my face, you would have seen a twinkle in my eye. I was kidding you, old friend. These pleasantries are not intended to be taken *au pied de la lettre.*'

He said he didn't know what *au pied de la lettre* meant, and I was supplying a rough diagram when an underling of sorts appeared and told him he was wanted at the front. He left me flat, departing without a backward glance, and I started hunting round for the port. There should be some, I felt, in this pantry. 'If butlers come, can port be far behind?' is always a pretty safe rule to go on.

I located it eventually in a cupboard, and took a stimulating swig. It was just what I had been needing. It has frequently happened that a good go in at the port at a critical moment has made all the difference to me as a thinking force. The stuff seems to act directly on the little grey cells, causing them to flex their muscles and chuck their chests out. A stiff whisky and soda sometimes has a similar effect, I have noticed, but port never fails.

It did not fail me now. Quite suddenly, as if I had pressed a button, there rose before me a picture of my aunt's bedroom, and in the foreground of it was the mantelpiece with its handsome clock, worth, I estimated, fully five quid on the hoof.

My aunt is a woman who likes to surround herself with costly objects of *vertu*, and who shall blame her? She has the price, earned with her gifted pen, and if that is how she feels like spending it, good luck to her, say I. Everywhere throughout her cultured home you will find rich ornaments, on any one of which the most cautious pawnbroker would be delighted to spring a princely sum.

No, Corky, you are wrong. You choose your expressions carelessly. It was not my intention to *pinch* this clock. The transaction presented itself to my mind purely in the light of a temporary loan. No actual figures had been talked by the representative of the Bottleton East Mammoth Palace of Pugilism, but I considered that I was justified in assuming that for such a post as announcer and master of ceremonies a very substantial salary might be taken as read. Well, dash it, my predecessor had died of cirrhosis of the liver. It costs money to die of cirrhosis of the liver. It seemed to me that it would be child's play to save enough out of that substantial salary in the first week to de-pop the clock and restore it to its place.

The whole business deal, in short, would be consummated without my aunt being subjected to any annoyance or inconvenience whatsoever. It shows what a good whack at the port will do, when I say that there was actually a moment, as I raced upstairs, when I told myself that, could she know the facts, she would be the first to approve and applaud.

I had modified this view somewhat by the time I reached the door, but I did not allow this to deter me. I flung myself at the handle and turned it with zip and animation. And you may picture my chagrin, Corky, when not a damn thing happened. Oakshott had locked the door and taken away the key, creating a situation which would have compelled most men to confess themselves nonplussed, and one which, I must own, rattled even me for a bit.

Then my knowledge of the terrain stood me in good stead. I had spent a considerable amount of time as an inmate of this house – it rarely happens that my aunt kicks me out before the middle of the second week – and I was familiar with its workings. I knew, for instance, that behind the potting shed down by the kitchen garden there was always kept a small but serviceable ladder. I was also aware that my aunt's bedroom had French windows opening on a balcony. With the aid of this ladder and a chisel I would be able to laugh at locksmiths.

Butlers always have chisels, so I went back to the pantry and had no difficulty in finding Oakshott's. There was an electric torch in the same drawer, and I felt that I might need that, too. I had just pocketed these useful objects, when Oakshott came in, and conceive my emotion when I saw that he was carrying a roll the size of a portmanteau. I presumed that he had come to the pantry to bank the stuff. A man in his position, with ready money raining down on him in a steady stream, would naturally wish to cache it from time to time, so as to leave room on his person for more.

The sight of me seemed to give him little or no pleasure. His eyes took on a cold, poached-egg look. 'You still here?'

'Still here,' I assured him.

'It's no good your waiting,' he said churlishly. 'You won't get a smell of that fiver.'

'I need it sorely.'

'So do I.'

'And how easy it would be to give of your plenty. With a wad like that, you'd never know it was gone.'

'It won't be gone.'

I sighed. 'So be it, Oakshott. You won't grudge me a drop of port?'

'You can have some port. I'll have some, too.'

'Shall I hold the money?'

'No.'

'I thought you might want to have your hands free while you poured. You've been doing well, it would appear. Business is good?'

'Fine. Well, mud in your eye.'

'Skin off your nose,' I replied courteously and we quaffed. He then left me, and I made for the garden.

Passing the drawing-room I could hear sounds of mirth and merriment as the multitude took its pop at the games of chance, putting more cash into Oakshott's pocket as it did so, and I was in two minds about pausing to bung a brick through the window. But this, I saw, though a relief to my feelings, would not further my business interests, so I let it go. I found the ladder and climbed to the balcony, and I was just about to get to work with the chisel when the lights in the room suddenly flashed on, giving me a bit of a jolt.

Speedily recovering, I shoved my nose against the pane and saw Oakshott. He was standing by the chest of drawers, still clutching the roll, and one sensed that, finding me in the pantry, he had decided that this would be a better place to put it. But before he could make his deposit there came a sudden change in the character of the sounds proceeding from below, and he stood listening, rigid like a stag at bay.

My aunt's bedroom, I must mention, is just above the drawing-room, and if there are routs and revels going on in the latter apartment you hear them clearly on the balcony; and inside the room, of course, they come up through the floor. What had arrested Oakshott's attention was the fact that at this juncture there was an abrupt increase in the volume of the noise, together with a feminine scream, or two, followed by a significant silence.

Well, it did not take a man of my experience long to gather what had occurred. I have participated in raids in my time as a patron, as a waiter, as a washer of glasses, and once, in America, actually as a member of the squad conducting the operations, and I know the procedure. What happens is that there is first a universal yell of consternation and the girls all scream, and then all is hushed and everyone stands peering bleakly into the future, trying to think of names and addresses which will sound reasonably plausible to the gentleman with the note-book.

Briefly, old horse, doom had come upon The Cedars, Wimbledon Common. The joint had been pulled.

V

That Oakshott, also, was able to put two and two together and form a swift diagnosis was shown by the promptness with which he now acted. There was a wardrobe not far from where he stood, a handsome piece in old walnut, and he dived into it like a seal going after a chunk of halibut, taking his roll with him.

And I popped in through the French windows and turned the key in the wardrobe door.

Why I did this, I cannot say, except that it seemed a good idea at the time. It was only some moments later that that extraordinary vision for which I have always been so remarkable suggested to me that not only clean fun but solid profit might be derived from the action. Here, it suddenly flashed upon me, was where I might make a bit.

You see, I had studied this Oakshott's psychology, and my researches had left me with the conviction that he was one of those who, finding themselves locked in a wardrobe by a police-man during a raid on premises which they have been employing for illegal purposes, will endeavour to make a dicker with that policeman. On these occasions, as you are probably aware, while the patrons may hope to get off with a fine, mine host himself is in line for the jug, and a butler's liberty is very dear to him. It seemed to me that I was entitled to assume that if Oakshott supposed that matters could be settled out of court, he would not count the cost.

At any rate, the thing seemed a fair sporting venture, so I approached the wardrobe and proceeded to address myself in a crisp, cultured voice – the voice of the younger son of some aristocratic family who, after a year or two at Oxford, has entered the Force *via* the Hendon Police College.

'What,' I inquired, 'are you doing they-ah, Simmons?'

To which I replied, this time using the bass clef and adopting a bit of a Ponder's End accent – for I pictured this Simmons as just some ordinary flatty who had graduated from a board school – 'I've got one of 'em locked in 'ere, sir.'

'Oh, reall-ah?' I said. 'Good work, Simmons. Guard him well. I'm off downstairs.'

I then went to the door, slammed it and paused for a reply.

It did not come immediately, and for a moment I feared that my knowledge of psychology might have let me down. But all was well. I can see now that Oakshott was merely thinking it over and fighting a parsimonious man's battle between his love of liberty and the lust to retain his ill-gotten wealth. Presently there came from within a deprecating, 'Er, officer,' followed by a rustling sound, and there stole out from under the door a fiver.

I gathered it in, and there for a while the matter rested.

I suppose Oakshott realized that when you are buying a policeman's soul you cannot be niggardly, for a few moments later another fiver came stealing out, and I pounced on that, too. After this had gone on for some time, with my current account going up by leaps and bounds, I decided to take my profit and retire from the game. At any minute a systematic search of the premises might be instituted – I couldn't imagine why it hadn't been done already – and if I were to be found on them my presence might be hard to explain. The pure heart and the clean conscience are all very well, but they pay few dividends during a gambling raid, and it seemed to me that I would be better elsewhere. It would not, I felt, be beyond the scope of Oakshott's subtle mind to make the constabulary believe that it was I who had been master of the revels.

So I unlocked the door and nipped out of the window and down the ladder. I have often wondered what Oakshott's reactions were when he stole out and found the place entirely free from P.C. Simmonses.

It was a lovely night, with the stars twinkling away in the firmament, and the garden was very cool and peaceful. I would gladly have lingered and drunk in its fragrance, but I could not but feel that this was not the moment. Many people have complimented me on my nerve of steel, and rightly, but there is a time for reckless courage and a time for prudence. I don't mind admitting that at this particular juncture, with the troops of Midian prowling around, my emotions were those of a cat in a strange alley, and I was anxious to get away from it all.

So marked was this feeling that, as I came abreast of the big water butt outside the kitchen door and heard a noise somewhere in the neighbourhood, as of regulation official boots trampling in the night, I halted with beating heart and raised the lid, intending to get inside. Whereupon, a hand came out and slid a banknote into my grasp. Seeing that my dugout was already occupied, I passed on.

This incident, as you may imagine, made a deep impression on me. It suggested to me that in following the policy of safety first, and concentrating on the swift getaway, I might be passing up something good. If there was gold in the water butt, there might be the same elsewhere. I decided to draw another covert or two before leaving. And to cut a long story short, at the end of ten minutes my balance had substantially increased.

Apparently not all the patrons of The Cedars had been content to remain supinely in the drawing-room when the gendarmerie came popping up through traps. There were those who had acted with that mettle and spirit which one likes to feel is the birthright of Englishmen, and had hopped out of the window, to distribute themselves here and there about the grounds. One splendid fellow, who came across with a tenner, had snuggled into the cucumber frame. You felt it was the sort of thing Drake or Raleigh would have done.

But now I was naturally anxious to count the takings. A methodical man always likes to know where he stands. It seemed to me that the potting shed was far enough away from the house to be out of the danger zone, so I made for it. And I was crossing the threshold with a gay, if *sotto voce*, song on my lips, when there was a sharp squeal from its dark interior, and I knew that here, too, some poor human waif had found and taken sanctuary.

The next moment the rays of the torch, of which I had quickly pressed the button, revealed the well-known features of my Aunt Julia.

VI

There are times in life, Corky, when the man of iron self-control may be excused for momentarily losing his phlegm. It is a very unnerving thing to find an aunt whom you know to be in the south of France nestling in a potting shed in Wimbledon. A sharp 'Gorblimey!' escaped my lips, and it was at once evident that the ear of love had recognized the familiar voice.

'Stanley!' she cried.

Usually when my aunt says 'Stanley!' it is a tone of refined exasperation, the ejaculation being preliminary to a thorough ticking-off. But now the general effect was vastly different. Her 'Stanley!' on the present occasion was roughly equivalent to the 'Gawain!' or 'Galahad!' which a distressed damsel in difficulties with a dragon would have uttered on beholding her favourite knight entering the ring with drawn sword.

'Aunt Julia!' I exclaimed. 'What on earth are you doing here?'

In broken accents and in a hushed whisper, starting from time to time at sudden noises, she told her story. It was, after all, quite simple. At Cannes, it seemed, she had met a friend, a recent arrival on the Riviera, who knew a man who had told her, the friend, that dark doings were in progress in the old home. And so arresting was this crony's report of the big evenings at The Cedars that my aunt had leaped into the first plane, intent on catching the miscreant responsible on the hop.

'I thought at first it must be you, Stanley.'

I drew myself up with a touch of hauteur. 'Indeed?'

'But my friend said no.'

'I should hope so.'

'She said it was the butler.'

'She was right.'

'And I trusted him implicitly!'

'A pity you did not consult me. Aunt Julia. I could have given you the lowdown on the man's true character.'

'He looks so respectable.'

'Many a man may look respectable, and yet be able to hide at will behind a spiral staircase.'

'You saw through him?'

'Like an X-ray. I suspected that, the moment your back was turned, he would be up to some kind of hell, and I was correct. I came here to-night in the hope of being able to protect your interests.'

'You were gambling?'

I switched on the torch, switching it off again immediately when she asked, with a momentary return to her normal brusque manner, if I wanted to bring every policeman on the premises to the spot.

'If,' I said, 'you were able in that brief instant to get a dekko at my person, Aunt Julia, you will have seen that I am not dressed. At functions like the one at which you have been assisting, the soup-and-fish is obligatory. I possess no soup-and-fish. What happened when you got here?'

'I went into the drawing-room and was just going to order those people out, when a policeman came bursting in and told us we were all under arrest. I promptly jumped out of the window.'

'Stoutly done, Aunt Julia. The true Ukridge resource.'

'And I took refuge here. What am I to do, Stanley? I must not be found. If I am, how can I convince the police that I am not responsible for the whole thing? The scandal will ruin me. Think, Stanley, think.'

I felt that it would be judicious to rub it in a bit.

'It is an unfortunate state of affairs,' I agreed. 'And while it is not for me to criticize the arrangements which you may see fit to make where your own house is concerned, I cannot but feel that you have brought this on yourself. If you had placed me in charge during your absence ... However, we can go into that later. What I propose to do now is to have a look around to see if the coast is clear. If it is, you will be able to do a quiet sneak over the garden wall. Wait here until I return. If I do not return, you will know that I have fallen a victim to a nephew's devotion.'

Whether or not she said, 'My hero!' I am not certain. It was what she ought to have said, but she is a woman who is apt to miss her cues at times.

However, she did clasp my hand in a fevered clutch, and with a brief word bidding her keep her tail up I went out.

I hadn't gone more than fifty yards when I barged slap into a substantial body. It was coming around a tree, heading east, and I was going around the tree, heading west. We collided like a couple of mastodons mixing it in a primeval swamp. Recovering its balance, it flashed a torch on me and a moment later spoke.

It said: 'Hullo, Ukridge, old top. You here? What a night, what a night, what a night?'

I recognized the voice of Looney Coote. And picture my astonishment, Corky, when, flashing my torch on him, I perceived that he was wearing a policeman's uniform. When I commented on this, he laughed like a hyæna calling to its mate and told me all.

Chagrined at losing his money on the previous night at The Cedars, he had decided to fit himself out at a costumier's and go and raid the place; thus, as he himself put it, giving it the salutary lesson it had been asking for and making it think a bit. Such, Corky, is Looney Coote, and always has been. I felt, as I had so often felt in my earlier dealings with him, that his spiritual home was definitely Colney Hatch.

Slowly I adjusted my faculties. 'You mean there aren't any cops here?'

'Only me.'

I had to pause at this to master my emotion. When I thought of the intense nervous strain to which I had been subjected and recalled the way I had been tiptoeing about the place and quaking at sudden noises and not letting a twig snap beneath my feet, and all because of this pie-faced half-wit, the temptation to haul off and bust him in the eye was very powerful.

I succeeded in restraining myself, but my manner was cold and severe. 'And the next thing that will happen,' I said, 'is that a bevy of genuine constables will blow in, and you'll get two years hard for impersonating a policeman.'

This rattled him. 'I never thought of that.'

'Muse on it now.'

'The Law gets a bit shirty, does it, if you impersonate policemen?'

'It screams with annoyance.'

'Well, well, well, I'd better leg it, you think?'

'I do.'

'I will. Listen, Ukridge, old man,' said Looney, 'there's something you can do for me. I locked an abundant multitude of the blighters in the drawing-room. I should be vastly obliged if, after I've gone, you would let them out. Here's the key. And, by the way, weren't you saying something this morning about wanting me to lend you money, or something?'

'I was.'

'Would a tenner be enough?'

'I could make it do.'

'Then here you are. Talking of money,' said Looney, 'there was a strong movement afoot among the blighters to bribe me to let them go. A good deal of feeling was shown. Amused me, I must confess. Well, good night, old man. It's been nice seeing you. Do you think, if I'm stopped by a cop, I could get away with it by saying I was on my way to a fancy-dress ball?'

'You might try it.'

'I will. Did I give you that tenner?' he said.

'No.'

'Then here you are. Good night, old man, good night.'

I went back to the potting shed and told my aunt that a quick burst from the garden wall was now in order, and she thanked me in a trembling voice and kissed me and said she had misjudged me. She then popped off at a good speed, and I pushed along to the drawing-room, forming my plans and schemes with lightning rapidity as I went. What Looney had said about the inmates trying to bribe him had stirred me not a little.

And I am happy to say that he had not deceived me. I found them most anxious to do business. A few *pourparlers* through the keyhole and the deal was fixed up at so much per head. The money was placed in my hands by a stately bird with white whiskers. He looked as if he might be the President of the Anti-Gambling League or some equally respectable institution, and there was no doubt that he had been asking himself quite often during his vigil what the harvest would be.

There was champagne on the sideboard. When they had all gone, I sat down and opened a bottle. I felt that I had earned it.

Ukridge paused, and drew luxuriously at his cigar. There was a look of deep and sublime contentment on his face.

'So there you are, Corky. That is why I am now able to stand you lunch in this robber's den without a thought for the prices in the right-hand column. My aunt is all over me, and I am once more the petted guest in her home. This gives me a base from which I can operate while making up my mind how best to employ my enormous capital. For it is enormous. I'd hate to tell you, old horse, how much I've got. It would be tactless. You are a struggling young fellow who considers himself lucky if he snaffles thirty bob for an article in *Interesting Bits*, on 'Famous Lovers of History' or some such rot, and it would be agony to you to know how rolling I am. You would bite your lip and brood and get all sorts of subversive ideas about the unfair distribution of wealth. It wouldn't be long before we should have you throwing bombs.'

I reassured him. 'Don't worry. I'm not envious. It is enough for me to feel that after this magnificent spread you are going to pay the bill.'

There was a pause. I noticed that behind his gingerbeer-wired pince-nez his eyes had taken on an apologetic look.

'I'm glad you brought that up, Corky,' he said, 'for I was just wondering how to break it to you. I'm extraordinarily sorry, old horse, but I find that I have inadvertently left my money at home. You, I fear, will have to settle up. I'll pay you back next time I see you.'

TITLES IN THE EVERYMAN WODEHOUSE

This edition of P. G. Wodehouse has been prepared from the first British printing of each title.

The Everyman Wodehouse is printed on acid-free paper and set in Caslon, a typeface designed and engraved by William Caslon of William Caslon & Son, Letter-Founders in London around 1740.